The Determined Debutante

THE DETERMINED DEBUTANTE

A Zodiac Regency Romance

Book 1

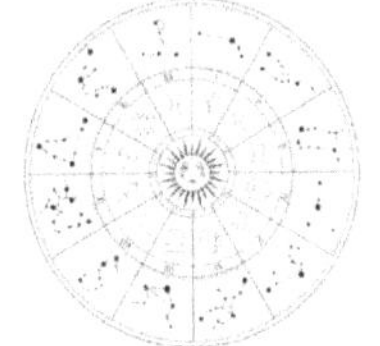

Meredith Bond

Editing by The Editing Hall
Cover Art by Briar Banerji

Published by Annessa Ink,
http://www.annessaink.com

Dedication

My great thanks go to Byron Buttery-Clements, who was kind enough to allow me to use his wonderful name. I hope I did it justice. Thanks, Byron!!

Aries (March 20-April 19): At their core, Aries do things their own way. They are unafraid of conflict, highly competitive, and honest. They throw themselves at the world eagerly and without fear. Aries are driven by a desire to prove themselves and their strength.

Gemini (May 21-June 20): Geminis are very intelligent and pick up knowledge quickly. They are perceptive, analytical, and often very funny. They have an unreserved, childlike curiosity, always asking new questions. Geminis have an uncanny ability to size up a person's character in a matter of seconds, even if they only just met them. They are great communicators because they tend to be very responsive and sensitive listeners. Geminis are versatile, comfortable being both introverts and extroverts.

CHAPTER ONE

"Ooof!" The pile of books Lady Rebecca Preston had been carrying dropped to the floor with a flutter of paper and one very loud *thud*.

"Oh! I do beg your pardon," a young woman said, immediately squatting down to pick up the fallen books.

"No, not at all," Rebecca said, joining her. "I'm not entirely certain it wasn't my fault. I'm afraid I wasn't looking where I was going."

The girl laughed. "I had my nose in a book and wasn't watching either."

Rebecca smiled at the pretty young lady. Her auburn hair was pulled up, but a few strands of wavy hair had escaped, and Rebecca could see that one of her hairpins was about to fall out. She reached out and shoved it back into place before smiling into the girl's surprised blue eyes.

"I do beg your pardon. Your hairpin was about to fall out, and I, well, I couldn't help myself."

The girl's cheeks flushed delicately. "I'm afraid my maid isn't very good at putting up my hair, but she's learning," she said, reaching to the back of her head to ensure her other pins were secure.

"It can be difficult to find someone experienced," Rebecca agreed.

"Er, yes," the girl said with hesitation.

They both stood up, now each holding a pile of books. Rebecca was surprised when the girl stood at her full height. She was extremely tall, taller than a number of men Rebecca knew. She was also, unfortunately, stick thin. Her gown hung on her like a sack—a sack made of good material and edged with lace, but a sack, nonetheless.

"I am Clarissa Ellison," the girl said.

"Lady Preston," Rebecca replied. "But you do know you shouldn't introduce yourself?"

"Oh!" The girl turned a deeper shade of pink. "Uh, yes, of course. It, er, just seemed the thing to do," she explained.

Rebecca smiled at her. Her eyes fell to the book at the top of the pile in her hands. "*The Ladies' Book of Etiquette and Manual of Politeness*," she read out loud.

"I believe that one's mine," the young lady said, snatching it back.

Rebecca gave a little laugh. "Yes, obviously." She could practically hear the girl swallow with embarrassment. "You wouldn't happen to be new to Town?"

She gave a little nod and lowered her gaze to the books in her hands.

"It's perfectly all right. I am not a such stickler for propriety," Rebecca reassured her.

Miss Ellison lifted her gaze with a grateful expression. "Thank you. My aunt would be mortified if she knew…"

"No need to tell her. This will be our little secret." Rebecca looked around. "Is she here, your aunt?"

"Oh, er, no. I snuck out of the house to come and purchase these books, I'm afraid. I do have my maid with me, though!" the girl added quickly. "I remembered to bring her."

Rebecca nodded slowly, trying her hardest not to laugh. "That's very good. You should never venture out without either your maid or a footman."

"Yes, I was warned of that."

Rebecca spied one of her own books in the pile the girl was holding. "I believe the Hutchins Almanack is mine."

Miss Ellison moved the top book to the bottom of the pile and opened the book that was now on top, as it had nothing on the front cover. "Hutchins Improved: Being an Almanack and Ephemeris of the Motions of the Sun and Moon for the Year of Our Lord 1809." She looked up with her eyebrows drawn down. "What is that—if you will excuse me for asking?"

Rebecca took the book and added it to her pile. "It's a book to help me calculate horoscopes."

She shook her head, not understanding.

"Have you heard of the Zodiac?" Rebecca asked.

"No, what is it?" Miss Ellison asked, clearly very curious.

"The position of the stars at your birth. They determine what sort of person you are and, some believe, can even be used to predict times when good things will happen and bad," Rebecca explained.

"Really? I've never heard of such a thing." The girl was clearly fascinated, which made Rebecca happier than it ought.

"Oh yes, it is something people have studied since biblical times. The Greeks studied it extensively, as have the Arabs, Chinese, and Indians."

"Goodness! And it is something you study as well?"

"Yes. It's a fun hobby of mine." Rebecca paused and then cocked her head a little. "Tell me when you were born, and I can tell you a little about yourself."

Miss Ellison's eyes widened. "March 27th."

Rebecca nodded. "You were born under the astrological sign of Aries. It means that you are very energetic and competitive. You're also very caring and an excellent leader. But you can be impulsive and not think things through before you act."

Her mouth dropped open.

Rebecca chuckled. "I see that I am right."

Miss Ellison just nodded.

"Are you in Town to make your debut, Miss Ellison?" Rebecca asked.

"Er, yes, yes, I am," she answered with a quick shake of her head as if to clear it for the change in topic.

Rebecca nodded. "Well, I should warn you, then, to try to wait until you have met a good number of gentlemen before choosing one to marry. I do hope your aunt is very levelheaded."

Miss Ellison frowned. "I suppose you could call her that. *Uninterested* would probably be more accurate."

The little snort of air escaped Rebecca as she tried to hold back her laughter. "Oh, dear. Well, if you need any assistance, please do not hesitate to call. I go to all the best engagements and know a great many people." She fished a calling card from her reticule. "If you'll accompany me to the counter, I'll write my direction on the back."

"Thank you! You are so very kind, ma'am," the girl said as she followed in Rebecca's wake.

Clarissa was let into her uncle's town house by Tom, the footman. "Lady Morley has requested your presence in the drawing room, Miss Ellison," he told her in ominous tones.

"Oh, dear." She quickly handed off the books she was carrying to her maid Annie. The bookseller had been kind enough to wrap them in brown paper so no one could read the titles as Clarissa walked home.

"Please take these up to my room," she said, handing over her hat as well.

She started to jog up the stairs and then remembered that proper young ladies only walked with decorum, no matter what—or so said her aunt. She slowed and walked the rest of the way, her back held straight and her chin high just as she'd been taught.

"Good morning, Aunt Lily," Clarissa said as she breezed through the door to the drawing room.

Her aunt simply scowled at her as she looked up from her embroidery. Her hair was still the same wheat-blonde it had always been, but the lines on her face told their own story. "Where have you been, Miss?"

"At the bookseller's," Clarissa told her. She eyed the sofa and then remembered that she should probably wait to be invited to sit down before doing so. She stood in front of her aunt, trying her best to look innocent and demure with her hands clasped at her waist.

"And who gave you permission to go out on your own?" the woman asked.

Clarissa opened her mouth but had nothing to say to that.

"Did your uncle say that you could go out? I certainly did not," Lady Morley prodded further.

"No, ma'am. I took Annie with me," Clarissa put in for good measure.

"You may not leave the house without permission." It was a statement. A law. A command, even.

Clarissa clenched her jaw but nodded. "Yes, ma'am. I will not do so again." She hoped that sounded sincere despite the fact that inside her head she was screaming with rage. She'd never had to ask permission of anyone to do something so innocuous as going to a shop *with her maid* at home. No, at home, everyone asked *her* for permission to do things. But Clarissa wasn't the mistress of this house, she reminded herself for probably the one-hundredth time since she'd come to London a week ago.

She was not only *not* the mistress of the house, but she was a guest—one who was not appreciated by the mistress. Clarissa was well aware of this since her aunt had not hesitated to inform her. She was here by the kindness of Clarissa's uncle, the Baron Morley, who had been so generous to give her a Season—just one, as her aunt reminded her. And if Clarissa's father hadn't been a viscount, Aunt Lily had assured her, she would not even have been given that opportunity, for surely no one would deign to marry an ignorant girl who'd grown up in seclusion on her father's estate. Clarissa wouldn't have called being in the company of her eight siblings, her father, and a good number of tenants *seclusion*, but it was true that she had not exactly mingled among what society there was in Salisbury.

Her father, much to her uncle's chagrin, cared little for society. Instead, he devoted himself to the upkeep of his estate, which was quite large, to be sure. He did all he could, he informed his children, to keep the estate as profitable as possible so as to rebuild the family coffers. He would not leave Frederick, his heir, with nothing but an empty title. In other words, he was a miser and a bit of a hermit. He didn't believe in spending more than was absolutely necessary on himself or his children. Everything went into the estate.

If it hadn't been for the generosity of her uncle, Clarissa would never have been given the opportunity to have a Season—and her aunt reminded her of this daily.

Aunt Lily seemed satisfied with this response. She had just opened her mouth, probably to remind Clarissa that her presence was being suffered only because of Lord Morley's generosity, when the gentleman himself strolled into the room.

"Ah, here are my two lovely ladies," he said with a broad smile covering his cherubic face. His brown hair had only a few silver strands lacing through it, and his blue eyes twinkled as happily as they ever had. Although he was middle-aged, his height allowed him to carry his extra pounds well.

Clarissa turned and curtsied to her uncle. "Good morning, Uncle. I hope you are faring well today?"

"I am! I am indeed," he said, giving Clarissa a chuck under the chin. "But haven't I told you, you don't need to curtsy every time I walk into a room, my dear. We are *family*." He said the last word with a great deal of emphasis, as if it were the most wonderful thing in the world—and to Clarissa, it truly was.

She smiled at the sweet old man. "Yes, my... Uncle, I'm sorry, I forgot."

"That's a girl. Well, certainly no harm done." He turned to his wife. "And what are your plans for the day, madam? Taking our dear little Clarissa to your modiste?"

The woman scowled at her husband. "Yes," she snapped. "We've already ordered some day dresses. Today we'll see about a ballgown or two."

"Do make it three," her uncle interrupted. "Or even four!"

Lady Morley looked astounded. "My lord, the cost!"

He waved a hand in the air, as if he were brushing aside a foul smell.

The woman pinched her lips together for a moment before continuing, "We'll see if anything can be done for the girl. She is so skinny I worry that anything Madam Celeste makes will hang on her like that." She indicated the gown, which Clarissa had made herself.

Clarissa knew it wasn't the most flattering dress, but she only had three, and this was one of the better ones.

"Oh, I'm sure she will. I'm sure she will," Uncle Lawrence said with a chuckle. "We will see her transform into a real beauty once she is out of her chrysalis."

His wife snorted. "Chrysalis, indeed," she said softly. "Sack is more like it."

"Well then, I shall leave you to it. I simply came in to inform you that I was going out to my club. I shall be home later in the afternoon." He gave Clarissa's cheek another little tap and an encouraging smile before leaving the room.

Aunt Lily shook her head after he'd closed the door behind himself. "He goes to his club every morning, comes home every afternoon, and still, he informs me of it." She turned to glare at Clarissa. "You see? Even your uncle tells me when he is going out."

Clarissa lowered her gaze to the floor. "Yes, ma'am."

"Well, don't just stand there, girl. Go and take off your pelisse and then rejoin me here. We'll go through the magazines and see if we can't find some designs that will make you look less like a stick and more like a young lady who a gentleman would want to marry."

Jonathan, the Earl of Uxbridge, turned slightly to one side so he could eye the steep steps going down from the attic before he began to descend them.

"Do be careful, Jonathan," his mother said from below.

He paused to make sure of his footing.

"I wouldn't want anything to happen to that chest," she continued.

He chuckled. "And here I thought you were concerned for *my* safety. No, it is the safety of this chest that concerns you," he said as he reached the bottom.

His mother laughed. "Your bones are not nearly as fragile as a one-hundred-year-old chest."

He started down the next flight of stairs with his mother following as quickly as her bad knees would allow. His mother had always been a well-padded woman. Sadly, age, and perhaps a little too much added weight, made walking difficult for her. "I suppose you are right. I have never broken a bone, and this chest looks like it's ready to collapse in on itself."

"Oh, no! Do not say so," his mother said, sounding truly worried.

"Well, all right, perhaps it's not quite that bad, but mold is definitely growing on the sides and most likely the bottom as well. I shall have to see if there is a leak in the roof."

"Oh dear, I certainly hope not." She then called out, "Robert, is the door to my sitting room open?"

"Yes, my lady," the footman called back.

Jonathan, or Ox, as most everybody called him except for his mother, carried the chest into the room and set it down carefully next to the settee.

His mother hurried in after him. He took out his handkerchief and was wiping the cobwebs and mold from his hands when she said, "Hmm, no. I've changed my mind. Robert, can you take it into my bedchamber? I think it would be better to go through it there."

The footman, nearly as tall as Ox and quite broad in the shoulder, situated himself in front of the trunk so he could lift it up. But the thing didn't budge. The man stood up and tried to lift just one handle, perhaps to drag it into the other room, but he could barely lift it an inch off the floor.

Laughing, Ox pocketed his handkerchief and lifted the chest once again to take it into his mother's bedroom. He could hear her chuckle and say consolingly to the footman, "It's all right, Robert. There are few men as strong as his lordship."

"Yes, my lady. It is quite, er, remarkable," he said tactfully.

Unnatural was what many had called him, but he rather liked *remarkable*. Ox had earned his nickname not because he was stubborn or bullheaded, but due to his size. He'd always towered over all the other boys in school and had the strength of a full-grown man by the time he was eleven—and it had only increased from there.

"I beg your pardon, my lord," said Andrews, their butler, stepping into the open doorway.

Ox put down the trunk once again, this time at the foot of his mother's bed. He looked toward the man as he straightened up.

"The Duke of Drayton is here, sir. I've shown him into your study."

CHAPTER TWO

Ox started to nod and then stopped. His study? Had he closed the door to his studio? He didn't think so. He'd been in there when his mother had requested he come to carry the chest down. "Excuse me," he said to his mother as he bolted from the room. The butler jumped out of his way, and he took the steps down to the ground floor two at a time.

"Drayton!" Ox said, bursting into his study.

"My God! I thought there was a stampede for a moment. It sounded like an entire herd of cattle was coming down the stairs. Was that you?" said Ox's closest friend, from the time they were boys together at Eton. He stood at the side table, clearly about to help himself to a glass of brandy, the decanter in one hand, its top in the other.

"I do beg your pardon," Ox said, coming forward. "I was, er, excited to hear that you'd come to visit." He put his arms around the other man's shoulders and gave him a pat on his back in a friendly manner as he gave the door to his studio a push with his other hand to close it. A moment later, there was a soft click of the latch catching just as Dray extricated himself from Ox's embrace.

"Now, I say! Er, happy to see you and all that, but..." Dray protested. He went back to pouring himself a drink.

"Sorry. It's just been so long," Ox said, trying to think quickly.

The other man looked at him sideways as he started to pour another glass for Ox. "We saw each other at Parliament last week.

"Was it really only a week ago? It somehow feels like a great deal longer." Ox accepted the glass and then gestured for Dray to take a seat in front of the fire. It might have been mid-April, but there was still a chill to the air.

"What have you been up to? You're covered in... what is that, cobwebs?" Dray, always fastidiously dressed, peered at Ox's sleeve.

He quickly brushed it off. "My mother asked me to bring a chest down from the attic for her."

"Ah. Does that also explain the odd smell?" Dray lifted his nose into the air and gave a sniff. "It seems to be gone now, but it smelled like turpentine."

"It must be," Ox lied. Surreptitiously, he glanced over at the door to his studio to ensure that it was, in fact, closed. The small room with a large window facing the garden had probably been intended to be an office for a secretary, but he had no need of one, and he loved the light that streamed in all morning long. "Well, my friend, tell me what has been happening with you," Ox said as he sat in the chair opposite the one Dray had taken.

"Ah! Exciting news. That's what I came to tell you." Dray sat forward in his chair and lifted his glass. "A toast, if you please."

Ox dutifully lifted his glass. "To?"

"Me! I am getting married!" Dray took a sip of the brandy in his glass, but Ox just lowered his.

"Married? To whom? When?"

"Oh, I don't know the particulars yet. Have to find the girl who will have me first, you know." Dray chuckled and sat back.

"Ah." Ox breathed a sigh of relief. "Then you are going to look for a wife this Season."

"Yes, that's it. Precisely."

"Your sister finally twisted your arm hard enough?" Ox asked with a little laugh.

Dray nodded. "Pointed out that as it now stands, Cousin Alfred is my heir." He looked up from his drink and added, "No one likes Cousin Alfred."

Ox nodded, still chuckling as he took a sip of his own drink. "I see."

"So, will you help me?"

Ox's gaze snapped to Dray. "Help you?"

"Yes. Help me find a wife," Dray clarified.

"You cannot possibly think I know the first thing about such business, my boy," Ox protested.

"Well, damned if <I>I</I> do!"

Ox sighed. "What sort of girl do you like?"

"Er, the female kind?" Dray tried.

Ox said nothing.

"Yes, yes, I know," Dray said quickly. "But that's the thing. I don't know."

Ox thought for a moment. "Well then, I suppose you'll just have to meet as many as you can to figure that out," he finally said with a shrug. "And I assure you, once word gets out that the Duke of Drayton is looking for a wife, you will have no issue in meeting quite a few."

Dray ran a hand through his dark-brown hair, ruffling the straight locks so they stood at odd angles. If he only knew what he'd done, he'd be horrified. "I'm going to be swarmed, aren't I?"

"Oh, yes!" Ox chuckled. "Better you than me."

Rebecca looked across the table at Lady Malton. "Would you care for another scone?" she asked politely.

"Thank you, no. They are quite delicious, though. You must have an excellent cook."

The lady was the wife of one of the twenty-eight Irish representatives to the British Parliament. Rebecca knew well what that was like. Her own husband had been one of the first elected. He'd been so proud to represent his homeland, and Rebecca had been thrilled at the prospect of living in London. Dublin was a fine place to live, but nothing could compare with the excitement of London and English society.

"I have been most fortunate," Rebecca agreed. "More tea?" she offered, lifting the teapot.

"Yes, thank you." Lady Malton handed over her teacup. "I am so pleased to hear that you are enjoying yourself here in London, but honestly, I can't imagine how you can suffer through the parties of the *ton*. They are always such crowded affairs."

Rebecca gave a little shrug. "I enjoy meeting people. And yes, they are crowded, but I don't mind. Are you not missing society?"

"No. Even in Dublin, we lived a quiet life," the lady admitted. "Are you still in touch with anyone there?"

"Only my family," Rebecca admitted. She'd never quite fit in with society in Dublin. She didn't know why that was.

Lady Malton nodded. "It's good to maintain family ties, even from a distance. They aren't encouraging you to remarry, now, are they?"

"No, not at all. They know that I'm very happy living as I am."

"So, you have no intention of remarrying?" the woman asked curiously.

"My husband's only been gone for two years, and still I miss him every day," Rebecca told her.

"I'm sure, but you don't feel the need?"

"For a husband? No, not at all."

"But then, what do you do with your time, aside from going to these parties?" the woman asked. "You have no children, and such a small household can't take much to keep it running smoothly."

Rebecca gave a little laugh, but she had the suspicion that her brother-in-law, Eoin, had put Lady Malton up to this. He'd probably written to Lord Malton to find out what Rebecca was doing and, more importantly, when she was going to remarry. It wasn't that she was too much of a responsibility for her brother-in-law. He gave her only a very small quarterly allowance, but still, she was here and continued to carry the title. Eoin was now the Earl of Preston, but perhaps he was thinking of marriage himself. She imagined he believed it would be easier for him to find a wife if Rebecca were remarried.

"I have my studies and my hobbies." Rebecca found that she'd crumbled her own scone into little bits on her plate. She wiped the crumbs off her fingers with her handkerchief.

"Oh, yes. I've heard you dabble in... what is it? Not witchcraft, but something like it."

Rebecca bristled. "Astrology has nothing at all to do with witchcraft," she stated with a little more force than she probably should have. She refolded the handkerchief into a tiny square.

"Astrology, right, that was it."

"Yes. It is a noble science, and one that has been studied by the ancient Greeks and even as far back as the ancient Israelites."

The woman reared back as if Rebecca had hit her. "You… you…"

"I read Greek, Hebrew, and a bit of Aramaic. There have been a good number of writings that come from India, but I'm afraid those languages are simply beyond me. It would take a great deal of study to be able to read and understand them." Rebecca went on, knowing full well that the more she spoke of her studies, the more repulsed Lady Malton became. It tickled her to see this, but she reprimanded herself; she really shouldn't tease the woman so—not that anything she'd said wasn't true, but still.

"I… I see," Lady Malton said. "So, you've not found a gentleman who shares this… this uncommon interest with you? I must admit that I'm not surprised."

"It is an unusual hobby," Rebecca admitted. "My dearest Preston enjoyed it as well. But then, anything with an intellectual bent fascinated him. Anything that involved learning a new language or something of the sort."

"Yes, I remember. He was an odd one, wasn't he?"

"I don't believe I'd call him odd," Rebecca protested.

"Oh, no! I didn't mean… I would never speak ill of the dead," Lady Malton said quickly. "Er, oh, look at the time." She stood. "Thank you ever so much for tea, Lady Preston."

Rebecca led the way to the door. "Of course, it was my pleasure." She opened it to allow Lady Malton to leave, but as the woman passed her, she couldn't help herself. "Do give my regards to my brother-in-law when you write to him." The woman looked back with such a startled, guilty expression that Rebecca didn't hold back but allowed herself to burst out laughing. She was still giggling when she closed the door and started toward her study.

Uncle Lawrence strolled into the drawing room the following day, where Aunt Lily was writing a letter and Clarissa was working on her embroidery.

"I'm off to my club, my dear," he said.

"Ah, I shall be leaving very soon myself," Aunt Lily replied.

"Excellent. Going to introduce Clarissa about? So glad to hear it," he replied with an approving smile.

Aunt Lily's eyes snapped to Clarissa, but the frown on her face told her that she hadn't been thinking of doing that at all. "Well, I..." Aunt Lily hedged.

"It's so wonderful of you to see to the girl. And you know, the sooner she meets more people, the more likely it is she'll find just the right gentleman to marry," Uncle Lawrence added. Was that a calculating look in his eye? Clarissa wondered.

"Of course, my lord. You are absolutely correct." Aunt Lily turned toward Clarissa. "Go and change into a more suitable gown for visiting, Clarissa—one of the new ones we received from the modiste yesterday."

Clarissa immediately set aside her sewing and went to do so. As she passed her uncle on her way out the door, he gave her a little wink. She was hard-pressed not to giggle. He knew exactly how to get Aunt Lily to do what he wanted.

Forty-five minutes later, they were shown into Viscountess Pemberton's drawing room.

"Ah, Lady Morley, how lovely to see you this afternoon," the lady said, greeting them.

"And you, my lady," Aunt Lily said with a little curtsy. "And may I present my niece, Miss Clarissa Ellison?"

"Of course. It is delightful to make your acquaintance. Are you making your debut this Season, Miss Ellison?" Lady Pemberton asked.

"I am, my lady," Clarissa answered after curtsying to the lady.

"Well, in that case, you will certainly want to speak with my daughter Eloisa. She is just there speaking with Miss Ricketts." The lady pointed to two girls, one with dark blonde hair, one whose hair looked like spun gold. "Come, I will introduce you."

"You are very kind, my lady," Clarissa murmured as she followed the lady to the girls.

"Eloisa, Miss Ricketts, may I present Clarissa Ellison? She will be making her debut this year. I'm certain you'll make her feel welcome." The lady gave both girls a commanding smile.

"Of course, Mother," the girl with the darker hair said. She then motioned for Clarissa to sit next to her on the sofa.

"Thank you. It is very kind of you," Clarissa said as she took a seat. "Are you also making your debuts?" she asked the two girls.

They looked at each other, as if they found her question amusing.

"No, Miss Ellison, we were both introduced to society last year," Miss Ricketts told her.

"Oh, well, that is fortunate for me, I suppose. Perhaps you can give me some advice on how to proceed. I am new to London, you see, and am not quite sure how to go on."

"Of course! We would be more than happy to do so," Miss Pemberton replied. "Have you been to any parties yet?"

"No, I've only been in Town a little over a week, and we're still waiting for most of my gowns to be delivered by the modiste. I believe I will be receiving one of the ball gowns either today or tomorrow. My aunt insisted on one being made as quickly as possible."

"Is your modiste not to call upon you to for the final fitting?" Miss Ricketts asked with a slight frown.

"Er, no. We went to her. She has a shop on Bond Street," Clarissa answered. She'd never thought that a modiste would come to her.

"Oh," Miss Ricketts replied, as if she found the concept alien to her.

Chapter Three

"Well, in any case," Miss Pemberton continued, "I do hope you will be attending Lady Midton's ball. It will be the first of the Season, and positively everyone will be there.

"I do believe we have received an invitation and are planning on going," Clarissa replied, trying to remember the list of parties her aunt had informed her they'd be attending.

"Yes, Lady Midton is very generous and extends invitations to just about everybody," Miss Ricketts replied.

Clarissa wondered if that was meant to be an insult, but since she didn't even know who Clarissa was or who she was connected to, why would she deliberately be mean? No, Miss Ricketts must have meant it innocently.

"I am looking forward to seeing who among the gentlemen will be looking out for a wife this year," Miss Pemberton commented.

Miss Ricketts leaned forward and said quietly, "I hear the Duke of Drayton will be looking for a wife."

"No! Wherever did you hear that?" Miss Pemberton answered, as if this was the most exciting news she'd ever heard.

"My maid heard it from her cousin whose good friend works for him."

"My goodness," Clarissa said, nearly laughing. She held it back only because the girl seemed so very serious, and even a little smug at having obtained her information in this way.

"You will soon learn, Miss Ellison, that the servants have all the best gossip," Miss Pemberton informed Clarissa.

"If you don't hear it from Lady Findlater or Lady Wrexley," Miss Ricketts agreed.

"Yes, of course," Miss Pemberton said.

"I have yet to meet these ladies," Clarissa commented. "But it sounds as if I should be careful what I say around them. Are they terrible gossips?"

"Oh, ye—" Miss Pemberton started, but Miss Ricketts cut her off.

"No, not at all! They are simply very well-known by absolutely everyone in society. They are, indeed, probably the most trusted ladies."

Miss Pemberton frowned at her friend, and Clarissa had the feeling she was being teased.

She glanced away to hide her expression of annoyance and happened to notice a girl standing off near the wall all by herself. She was tall, like Clarissa, but plump where Clarissa was slender and much more shapely. Clarissa looked back to Miss Pemberton. "Who is that?" she asked, nodding toward the girl.

"That is nobody," Miss Ricketts answered immediately.

"It's Miss Buttery-Clements," Miss Pemberton said at the same time.

"Why is she there—" Clarissa started.

"We do not speak with her," Miss Ricketts informed Clarissa.

"We do not?" she asked, looking at Miss Pemberton for confirmation.

The girl just kept her eyes lowered.

"Well, if you do not, I shall," Clarissa said, standing.

"If you do, you will in all likelihood destroy your reputation before you've even had the opportunity to establish one. On the other hand, if you would like the best reputation, to be seen with the best people, you will stay right where you are," Miss Ricketts said with an unmistakable hint of command in her voice.

"Ah, well, I suppose I'll just have to take the chance. If you'll excuse me." Clarissa hated girls like Miss Ricketts, she decided. Miss Pemberton was only guilty by association. Clarissa wouldn't make any judgment about her yet.

She strode up to Miss Buttery-Clements. "I am Clarissa Ellison," she said, holding out her hand. The girl stared at it for a moment before taking it in her own for the briefest moment.

"I'm Katherine Buttery-Clements," she said in a near whisper. "Are you certain you wish to be speaking to me?"

"Of course! Why wouldn't I?" Clarissa asked with a tilt of her head.

The girl lifted one shoulder. "Only because you were just speaking with Miss Ricketts. She, er, doesn't like me very much."

"To be honest, I'm not entirely certain I like her," Clarissa said quietly.

The girl's round face immediately brightened into a smile, her blue eyes dancing with mirth. "You shouldn't say that too loudly. Miss Ricketts is quite well-known in Society."

"Is she? Then how is it that she hasn't found a husband yet? I understand this will be her second Season."

The girl's eyes widened as she stared at Clarissa. "I... I don't know. From what I've heard, she was considered a diamond of the first water. I'm certain she received quite a number of proposals."

Clarissa lifted her eyebrows. "Are you certain? I have the feeling that gentlemen may have found her quite pretty on the outside, but perhaps not so on the inside."

Miss Buttery-Clements's eyes laughed, but she somehow managed to keep her expression neutral. "You should not say such a thing, I'm sure."

"I'm certain you're right. I've only known Miss Ricketts for about fifteen minutes. My apologies, Miss Buttery-Clements."

"Oh, don't apologize to me! I happen to agree with you, but you should not *say* so. Or at least, you should be careful who you say it to," the girl clarified.

"Ah, I see. Thank you for the warning. I am new to all this, you see, and I fear I have a lot to learn."

Ox had a love-hate relationship with parties. He loved being social, and where better to meet members of the *ton* than at a party? On the other hand, he refused to dance. It wasn't that he didn't know how—it was that he was too large and too heavy. If he were to accidentally step on a lady's foot, it would break into a hundred pieces. He couldn't risk hurting anyone, and he didn't have enough confidence in his dancing ability to take the risk.

Dancing was one of the preeminent activities at a party.

"You have to go, Ox." Dray's voice had nearly become a whine.

They'd been sitting at their club, Powell's Exclusive Club for Gentlemen of Refinement, sipping ale and alternating between chatting and reading the papers that were scattered about the Reading Room. It was a pastime they'd enjoyed doing together for the past few years whenever they were both in Town.

"But I don't dance," he reminded his friend.

"Then don't ask anyone."

"At a ball?" Ox looked at Dray as if he'd lost his mind.

"Forget that it's a ball. Ox, I need you!" Dray was beginning to sound desperate.

"For all that is holy, why?" Ox nearly exploded. He hated the fact that he couldn't just go to a ball like any other fellow and enjoy himself. Speaking with people, meeting new people, it was one of life's joys.

"Because I've got to find a wife. As soon as it gets around, I'm going to be surrounded."

The picture in Ox's mind made him laugh. "You're going to drown in young ladies and their mamas."

Dray dropped his head into his hands. "Please, Ox."

Ox sighed. "Very well. I'll go."

Dray perked up immediately, lifting his head and smiling at him. "You go before me and scope out the territory. I'll join you maybe a half an hour later, and you can give me the lay of the land."

"This isn't a battle, Dray," Ox said, chuckling.

"Oh, but it is. I am absolutely certain it is."

That evening, Ox strolled as casually as he could through the ballroom Lady Midton had rented for the occasion to celebrate the start of another Season. He nodded to a few gentlemen he knew from his club who were huddling together, probably for a respite from the ladies.

He caught sight of Lady Lonsdale. Her daughter had married a few years ago, and he didn't think she had another. But she was speaking to Lady Debenham, who had a daughter of marriageable age. Yes, she was standing just there, partly behind her intimidating mother. She looked pretty enough, with her brown hair pulled up into some complicated coiffure and wearing a demure gown of pale pink with roses embroidered along the neckline. Her silk gloves had matching roses embroidered along the top of them, just past her elbow.

Ox stopped before the three women. "Good evening," he said, bowing to them all.

"Oh, good evening, my lord. How surprising to see you here," Lady Lonsdale said, holding out her hand for him to kiss. "I don't believe I've ever seen you at a ball before."

He saw Lady Debenham's daughter staring up at him, her mouth hanging open a touch. He ignored it and kept his eyes on the older ladies. "Well, I thought I'd see what I've been missing. Since it clearly includes meeting lovely ladies like you, I think you might be seeing me at more of these events in the future."

The two older ladies giggled, and Lady Debenham even snapped open her fan and waved it slowly in front of her.

"My lord, may I introduce my daughter, Miss Liza Lomax?" the lady asked.

"I would be delighted," Ox said, turning toward the young lady.

"Liza, this is the Earl of Uxbridge," she told her daughter.

The girl curtsied, mumbling, "It's a pleasure to meet you, my lord."

"Are you enjoying the ball, Miss Lomax?" he asked.

"I, er, yes, my lord," she said quietly.

"Excellent. And, er, have you been in London long?"

"No, my lord, for a month only," she said. He practically had to bend down to hear her. She was clearly terrified of him. He could practically see her hands shaking, and she had become quite pale. Was she merely scared of his size or the possibility that he might ask her to dance? In either case, he would not impose himself on her any further.

"I see. Well, I do hope that you enjoy the rest of your evening. It was very nice meeting you." He gave her a slight bow and a deeper one to the ladies. "A good evening to you all."

He continued on his way. No, she wouldn't do at all. Dray needed a duchess, not a mouse.

He found a spot near a potted plant, not too far from the wallflowers, from where he could look around and watch the people of the beau monde doing what they did best—having fun.

The first ball of the Season was always an exciting event. So many people returned to Town from a winter of relaxation, holidays, and planning for the coming Season.

New faces mixed in with the familiar. There were girls in their first Season filled with equal parts excitement and trepidation, and their mothers anxious and hopeful. Young ladies in their second or third Season were worried they would be outshone by the newcomers but still hopeful they could make a good match. And, of course, there were the well-established members of Society, like Rebecca, simply here to watch with amusement and, of course, to see old friends.

Rebecca sighed happily.

As her eyes scanned the assembled beautiful people of Society, her gaze landed on one gentleman in particular. Of course, he was hard to miss, being without a doubt the largest person in the room.

The Earl of Uxbridge, standing at least six feet and three inches tall, towered over nearly every other man in the ballroom. His height was balanced by his powerful shoulders and arms, currently encased in a coat of black wool, and his long legs in black trousers which did nothing to hide his well-defined calves. His blond hair was cut stylishly, and his pale green eyes were scanning the crowd very much like Rebecca's. But while she was standing at the edge of the dance floor, Ox—as the earl was known to his friends—was standing with his back to the wall, just next to an arrangement of potted greenery.

It was usually the shy young ladies who were to be found in such a position, but Ox had clearly displaced them. They were standing a few feet away, every now and then peering curiously at the enormous man.

As she stood there looking at her friend, Rebecca's mind wandered back to the young lady she'd met the previous week at the bookshop. Her fingers began to tingle, and her feet moved almost of their own volition—heading straight for Ox.

"Good evening, my lord," she said as she approached him.

He turned and his face lit up, making the handsome man practically glow with joy. "Lady Preston." He took her outstretched hand and bowed over it. "How wonderful to see you again. I do hope you have been keeping well?"

"I have indeed. And you? Did you have a good winter?"

He gave a brief nod. "It is always, er, interesting to return to my estate."

Rebecca gave a little laugh. "Oh dear. That doesn't sound very good."

He smiled. "No, no, it's fine. It's just that no matter how diligently I work on estate matters during the Season, there always seems to be so much more that needs to be done."

"Ah, yes. I understand."

He gave a little shrug. "That is not to say I don't enjoy being home. Indeed, I do. And I even find some satisfaction in seeing the fruits of not only my labor, but all who work there. I, certainly, could never claim even a small portion of the accolades, due to an estate as well run and productive as mine."

"Well, I am happy to hear things are going well," she said.

"They are indeed."

"And so, with such happy news, can I ask you a question?"

His smile wavered a bit as his face took on a wary expression. "You're going to ask whether I plan to find a wife this Season, aren't you?"

She laughed and shook her head. "You know me very well, indeed, my lord. But in fact, I was merely going to ask you to remind me of your astrological sign."

"Oh!" he said, surprised at the turn in conversation. "I do believe you determined that I was a Gemini," he told her.

"Ah, yes, er, born in June if I'm not mistaken."

He nodded.

"You do enjoy a social gathering and experiencing new things, is that not right?"

He nodded again, this time even more warily. "Are you going to have me experience something new this evening? Perhaps in the form of a young lady?"

Rebecca burst out laughing. "Oh, how you *do* know me well!"

He chuckled. "Lady Preston, how many young ladies have you attempted to introduce to me?"

"Oh, I don't know. Quite a number, I imagine," she admitted.

"And do you see me married this evening?"

"Alas, I do not. But that doesn't mean you might not change your mind if you were to meet the right girl."

"It is highly unlikely. But, say—I could probably use your assistance with my good friend Drayton. He is looking for a wife this year," he told her.

He was clearly trying to distract her, but it wasn't going to work. "That is excellent news. However, there is a young lady I'd like *you* to meet. She is new to Town and—"

"Looking for a husband," he finished for her.

"Well, yes. But aside from that, she is in need of friends," Rebecca finished, knowing there was nothing a Gemini liked better than making new friends.

To her joy, Ox did raise his eyebrows at that.

"Come, allow me to introduce you, and perhaps you may ask her to dance."

"You know very well that I do not dance," he reminded her.

"Oh, well, a walk around the ballroom, in that case," she suggested, taking his arm. She led him toward the spot where she had seen Miss Ellison standing, looking about the room with wide eyes.

Chapter Four

Clarissa scanned the ballroom in fascination. There were so many beautiful people and such a show of wealth Clarissa had never imagined possible. And here she was, amongst these happy, rich people in her brand-new ball gown.

She had no idea how much her uncle had paid for the dress. Money was not discussed at the modiste's. Clarissa had tried asking, but her aunt had stopped her with a glare and the sharp words, "Don't be vulgar." So, Clarissa could only guess, and what she figured was that it cost enough to clothe all her siblings for a good long while—although maybe not Frederick. At 14, he had suddenly started growing like a weed.

Looking around the room, she saw so many other young ladies making their debut. They were easy to spot—they either looked around wide-eyed like she was doing, or they looked terrified. But they, she thought bitterly, probably didn't have their entire family relying on them to make an advantageous match. If Clarissa couldn't find a wealthy gentleman to marry, her brothers would never go to school, and her sisters would never have the opportunity to make matches of their own. Her father would continue to rule his house with an iron fist, which held all the resources they all needed, and not let so much as a penny escape from it.

With an internal shake of her head and a lift of her chin, she decided there was no point in worrying about not making a match until later—much later. She had the entire Season ahead of her. She was intelligent, passably pretty, and from a good family. Surely a good number of gentlemen wouldn't care that she had a tiny dowry. There had to be wealthy gentlemen and those who wouldn't mind that marrying her meant getting not just a wife, but an entire family.

Clarissa's shoulders sagged. She was deluding herself if she thought she could find someone like that. However, perhaps she would meet a man who wouldn't care how she spent his money and would be able to turn a blind eye to all her siblings. Yes, there had to be a gentleman like that here.

"Well, it looks as if you will have your work cut out for you, Clarissa," her aunt said, her gaze wandering the ballroom.

Clarissa could feel her blood begin to rush through her veins in excitement at the implied challenge. There was nothing she liked better than a competition. She always rose to the opportunity, and losing was simply not something she did.

"In what way, my lady?" Clarissa asked as mildly as she could.

"Just look around, girl. A great number of young ladies here are prettier than you and with dowries much, much larger than yours," her aunt said. Clarissa knew she was just trying to dissuade her from continuing with this nearly impossible task. She knew her Aunt Lily wanted nothing more than for Clarissa to slink back to her father's estate and leave her to enjoy herself with her friends.

"Yes," Clarissa agreed, "however, there are also a good number of gentlemen who, I'm certain, do not care so much for a girl's dowry as he does for her intelligence and excellent skills in economy."

Her aunt huffed a laugh. "Well, if you didn't have the latter, I would be shocked, considering what a miser your father is."

"My father is simply attempting to refill the family's coffers," Clarissa said defensively.

"From the destruction your—"

"Miss Ellison," a kind voice interrupted Aunt Lily.

Clarissa turned and found the kind lady she'd met at the bookshop approaching her with a very tall, handsome gentleman on her arm. Clarissa smiled at her newfound friend and then even wider when she noticed her aunt's expression of surprise.

"Lady Preston, how lovely to see you again. May I introduce my aunt to you?" Clarissa asked, remembering the etiquette books she'd spent hours poring over. She had looked up Lady Preston in her aunt's copy of Burke's Peerage and discovered that she was a countess and, therefore, a higher rank than her aunt, who was merely a baroness. One always introduced a person of lower rank to one of higher rank.

Lady Preston nodded and turned toward Aunt Lily as Clarissa made the introduction. "Lady Preston, my aunt, Baroness Morley. Aunt Lily, this is the Countess of Preston who I met at the bookshop last week."

Lady Preston nodded while Aunt Lily gave a little curtsy.

"What a pleasure to meet you, Lady Morley. You must be so happy to have your niece visiting for the Season," Lady Preston said.

Aunt Lily gave a polite smile. "Indeed."

Clarissa nearly laughed.

"And may I present my good friend, the Earl of Uxbridge?" At Aunt Lily's nod, she continued, "My lord, Lady Morley and Miss Clarissa Ellison."

Clarissa curtsied. "It is a pleasure, my lord," she said quietly. She noticed that he was reaching out for her hand and quickly proffered it.

He placed a feather-light kiss on the back of her gloved knuckles. "The pleasure is mine," he said, his deep voice a rumble that seemed to pass straight through Clarissa's heart.

"Madam," he said, turning to Aunt Lily. He nodded politely while Clarissa's aunt curtsied again. "Might I have the honor of escorting your niece on a promenade about the room?"

"Oh! Of course, my lord," Aunt Lily said, her voice coming out at a much higher pitch than normal. "I'm certain she will be delighted."

He turned to look for confirmation of this from Clarissa—something which she appreciated a great deal since, according to her books, he didn't need to, as her aunt had just given her permission.

Clarissa curtsied and then lightly placed her fingers on his outstretched arm. It was such a lovely change to accompany a gentleman taller than she. Sadly, Clarissa had inherited her father's height and stood nearly as tall as most of the gentlemen in the room. But this man was probably half a foot taller than she was.

She looked up at him with a smile as he led her away.

Miss Ellison's touch was lighter than that of a butterfly. He could barely feel her hand as it rested on his arm. She was delightfully tall, but so thin she looked like would break if he just looked at her strongly.

"Lady Preston tells me you are new to Town," he began as they sauntered away.

"Yes." Her answer was precise and short. She seemed to realize that more was required of her, so she added, "I have never been to London before. Have you lived here long?"

He smiled at her naiveté. "I stay here if Parliament meets in the autumn and for the Season. Otherwise, I live at my estate. It's about two hours from London."

"Oh! Of course." Her cheeks took on a pretty rosy hue.

"Lady Preston also mentioned you were in need of friends," he said as gently as he could.

The girl's cheeks pinkened further, but she sighed. "Yes, I suppose she's right. I really don't know anyone—aside from Lady Preston and my aunt. I did meet a few young ladies the other day, but only with one of them would I wish to form a friendship."

"I see," Ox said. He smiled at her. "But I can see now why Lady Preston felt you needed friends."

"Yes," she said softly.

"Well, I am more than happy to be one of the very many friends you are bound to make during your time here."

"Thank you, that is very kind of you." Before she had even finished her sentence, her head was turned by a small crowd gathering near the entrance to the room.

"Ah, that must be a friend of mine," Ox said with a chuckle.

Her gaze snapped back to Ox.

He could barely contain his laugh. "I am good friends with the Duke of Drayton. He always gathers a crowd like that when he enters a party. And it is even worse this year because he has made it known that he is looking for a wife."

"Oh, yes. Miss Ricketts told me this. I have to admit I didn't understand the implication then, but now..." She turned back to look at the crowd.

"He is quite the catch, as you can imagine," Ox explained.

She nodded absently, still watching the crowd of young ladies and their mamas who had swarmed Dray. "So, he is the one to win," she said almost thoughtfully.

"Oh, indeed," Ox agreed. She could hardly take her eyes from the crowd—it was impossible to see Dray, himself, for all the women around him. "I say, would you care to meet him?"

The girl's mouth dropped open a touch, but she quickly snapped it closed again. "I would indeed, that is... would it be..."

"It's quite all right. Despite Lady Preston's hopes, I am not looking for a wife, and since my friend is, I am more than happy to make things easier for him and help you in the process as well."

"You are too kind, sir—er, my lord," she quickly corrected.

"Come along. Let's see if we can't part the waters without stepping on any toes." It sounded as if he were funning, but in truth he was terrified of doing just that.

Clarissa couldn't believe her good luck! Lord Uxbridge, aside from being an incredibly kind and thoughtful gentleman, knew the man who was clearly the biggest catch in the marriage mart. In moments, she will have gone from knowing no gentlemen to knowing—and being known by—the two most handsome gentlemen of the *ton*. They were clearly the most sought-after, as well, judging by the fact that heads turned nearly every time Lord Uxbridge passed someone and, of course, the enormous number of young women who had surrounded the duke the moment he'd walked into the room.

An earl and a duke! And Aunt Lily had said she'd be lucky to attract a knight or a baronet.

But then it hit Clarissa like a cricket bat to her head—she had no idea how to attract a duke, nor even an earl, even though he'd clearly stated he was not looking for a wife. A man could surely be persuaded otherwise, couldn't he?

And here they were, Clarissa and Lord Uxbridge heading straight toward the Duke of Drayton. Clarissa's pace slowed as thoughts and fears inundated her until she finally stopped not twenty feet from the crowd surrounding the duke.

"Miss Ellison?" Lord Uxbridge asked as she pulled him to a halt. "Is everything all right?"

She looked up into his green eyes, so filled at the moment with concern for her. Oddly, she was struck once again by how tall this man was. She actually had to look up at him despite how tall she was, herself. It gave her a warm feeling, as if he were there to protect her, and goodness knew she needed protecting just now. And help.

"I... I don't know the rules of this game," she told him honestly.

One side of his lips quirked up. "Game?"

She nodded. "How to win a gentleman's interest. How to make him want to propose. How to win the marriage game."

He tilted his head in curiosity. "Is this just a game to you?"

"It's not *just* a game. It's a very serious game. A life-changing game. And I don't know the rules. I don't know what strategy to adopt to win."

He looked at her with renewed interest. "What a fascinating way to look at it. Has your aunt not proffered any advice?"

Clarissa nearly laughed at the thought. "My aunt only wants to help me find a husband in order to get me out of her life, but she wants to do so with as little effort on her part as possible."

Lord Uxbridge drew his eyebrows down over his deep-set eyes. "So, not the most helpful or concerned relation."

Clarissa shook her head. "She is only sponsoring me because my uncle is forcing her to. It is my uncle who is the true relation. He was my mother's younger brother."

"*Was* your mother's...?" he asked hesitantly.

"She died in childbirth two years ago."

"I am sorry."

"Thank you. But now you understand how difficult this is. I've got no one to teach me how to play." She felt nearly ashamed to admit as much to this gentleman, but there was just something that made her trust him.

She was relieved when his face lit up into a smile again. He took her hand in his own large one. "I would be more than happy to teach you how to attract a gentleman or, at least, how to get Dray interested since, naturally, every man is different."

Clarissa breathed a sigh of relief. "Thank you, my lord. You are so kind and understanding."

He smiled. "Well, don't thank me yet. I haven't even introduced you."

"No, but I have a great deal more confidence now that I know you're on my team."

This made him laugh. "I do like the way you think, Miss Ellison."

She turned to face the throng still surrounding the duke. "So, what is the strategy here?"

Lord Uxbridge, too, looked over at his friend. As he did so, a worried expression covered his face. "I think you need to wait here while I extricate Dray from those women. I will bring him over, introduce you, and he will, in all likelihood, ask you to dance."

Clarissa nodded. "And then?"

He looked at her blankly for a moment. "And then you treat him as you would any other gentleman. Be amusing and charming." He gave a little shrug. "Just be yourself."

Clarissa was about to protest that she was neither amusing nor charming, but the man was already striding toward the duke. Well, she supposed she would simply have to do the best she could.

Chapter Five

Much later that evening, Ox sat in companionable silence with Dray in the Reading Room at Powell's. Ox was sipping on a glass of the club's famous rum. Dray had gone for something with a little more potency and was enjoying a good Scottish whiskey.

"Any prospects this evening, old man?" Ox asked after watching Dray's expression for a few minutes.

"Eh? Oh, er, yes, I suppose so." Dray took another sip of his whiskey. "Say, who was that girl you introduced me to? Dashed fine dancer."

"Miss Ellison," Ox reminded him.

"Yes, that was it. Miss Ellison. Not my type really, but a sweet girl."

"Well, since I don't know what your type is—and I'm not entirely certain you do either—you might consider her. She seems to be quite lovely."

"Yes. Has excellent conversation," Dray said.

"I enjoyed speaking with her before I introduced you. In fact, it's *why* I introduced you."

"Right." Dray frowned a moment before taking another sip. "And where did you meet her?"

"Lady Preston introduced us," Ox told him.

"I see." He nodded. After a moment, he turned a smile onto Ox. "She's always trying to match you up with someone, isn't she?"

Ox could only sigh and nod his head. "I have told her time and time again I am not looking for a wife, but—"

"She ignores you, just like any good friend would. You really should, you know."

"Should ignore me?" Ox asked, wondering if either he or Dray had already had too much to drink.

The duke laughed. "No, should look for a wife."

"Oh! No, my friend. You and I both know very well that it wouldn't work at all."

Dray scowled at him. "Honestly, Ox. You aren't still afraid you might hurt someone."

"Women are darned delicate creatures," Ox said in his own defense. "And I am a big oaf. If I were even to accidentally step on a lady's toes, she wouldn't come away whole."

"Then don't step on her toes," Dray argued.

Ox just looked at him, his mouth set in a firm line.

"No, truly, Ox. I don't think you're as clumsy as you claim. I've seen you play cricket. You are as light on your feet as anyone and can catch and hit better than most."

"That's cricket, not dancing or... or..." He waved a hand. "Anything else one does with a woman."

Dray chuckled, understanding Ox's meaning, but then suddenly bolted upright. "Wait a minute! Do you mean to say you haven't... you don't..." He lowered his voice to a soft whisper. "You haven't slept with a woman?"

Ox could feel his cheeks burning. "Of course I have!" he protested immediately, but at the same volume as his friend. "But I was as gentle as I could be, and I, well, she..." He swallowed. "I insisted that she be on top. To make sure I didn't squish her, you know," he added.

Dray sat back, laughing. "I'm sure you wouldn't have. I mean, you don't need to put your weight on her at all. Hell, I'd probably squish a woman if I did that."

Ox just shrugged. While he had slept with a woman, it was precisely that—*a* woman, as in once. And she'd been a professional, so she'd known what she was doing—which was good, because Ox certainly hadn't. But he could tell that she'd been frightened of how big he was. She had commented on how broad his shoulders were (as she took off his shirt), how sturdy his legs were (as he'd lowered his breeches), how heavy he must be (when the bed had dipped with his weight as he'd lain down on it). In truth, she'd been the one to suggest their respective positions, and he had readily agreed. It had been one of the most embarrassing experiences of his life, and he hadn't repeated it.

"We weren't talking about women who I might marry, old man," Ox said, deliberately changing the topic. "We were discussing you. You said you were going to take a wife this year."

Dray nodded, not very happily. "I have to. The family is getting anxious about an heir."

"You're only twenty-nine!" Ox objected.

His friend shrugged. "Apparently, when my father was my age, he'd had not only my older sister, but me as well. Susan didn't come along till later."

Ox *harrumphed.* "Well then, you need to get to know some more young ladies."

"I'm trying!" Dray protested. "But they all swarm me so I can hardly have a word with anyone. And even when I've got just one who I'd like to speak with, her mother interrupts and speaks for the girl."

"It's not easy for you," Ox agreed. "How about if you arrange to take one out for a walk in the park?"

"We'd have twenty following us," Dray pointed out.

"A drive? In your high perch phaeton," Ox suggested.

Dray nodded at that. "Yes, that might work."

"And you can speak with her while you're dancing. No mothers there."

"Excellent idea! I like it." He slapped Ox on his shoulder. "That's why I have you as a friend, Uxbridge. Damned smart!"

Clarissa entered the breakfast room the following morning to find her aunt and uncle already at the table. She wasn't surprised to find her uncle there—he was an early riser—but she wondered what had made Aunt Lily pull herself from bed so early.

"Good morning," she greeted them both.

Her aunt didn't say anything, barely looking up from her cup of cocoa. Her uncle, meanwhile, lowered his paper and smiled at her. "Good morning to you, my dear."

Clarissa went to the sideboard, where there were hard-boiled eggs, ham, and toast. She helped herself and then sat down across from her aunt, on her uncle's other side.

"So, I have had your dear aunt's version of events from last night, but I would like to hear your opinion. How do you think it went?" her uncle asked as he set down his now folded paper.

"I think it went very well," Clarissa told him. "What is your opinion, Aunt?"

Aunt Lily stifled a yawn. "Oh, indeed! I still can't believe you managed to get an introduction to the Duke of Drayton."

"And a dance," Clarissa reminded her with a smile before she took a large bite of her toast, now smeared with butter and egg.

"And a dance," her aunt agreed. "Who else did you dance with? I cannot recall."

"Lord Portland and Lord Featherington," Clarissa reminded her.

"Oh, yes. Well, Lord Portland is poor as a church mouse, and Lord Featherington dances with everyone," her aunt said.

"But the duke!" her uncle pointed out.

His wife just gave him a disbelieving look. "Was a quirk of fate and nothing significant. He danced with a great many young ladies. I'm sure if Clarissa was to stand in front of him today, he would not be able to recall her name or, quite possibly, that you'd even met."

Clarissa could hardly believe her aunt's callousness and clearly her uncle couldn't either, for he immediately protested. "Oh, come now, my dear. I'm certain he would."

"Well, if he did, it would be because he has a good memory for names. Clarissa couldn't have made any sort of impression on him to begin with, and secondly, she is not the sort he is looking for. He is a duke for goodness' sake! Do be intelligent about this, Morley."

"What sort of girl do you think he is looking for?" Clarissa asked.

Her aunt turned toward her with an expression of boredom. She raised one finger in the air. "Someone who is pretty." She raised a second finger. "Someone from an excellent, titled family—yes, yes, your family is quite old, but your father is a viscount. I'm certain the duke will marry no one lower than the daughter of a marquess. And..." She raised a third finger. "Someone with a dowry whose family hasn't lost all their money."

Clarissa swallowed. Doing her best to keep her anger from showing in her voice, she responded, "It is not my father's fault the family fortune was lost. And why would a duke need to marry someone with a large dowry, anyway? I'm sure he's as rich as Croesus."

"Oh, I'm certain he is," her aunt agreed. "But he also wants to stay that way. A dowry would be important even to Croesus." She leaned forward a little. "Clarissa, lower your expectations. If you find a husband at all, it will be someone without a title, or if he has one, he will be of the lower nobility. If you think you can bring the duke up to scratch, we might as well confine you to Bedlam now." She gave a bark of laughter.

Clarissa's hand, sitting by the side of her plate, curled into a fist.

Her uncle must have noticed, for he gently patted it. "Now, now, my dear," he said. Clarissa wasn't certain if he was speaking to her or his wife since he was looking at both of them. "Clarissa is quite pretty," he began, speaking to Aunt Lily. He turned and looked at Clarissa. "But I agree, you should probably set your sights a bit lower than the duke."

Clarissa couldn't stand this any longer. She stood up. In her mind, she screamed, *Challenge accepted!* but had the intelligence not to say it out loud. Instead, she simply walked from the room.

It made life so much easier that Ox had chosen miniatures as his favorite form of painting. They were easier to carry, wrapped in a little tissue paper and tucked inside a small satchel, than large canvases would be.

He descended from his phaeton after reaching Gladwell's Art Gallery on Queen Street, leaving it with his groom. The shop sold only high-quality paintings and, therefore, was frequented by many in society. Going this early in the morning, however, he was certain not to run into anyone he knew.

"Ah, good morning, Lord Uxbridge," Mr. Gladwell, himself, greeted him.

"Good morning," Ox said, strolling up to the counter.

The man clapped his hands together and rubbed them greedily. "Do you have something for me today?"

"In fact, three things," Ox said. He pulled out the three small canvases he'd recently completed and laid them on the counter.

The man gingerly picked one up and unwrapped it. Blindly reaching for a magnifying glass while staring at the tiny painting, he made a humming sound in the back of his throat.

Mr. Gladwell held the glass in front of the painting, carefully inspecting Ox's work. His humming turned into an *ooh* and then, "Very nice, oh, very nice!" He finally looked up, smiling at Ox. "As always, my lord, your work is impeccable. How you manage to get such detail on a painting so small..." He just shook his head.

He put down the first painting and picked up the second.

"That is the stormy sea you asked for," Ox told him.

"Ooh, yes, I see, I see," Mr. Gladwell said, once more holding the glass up to the painting to see it better.

"And the third is a portrait of the Queen, which I thought might not be so difficult to sell. What do you think? Would you be interested in that as well?"

Gladwell unwrapped that one as well but didn't inspect it so closely. Instead, he merely glanced down at it lovingly, as if it were a child. "Oh, indeed, my lord, indeed. These are quite magnificent."

"Thank you." Ox gave a slight nod of his head.

As always, Mr. Gladwell looked up at him in wonder. "And to think such fine work comes from your hands. You are certain you are the one who painted these?" he teased.

Ox just smiled. "Do you have any other commissions you'd like me to carry out?"

"Ah, yes. I received one last week. Lord Roseberry would like a miniature of his family home."

Ox frowned. "Roseberry... Isn't his estate in the north?"

"Er, yes. North of York, I'm afraid."

Ox just shook his head. "I'm very sorry, I don't think—"

"Oh, but he said he had a larger painting of it that he would be willing to lend you. You could use that as a reference."

"So, he just wants a miniature of a larger painting?" Ox asked as the bell over the door rang behind him. He briefly glanced back to see who had entered the shop and then quickly turned back. *Blast it all!*

"Ox, is that you?" Dray asked, coming up beside him. "Ha! Well met, my friend."

Ox could do nothing but nod. "You are up and out early, Dray. What brings you here?"

Dray was staring down at the miniatures sitting on the counter. "I, er, wanted a painting, oddly enough." He picked up one of the Queen.

"I was just deciding—" Ox started.

"Do you sell these here? Your work is excellent," Dray said, interrupting him.

"What?"

Dray studied him. "Oh, don't play the innocent with me. I know you paint. I hadn't realized how good you were, though. This is exquisite."

"You knew?"

Dray looked at him in a funny way. "Ox, we've known each other since we were children. Shared a room in both school and at university. Of course I know!"

"But you never said anything!"

"Why should I? Every man is allowed his hobbies," Dray said with a shrug. He put down the painting and picked up the one of the stormy sea. "Can't say I like this one overmuch."

"It was done on commission," Mr. Gladwell put in. "A gentleman wanted it for his watch."

"Really?" Dray looked up at the man.

Mr. Gladwell shrugged. "I believe it has a glass cover, and he wanted that inserted behind the glass."

"How very unusual." Dray put the painting back down. He turned to Ox. "So, you do commissions?"

Ox cleared his throat. "Er, yes."

"Excellent! Then I'd like to hire you."

Now it was Ox's turn to look perplexed.

"I need a miniature done of my sister Louise. My brother-in-law is dicked in the knob and has bought a commission to fight on the Continent. I thought, as a going-away present, I'd give him a painting of the wife he's leaving behind."

"Oh, I can certainly do that," Ox said with a shrug.

"Brilliant. How much do you charge?"

Ox nearly choked. "Nothing! For you, I wouldn't—"

"Yes, you will. Otherwise, it will be a present from *you*, and I'd like it to be a present from me," Dray explained.

"Oh. Well then, how about a guinea?"

"You must charge more than that for these," Dray protested.

Ox just shrugged.

"I pay him anywhere from five to ten pounds, depending on how detailed the piece is," Mr. Gladwell offered.

"Good. Ten pounds it is." Dray put out his hand to shake on the deal.

Ox didn't see that he had very much choice in the matter. Dray could be stubborn at times, so he took his friend's hand. "Er, just so you know, whatever I earn from my paintings goes directly to Lord Welles, who then distributes the money to those in need."

"Do you? That's very good of you, but honestly, I don't care what you do with your money," his friend said.

"Well, I suppose not, but…"

"Don't worry, my friend, have no fear. I know you're not in desperate straits."

"Not in the least," Ox confirmed. "This is just a hobby."

"And one at which you excel. Just let me know when you can come over to begin, and I'll be sure Louise is there to sit for you." With that, he gave Gladwell a nod and left the shop.

Well, thought Ox, *that was both embarrassing and rather liberating.* His secret was now out in the open between him and Dray. And he had no concern whether his friend would keep his little secret—he had for the past ten years or more, even from Ox himself.

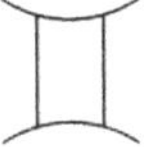

Chapter Six

Because of his early morning outing, Ox had missed his morning ritual with his mother. Every day after breakfast, they took their tea to the drawing room, where he went through the day's post, and they discussed the events of the day. Since she wasn't able to get out much because of her bad knees, she lived vicariously through him. He knew how important their mornings were to her, so he determined he wouldn't miss it altogether.

He was let back into the house by the footman, Robert. "Thank you. Where is today's post?"

"In the drawing room, as always, my lord."

"Excellent. And Lady Uxbridge?"

"I believe she is there as well."

Ox gave him a nod and went straight up, leaving his satchel with the man to put away for him.

"Good morning, Mother," he said as he breezed into the drawing room.

"Oh, Jonathan. I received your message this morning. Were you successful in selling your latest creations?"

He bent down and gave her a kiss on the cheek. "I was and got another commission as well—from Dray. Do you know that he's known all this time that I paint?"

She chuckled. "I'm not surprised. You did live together for many years."

"Well, yes, but I didn't really get into painting until university when we merely lived down the hall from each other. And I'd thought I'd hidden it well."

"You're very talented, Jonathan. I don't know why this is such a big secret."

"Because gentlemen do not paint, and if they do, they certainly don't paint pretty little miniatures," he informed her.

"Well, I think you're wrong, but let us get on with the mail, shall we? I did wait for you."

"Thank you. That was very considerate." He picked up the pile of letters. "And you didn't even peek to see what was here?"

She looked guiltily off to her left. "I might have. But just a peek!"

Ox laughed. "Well, let's see what we have here."

He handed her all the invitations—she would go through them and decide which ones he should accept. On the odd occasion, she would accept an invitation as well, but it had to be a very special event to draw her out of the house.

Ox corresponded with a few of his relatives, but there weren't many since his father's two brothers had already died, and his mother was an only child like him.

There was the letter from his estate manager and then one from his solicitor. No, wait, that wasn't his solicitor. It was another who he'd never heard of.

Ox broke open the seal and read,

My lord,

It is with great sadness that I write to you today to inform you of the passing of your great-aunt, Lady Agnes Werthington.

Please accept my condolences on your loss.

Since Lady Agnes included you in her will, I am most humbly requesting an audience with you at your earliest convenience. I will be more than happy to call upon you in your home.

Thank you…

Ox lowered the letter. Dear, sweet Great-Aunt Agnes. What a shame.

He passed the letter on to his mother to read.

"Oh, the poor thing. What a shame," she said as she read. "She had to have been nearly eighty if not older. But it was kind of her to think of you and leave something."

"It was," Ox agreed. His great aunt was one of those relatives he'd regularly corresponded with. Ah, well...

Ox pulled forward the writing slant that was kept nearby so invitations could be responded to promptly. This time, he pulled out a piece of paper, dipped his pen in the ink, and quickly jotted down a response to the solicitor. He asked the gentleman to come by the following afternoon at two. A pull on the bell and a footman was dispatched with the note.

He then turned his attention to whatever Cartright had to tell him of his estate.

It turned out the man had a great deal to say. The seeds for this year's crops were in the ground, including in the newly drained east field, and it looked like the drainage system was working just as it ought. Ox hoped it continued to do so. Having another field of wheat would perhaps give Ox the funds to make some investments he had his eyes on.

Unfortunately, the next paragraph sank all his hopes.

He read it aloud, knowing his mother would be interested as well.

"The Browns' cottage was struck by lightning during a particularly violent storm. The house was set ablaze. Thank the Lord, everyone got out safely, but the building burned to the ground.

"With the cost of seed and the new drainage system, and now having to build a new home for the family, funds are going to be tight for some time."

Ox sat back in his chair. "How awful. I do hope the Browns have someplace to stay while a new home is built for them." And then, as the thought came to him, he added, "If I remember correctly, Mrs. Brown's brother lives in the village. Perhaps he could put them up for a while."

"Yes. I'm sure they'll be fine. It's just such a shame," his mother said, looking up from the newspaper she was now reading.

Well, there went his plans for investments. Now it was especially important that the east field be productive.

At precisely two the following afternoon, there was a knock on the door, and Mr. Price, the solicitor, was shown into Ox's study. Ox was still wiping the turpentine from his hands—but had remembered to close the door this time—when the man bowed to him.

"Thank you for coming, Mr. Price," Ox said, indicating the man take the chair on the opposite side of his desk.

"Of course, my lord. No problem at all. Oh, and please do accept my condolences," the little man said. Well, Ox supposed he was of an average height, but since Ox was so tall, he looked quite short in comparison.

"Thank you." Ox folded his hands on top of his desk. "I understand my aunt has left a small bequest?"

he asked as the man got some papers out of the case he was carrying.

"Er, I don't believe one would call it small, my lord," the man said, placing a folder onto his lap. He opened it and, after rifling through it for a moment, pulled out a piece of paper. "Here we are." He finally looked up and gave Ox an apologetic smile.

"Your aunt's will states, and I quote:

"*To my dearest great-nephew Jonathan, Earl of Uxbridge, I leave the sum of thirty thousand pounds to be given to him as a wedding present on the day of his marriage, so long as he marries in this year of our Lord 1809. If he does not, the money will go to my grandson, the Honorable Theodore Burney. He is a spendthrift and a wastrel and will, in all likelihood, lose the money at the gaming tables, but hopefully Uxbridge with do the right thing and marry some wonderful girl.*"

The solicitor's cheeks had turned pink when he looked up at Ox once again.

Ox was silent for a moment and then asked, "It says that? That my cousin is a wastrel and a spendthrift?"

"Er, yes, my lord."

Ox chuckled. "And how did he respond?"

"I have not informed him as yet, and I won't unless you forfeit the inheritance," Mr. Price said. There was a slight pleading look in his eyes that told Ox that the solicitor truly wished he would not have to do so.

"Was any money or property left to Burney?"

"Yes, my lord. He inherited your great-aunt's home and everything within it."

"Oh, well, that's good. I wouldn't want…" Ox stopped as he recalled the conditions of the inheritance. He then leaned forward toward Mr. Price. "Did you say that I had to marry *this* year in order to receive the… er… what was it?"

"Yes, my lord. Thirty thousand pounds and, indeed, you do have to marry within the year." The fellow then smiled and added, "Convenient that she passed during the Season, eh?"

Ox sat back, frowning. That was a lot of money. He hadn't even realized his aunt had so much. She had lived comfortably, but he hadn't really given it much thought. But married! Within the year!

The man coughed and cleared his throat. "All you need to do is inform me of your wedding date, and I will arrange for the funds to be transferred to your bank, my lord."

Ox nodded. "Assuming I can find someone to marry a big… er… person like me."

"Oh, come now, my lord, you are young, titled, and soon to be much wealthier than you already are. Any young miss would jump at the chance, I'm sure."

"So long as she didn't mind… Well, that is my problem now, isn't it?"

"Er, yes, sir." The man slipped his folder back into his case and stood. "Well, there you are, my lord. I do hope I'll be hearing from you before too long." He gave a little bow and then left.

"Thirty thousand pounds," Ox whispered to himself. "But who could I possibly find to marry me? Who would be made of stern enough stuff not to be terrified of what I might accidentally do to her?" Broken bones were practically a certainty. Hell, he was afraid to even touch a young lady for fear of hurting her. Women were such fragile creatures.

Well... not all of them. His mother was a strong woman. He'd never hurt her in his life. But she was also on the larger side. Yes, perhaps that's what he needed, a larger woman. One who wouldn't be so delicate. And perhaps she would even be comely, and intelligent, and charming—like Miss Ellison.

He laughed. Where would he ever find such a girl?

"I say, Clarissa," Uncle Lawrence said, popping his head around her bedroom door after a brief knock.

"Good afternoon, Uncle," she responded.

"Er, yes, good afternoon." He straightened up but still stayed in the doorway. "I was just wondering if you wouldn't enjoy a ride in the park?"

"With you and Aunt Lily?" Clarissa asked, thinking about it.

"Well, no, just me. Your aunt is, er, otherwise engaged."

"Oh! In that case, yes, I would love to," she said, standing with enthusiasm.

Her uncle chuckled. "Then get changed lickety-split and I'll order the carriage."

Clarissa had never been to the park at the fashionable hour before. Her uncle reached across and pushed her chin up so her mouth closed, laughing as he did so.

"I've never seen so many carriages, and riders, and goodness, look at all the people walking too!" She could hardly keep her eyes in one place for very long. They were darting here and there, trying to take in everything at once.

Her uncle, who had been so kind as to take the backwards-facing seat, turned to look about. "It is quite a sight, is it not? I expect there are more people than usual because it's the first really nice day we've had in a little while."

Clarissa nodded. "It is lovely—and so are all the people. It looks like the very best of society is out enjoying the sunshine."

"I do believe you're right—and we are among them."

Clarissa could only shake her head in wonder. A quiet country girl like her, here in this great metropolis among the *haut ton*.

Her uncle called out a greeting to a gentleman on horseback. "Ho there, Easton!"

"Lord Morley, what a pleasure to see you out today and with such a lovely companion too," the handsome, blond man said after pulling his horse to a halt beside them.

"Ah, my niece, Miss Clarissa Ellison. Clarissa, my dear, this is Lord Easton, a fine fellow—good politics too," he added in a loud whisper.

Clarissa could do nothing more than nod her head as the gentleman gave her a slight bow.

"So lovely to meet you—and your uncle only approves of me this week because I'm backing his bill in Parliament," he said with a bright smile.

"Oh, I didn't know he had even proposed one," Clarissa said, feeling a little out of her depth. She supposed she should begin reading the newspaper each morning like her uncle did, although she was certain she'd never seen her aunt do so.

"No, no, you wouldn't. No need to, either," her uncle said with a laugh.

"Well, enjoy your day," Lord Easton said as he spurred his horse forward.

They too began moving, but only a minute later, they had to stop while the people in the carriage in front of them wished to speak with someone.

"There now, when you next go to a party, I'm certain Lord Easton will ask you to dance," her uncle said jovially.

Clarissa smiled. "Well, I think he has the right idea being on horseback. We are constantly having to stop for traffic."

"Yes, it is the nature of these things, but since we have nowhere in particular to go, does it really matter?"

"No, I suppose not," she said with a little laugh. It immediately died on her lips, however. Coming the other way, in an elegant high perch phaeton, was the Duke of Drayton with Miss Ricketts up beside him. The girl was looking around like a queen surveying her people. She had a very smug expression on her face, as if she knew she was to be admired.

The duke's gaze landed on Clarissa, and he pulled his carriage to a stop just beside them. "Good afternoon, Miss Ellison," he called down to her.

Clarissa had to crane her neck a little awkwardly since he was sitting so high in his phaeton, and she was in a low-slung landau. "Good afternoon, Your Grace. May I introduce my uncle, Lord Morley?" she asked.

The duke nodded as her uncle attempted to bow while seated.

"And Miss Ricketts," Clarissa added, turning her gaze onto the extremely bored-looking young lady.

"How do you do, Miss Ricketts," Uncle Lawrence said politely.

"Quite well, thank you," she answered, deigning to glance down at him. "What a day to be driving in the park. Why, everybody is here from the highest duke"— she turned and smiled to her companion—"to the merest riffraff," she finished, looking down at Clarissa.

Clarissa did her best not to narrow her eyes at the girl's implied insult.

"Oh, I believe it is all the best of society," Clarissa countered.

"Yes, I suppose you would," Miss Ricketts said, beginning to look bored once again. "Shall we continue on, Your Grace?"

Uncle Lawrence gave their driver the go-ahead to move on.

"It was very nice seeing you," the duke said as they moved away from each other.

"Well, if that is the man you plan on pursuing, I think I would advise you to reconsider," her uncle said with a huff.

"He was much more pleasant and polite when I met him at the ball the other night," Clarissa said, feeling as if she should defend the man. She wasn't quite sure why he'd said nothing to Miss Ricketts' denigrating remarks.

"You can tell what sort of person a man is by the company he keeps," Uncle Lawrence said with a shake of his head.

Clarissa stayed quiet. She wondered what had driven His Grace to invite Miss Ricketts out this afternoon. Well, whatever it was, it now evened the score between Clarissa and Miss Ricketts—one point each.

Chapter Seven

A few nights later, Ox found himself looking nervously around Lady Humesbury's drawing room. How was it that he had been able to speak so easily to anyone before, and now, when he truly needed to meet young ladies, his tongue felt glued to the roof of his mouth? He needed a drink, that's what he needed—and not this odd-colored punch that was being passed about. No, now he completely understood Dray's desire for whiskey—

"Is it warm in here, Ox?" a female voice sounded at his elbow.

He glanced down and found Lady Preston standing there, smiling up at him. Quickly, he pulled his handkerchief from his pocket and wiped his forehead. "I suppose it is, my lady. You do not feel the heat in your very pretty short-sleeved gown, but I am in a wool coat."

"You know, I never could understand why that was. Gentlemen, who are usually warmer to begin with, wear wool, and ladies, who are slighter and therefore feel the cold more acutely, wear short-sleeved gowns. Mine is silk, which to be sure, is quite warm, but clearly not as warm as your coat."

As she spoke, Ox gradually found himself relaxing. It was so nice to speak to a friend about such silliness as fashion.

"Now, you must tell me why you were looking like a scared rabbit a moment ago," she said, her moss-green eyes twinkling with mirth.

He chuckled. "Was I?"

"Oh, indeed," she confirmed.

"You know, I don't believe anyone has ever likened me to a bunny rabbit before. An ox, naturally. A bear quite a few times. But never a rabbit."

"You are stalling and attempting to change the subject."

He swallowed. He wasn't certain Lady Preston was the right person to divulge his new position. She loved playing matchmaker. On the other hand, perhaps she could help. He sighed. "Very well. I was informed recently that I have been left a bequest—a, er, rather significant one—to be given to me upon my wedding day, on the condition that it is within the year."

"On your—" Lady Preston's mouth dropped open for the briefest moment before it split into a brilliant smile. "You are looking for a wife? The man who said he would never, ever marry?"

"As I said, it is quite a significant bequest."

"Hmmm..." Lady Preston looked around the room.

Ox followed her gaze with his own. Miss Ellison was just entering the gathering with her aunt, who immediately abandoned her to her own devices. Ox frowned.

"You are seeing what I am, are you not?" Lady Preston asked.

"Miss Ellison?"

"Yes. She would be perfect—"

"No!" Ox said without a moment's hesitation.

Lady Preston turned to him. "But why ever not? Did you not enjoy her company when I introduced you? You looked to me like you were. Was I wrong?"

Ox frowned. "No, you were correct. I did enjoy her company. But look at her." He struggled to keep from pointing in her direction, which would have been incredibly rude.

Lady Preston did. "She is beautiful. Intelligent. Yes, a little green, but that can easily be remedied."

"She's like a deer—graceful, lithe, and so easy to break. Whereas I am a big elephant of a man."

"Oh, I think she's—"

"No, my lady. I would not take the chance. I need a young lady of more... substance. Like me," he insisted.

"Oh, come now, Ox," she protested.

"My lady, you are kind and probably the most intelligent person I know, but you are also incredibly stubborn. I am not going to marry Miss Ellison. Now, if you will excuse me. I think I will see if I can't find someone more appropriate." He strode off, feeling a horrible pinch in his stomach. He didn't like being so forthright, not even with a good friend like Lady Preston. And if he were completely honest with himself, he didn't like the candid truth he had just spoken. There was no way he could even consider marrying someone as beautiful and delicate as Miss Ellison, no matter how much he might enjoy being in her company.

Ox moved farther into the room. He stationed himself, as he always did, against a wall close to where the wallflowers stood, staring about like nervous mice. Wallflowers!

He turned to look at the girls standing nearby. A few were like Miss Ellison, and so slender, he could practically see through them. But at the end, there were two who looked much sturdier.

He turned toward the center of the room and caught sight of his hostess. When he returned with her a few minutes later, one of the girls was gone, but the other was still standing there, looking rather forlorn. Her deep-brown eyes were wide as she watched the dancers. Her coloring was unusual. Her skin was very pale, but so was her hair, being an almost flaxen blonde. Her eyes were the only thing about her with any color. Aside from that, Ox thought she might be sturdy enough for him, even though she was rather short.

"Lady Helena, may I make you known to Lord Uxbridge?" Lady Humesbury asked the girl.

Two bright pink dots bloomed on Lady Helena's cheeks as she stammered, "Ye-yes, my lady, of course."

"My lord, Lady Helena Hanley, daughter of the Marquess of Hartfell."

Ox bowed, holding out his hand for her to place hers into it so he could kiss her knuckles—or at least the air above them.

She did so but very hesitantly, as if he might disappear the moment they touched. "How—how do you do, my lord?"

"Very well, Lady Helena. It is a pleasure to make your acquaintance," Ox said as gently as he could, almost as if he were speaking to a child.

"Likewise," she said and then giggled. It seemed now that she'd established that he was, in fact, real, she was a little less nervous.

"Would you care to promenade, my lady?" he asked, holding out an arm for her to take and then, immediately, had to lower it for her diminutive stature. This was going to be a little awkward. At least she wasn't one of those young ladies who only spoke in a whisper. He had met a few of them, and it was extremely annoying to have to bend almost indecently close just to hear what the girl said.

"Are you enjoying your evening so far, Lady Helena?" he asked as they began to walk about the room.

She tittered. "Oh, yes, my lord."

"Excellent. I have to say Lady Humesbury's parties are always quite lovely," he said, looking down at her.

She fluttered her eyelashes.

"Is there something in your eye, Lady Helena?" he asked.

"What?" She began to giggle again. "Oh, no, my lord... unless, unless you'd like to look." She fluttered again.

He tried his best not to frown and even attempted to pull his lips up into a smile. "I'm certain I wouldn't be able to see very much in this light."

"Oh." She sounded rather disappointed then tittered again. "Well, perhaps we could go to a different room where... where there might be better lighting? The library, perhaps?" The eyelids fluttered yet again as she attempted to look up at him with a sidelong glance.

Was she trying to be suggestive? Did she truly want him to take her into another room where they would—

"We would be alone there," she said with another giggle and a flutter.

Ox cleared his throat. "Which is precisely why it would be most inappropriate, Lady Helena."

"Oh, who cares for that," she said with a wave of her hand.

This time Ox didn't even attempt to hide his frown. "I do. Is your mother or, perhaps, a chaperone here with you?"

The pink in her cheeks drained, and she looked startlingly pale all of a sudden. "My mother is here. I believe she is getting some refreshments."

"Ah, an excellent idea." Ox immediately turned them to head in the direction of the dining room.

The girl didn't say another word. And, thank goodness, she had stopped her incessant giggling and fluttering.

Ox left Lady Helena—looking even more unhappy than when he'd met her—with her mother. She was definitely not the one for him. No wonder she was a wallflower.

"Ah, Uxbridge!" He heard the voice coming from behind a group of ladies chatting away. He vaguely saw a man through the feathered headdress of one of them.

The fellow managed to get past the women, and Ox was confronted with a gentleman he'd seen at his club a number of times but had never actually met.

"It is Uxbridge, isn't it?" the man asked in a friendly manner.

"Yes, it is. I believe you're a member of Powell's, are you not?" Ox asked, extending a hand.

"Yes! Yes, that's right. Seen you there," the man said, shaking Ox's hand with a hardy pumping up and down.

"I'm afraid you have the better of me, sir," Ox said, grateful to have his hand back. The handshake hadn't hurt, naturally, but it was oddly disconcerting.

"Ah, so sorry. Aston. Byron Buttery-Clements, Viscount Aston," the fellow supplied. He was nearly as tall as Ox and had a good, strong, athletic build.

"How do you do?" Ox asked.

"Quite well, thank you. Say, I've heard you're looking for a wife," the man said.

Ox took a small step backward. "Who told you this?"

"Oh! Er, I do beg your pardon if I've been misinformed," the man said immediately.

"No," Ox admitted hesitantly. "I simply haven't mentioned this to very many people, so I was wondering..."

"Oh! Yes, I see. Er, it was Lady Humesbury, actually. She told me you'd asked for an introduction to Lady Helena Hanley."

"Ah, yes. Hadn't realized she would spread the news," Ox admitted.

"Oh, I don't know that she is, precisely. She told me, you see, because I have a sister who happens to be looking for a husband." The man gave him a big grin. "Lovely girl, I assure you—although I may be a bit biased."

Ox smiled. "I am glad to hear that you are. Not all brothers are on such good terms with their sisters."

"Oh, indeed. We are quite close. She's got a wicked sense of humor and is extraordinarily clever. May I introduce you?"

Ox didn't give it a moment's thought. "Thank you, I'd like that."

The man actually rubbed his hands together before turning and leading Ox across the room.

A few minutes later, he was bowing over the hand of Miss Katherine Buttery-Clements.

"It is a pleasure, Miss Buttery-Clements," he said. She was nearly as tall as Miss Ellison—in other words, the perfect height. Her round face was flushed, but her sparkling blue eyes looked to be filled with intelligence, just as her brother had said.

"The pleasure is mine, my lord," she said, lowering her eyes.

Lord Aston gave his sister a wink and then took himself off.

"So, how are you enjoying the evening so far?" Ox asked.

"It is well enough," she answered.

Ox couldn't help but chuckle. "Well enough? Are you not enjoying yourself?"

"I haven't spoken with very many people, my lord. Many tend to... stay away from me."

Ox tilted his head in curiosity. "Why is that? You are lovely, very well dressed, and the sister of a viscount. To me, it sounds as if you should be having to fend off the gentlemen vying for your attention."

She gave a little snort of laughter. "I believe you may need your eyes checked, my lord. I am larger than almost every other woman here."

He nodded and smiled. "And I am larger than any other man."

She looked up at him, a smile slowly creeping onto her face. "Yes, you are."

He held out his arm. "Would you care to promenade, Miss Buttery-Clements?"

"I would like that very much, thank you."

Chapter Eight

Clarissa had, as usual, been abandoned by her aunt the moment they'd walked in the door to Lady Humesbury's soirée. She couldn't imagine her aunt didn't know that she was supposed to stay with Clarissa, perhaps even introduce her to some eligible gentlemen. But, no, instead she disappeared immediately, weaving her way through the crowd to find her friends. Clarissa didn't think she could have followed her even if she'd tried.

She had done so at the first party they'd attended, but her aunt had simply ignored Clarissa's presence until her friend had said something. Only then had she actually stood with Clarissa until Lady Preston had arrived with Lord Uxbridge, so her aunt had been released to see to her own pleasures once again. Clarissa hadn't seen her for the rest of the night until she had been informed that Lady Morley was leaving.

Clarissa had tried, when she'd first arrived in London, to be helpful to her aunt, but the woman had taken it the wrong way and thought Clarissa was trying to encroach in her domain. Now Clarissa just did the best she could to stay out of her aunt's way. Happily, her uncle had given her permission to buy whatever she wanted at the bookshop and just had them send the bill to him. Reading was a passion of hers, so at least she had something pleasant with which to fill her time.

This evening, Clarissa didn't even make an effort to stay with her aunt. Instead, she wandered down the edge of the room, pausing to watch the dancers in the center execute the intricate designs of a country dance.

"Well, well," a voice said, coming up from behind her.

Clarissa turned and found Miss Ricketts looking at her as if she couldn't decide whether to give her the cut or actually demean herself to speak to her.

"Good evening, Miss Ricketts," Clarissa said, forcing the decision.

"Good evening." The girl inclined her head regally.

Clarissa didn't curtsy. "Are you enjoying yourself this evening?" she asked out of politeness.

"I am. Did you enjoy your drive in the park the other day—with your uncle," she added.

"I did. Thank you for inquiring. It was a lovely afternoon, was it not?"

Miss Ricketts sniffed. "It was indeed. From where I was, perched up so high on the duke's phaeton, I had an excellent view."

"I'm sure you did," Clarissa conceded.

"His Grace was so kind as to take me up beside him when he came upon me walking."

"Ah, so he hadn't actually invited you out for a drive, merely took you up out of the kindness of his heart."

"He is a true gentleman," Miss Ricketts said. "And he had to leave that enormous Lord Ox, or whatever his name is, to walk home on his own." She ended with a derisive laugh.

"Lord Uxbridge, you mean? Yes, the two men are good friends, so you might want to be careful what you say about him to the duke," Clarissa warned her.

Miss Ricketts sobered for a moment. "I did assume they knew each other. They were driving together. They are close friends, you say?"

Clarissa nodded. "They are."

The girl seemed to think about this for a moment. Clarissa gave a little laugh. "Why do I get the feeling that you said something unkind about Lord Uxbridge?"

"I..." Miss Ricketts shrugged. "It doesn't matter. Have a good evening, Miss Ellison."

She walked away and was soon lost in the crowd.

Hmm... score one point for Clarissa? Quite possibly, she thought.

Clarissa could only shake her head at the girl. As she did so, she noticed a crowd of women by the door. Oh dear, the Duke of Drayton must have just come in. The poor man was always mobbed by girls wanting to be his duchess and their mothers.

Clarissa had an idea.

CHAPTER NINE

She walked over to the crowd and shoved herself in. She had to push some women aside and step on a few toes, but she finally found the man at the center of it.

"Oh, Your Grace, you remembered," she exclaimed brightly and loudly as she pushed past the last girl.

"Miss Ellison, how delightful to see you," he said. "Er, I remembered—"

"Our dance. You are too kind, Your Grace. You promised me the first dance after you arrived this evening, and here you are."

"Oh! Er, yes. Yes, of course. Well, I would never promise something and then not follow through. Matter of honor, you know."

He held out his arm for Clarissa to take and then excused himself from the bevy of girls, leading Clarissa out onto the dance floor, where a country dance had just started.

"You, Miss Ellison, are a miracle. I cannot thank you enough for rescuing me. I am indebted to you."

"It was no problem at all, Your Grace. I'm sure you will do me a good turn at some point this Season, and we'll call it even."

They moved apart with the dance, but when they came together again, he had lost his smile.

"If you will excuse my impertinence, Your Grace, but you are looking entirely too serious for one who is dancing and supposed to be enjoying himself."

He momentarily smiled, but then said, "I'm afraid it is because I owe you and your uncle an apology."

"Whatever for?"

"For not speaking up yesterday. Miss Ricketts was unconscionably rude."

"Oh, well..." She paused as the dance moved them too far to speak for a moment. "I'm afraid you did not make the best of impressions on my uncle," she admitted when they were together again.

"I am not surprised," he admitted. "And I am rather ashamed of myself."

Clarissa was at a loss as to how to respond to this, so she thought that perhaps it would be better if she simply didn't.

"I was surprised at how crowded the park was the other day," she said, deliberately changing the subject. "Is it always like that?"

When the movements of the dance brought them together again, His Grace nodded. "Well, it was the first truly nice day we've had for some time."

Clarissa laughed. "That is precisely what my uncle said."

The duke smiled and then looked at her curiously as he turned another lady about. Clarissa allowed the gentleman who had been to the duke's left to do the same with her, but unfortunately, he wasn't exactly on time with the music and ended up stepping on the hem of her gown. She could hear the rip and stopped moving in an attempt to minimize the damage.

When she and the duke were partnered once again, he asked, "Was that your first time in Hyde Park at the fashionable hour?"

"It was."

"Well, in that case, it sounds as if you need a second visit to compare to your first," he said, before moving away for a moment. When they were close enough once again, he said, "Do you think your uncle would mind if I escorted you to the park tomorrow?"

"I believe tomorrow it is going to rain," she told him, remembering the threatening clouds that had already been gathering when they'd arrived at the soirée this evening.

"Hmm, perhaps the day after, then?"

She nodded. "I'm certain my uncle wouldn't mind at all. Thank you, Your Grace."

"It will be entirely my pleasure," he replied, but as he did so, his eyes strayed off somewhere over her shoulder.

As she turned around with the movement of the dance, she looked to see what he had seen. "Is it Lord Uxbridge who has caught your attention?" she asked.

"What? Oh! I do beg your pardon," he said quickly.

"No, not at all," Clarissa said, giving him a smile to show that she hadn't minded in the least.

"I was just... Do you know who the young lady is?"

This time Clarissa had to glance back to see. "That is Miss Buttery-Clements. She is the sister of the Viscount... I'm afraid I can't remember."

He seemed to find this amusing, but then he looked back over her shoulder. "So you know her?"

"I do. I met her last week when my aunt, and I paid a morning call. She's very sweet."

His eyes met hers once again. "Do you think... would it be very awful of me to ask for an introduction?"

"No, not at all. I would be happy to introduce you."

Miss Ricketts, one; Clarissa, three; Miss Buttery-Clements, one. This game was getting more complicated.

Ox was enjoying his time with Miss Buttery-Clements so well that he didn't even notice when Miss Ellison and Dray walked up. He'd seen them dancing as he and the young lady had completed their circuit of the room. Then he had turned his back on the dancers to listen to Miss Buttery-Clements finish telling him about her brother, who was reading everything he could find to learn more about agriculture now that he was the viscount.

"Oh, good evening, Miss Ellison," Miss Buttery-Clements said, interrupting herself.

Ox turned around and found his friend smiling in an odd way at Miss Buttery-Clements.

"Good evening. Miss Buttery-Clements, may I introduce you to the Duke of Drayton?" Miss Ellison asked.

"Oh, yes, of course," the girl breathed in a manner that surprised Ox. She hadn't sounded that way when she'd met him.

"Your Grace, Miss Katherine Buttery-Clements," Miss Ellison said, completing the introduction.

Miss Buttery-Clements curtsied deeply. "It is an honor, Your Grace."

"The honor is entirely mine," Dray answered smoothly as he placed a kiss on her knuckles.

The girl's cheeks turned pink with his attention. "I do hope you are enjoying the evening? I saw you dancing a few minutes ago."

"Yes, thank you. And you? You were promenading with my dear friend here," the duke said, not even sparing a glance at Ox.

"I was. We had a very enjoyable conversation." At least she looked at him as she said it. Even looked happy about it. "And you, Miss Ellison?"

"It has certainly been an interesting evening—with good parts and, er, not so good." She turned to Dray. "Dancing was most definitely a good part."

They smiled at one another in a way that gave Ox hope that his friend might indeed be considering Miss Ellison as his duchess.

"Oh, but Miss Ellison, I see that your hem has torn," Miss Buttery-Clements exclaimed.

"Oh, yes. I'm afraid the other gentleman who turned me about during the dance stepped on it. Is it very bad?" She tried to look behind her at the bottom of her gown.

"I do think we should get it pinned up, so it doesn't rip farther," Miss Buttery-Clements said. She then looked at Ox and Dray. "If you will excuse us, gentlemen?"

They both nodded, and the two young ladies headed off toward wherever it was that ladies' dresses could be repaired.

Ox turned back to Dray. He was still watching the girls walk away. "It's wonderful that you had a dance with Miss Ellison," Ox started. "It seems as if you're enjoying her company."

Dray started and turned back to him. "What? Oh, yes! She is a lovely young lady."

"Excellent."

Dray drew his eyebrows down. "I have to say I was surprised to see you with Miss Buttery-Clements."

"Ah, yes, well..." Ox started. He gave a little shrug. "Turns out I have to marry after all. This year, in fact."

Dray perked up a bit, his mouth quirking as he tried to hide a smile. "What's that? The man absolutely determined never to marry is going to—"

"It's a matter of an inheritance," Ox spat out. "My great aunt left me a very generous sum to be given to me as a wedding present so long as I married within the year." He still wasn't happy about the situation, but it was a lot of money.

"Thought you weren't in need of funds?" Dray asked with a skeptical raise of an eyebrow.

"I'm not, but I'm also not about to turn down an offer of thirty thousand, especially since if I don't get it, my cousin who is an inveterate gambler will."

"Ah... I understand. And so, you decided to start your search with Miss Buttery-Clements?"

Ox shrugged. "She seemed less likely to break should I take her hand too firmly or something."

"Oh, I see. Yes. She does look, er, sturdy."

Ox was about to agree when Dray continued much more softly, "And beautiful, with the loveliest smile, and those eyes." He ended on a whisper, his gaze straying in the direction the young ladies had gone.

Ox tilted his head curiously. It sounded as if Dray was enamored of the girl. But he had Miss Ellison. And besides, Miss Buttery-Clements was much better suited to Ox, at least in size. It wasn't that Dray was short or small in any way, he just wasn't as large as Ox. And Miss Buttery-Clements wasn't so much shorter than him. Of course, Miss Ellison was tall as well, but it just meant that she and Dray would see nearly eye to eye. That was all right.

"What do you say we look around for more possibilities?" Ox suggested, trying to divert his friend's attention.

"What? Oh, yes. Excellent idea. There are a good number of eligible young ladies here—and quite a few who won't break, I imagine." Dray gave a little chuckle.

Clarissa dressed in one of her pretty new carriage gowns for her drive with the duke. It was yellow—no, jonquil, she reminded herself—and had delicate white lace at the neckline. As Annie put the final touches on her hair, Clarissa noted that the color of her dress brought out the red mixed in with the light brown in her hair. She rather liked the effect, despite the fact that red hair was generally frowned upon. She gave a little laugh—as if someone could help what color their hair was.

"Is it all right, Miss?" Annie asked, looking worried. The poor girl was only just learning to be a lady's maid. Clarissa had brought her from Ellis Hall when she'd come to London because Aunt Lily had told her to bring a maid. Clarissa hadn't had one—she and her sisters simply helped each other to dress should the need arise—so she'd brought one of the housemaids. They only had two, and the other hadn't wanted to go to London, but Annie had jumped at the chance.

"Yes, it looks wonderful, Annie," Clarissa said to the girl with a reassuring smile. "You are learning so quickly and doing an excellent job."

The girl blushed and curtsied. "Oh, thank you, miss, I'm trying, really, I am."

"I can tell. Now, I suppose I should take my new lace parasol. Could you find it for me?"

"Yes, Miss. I know right where it is." She hurried to the wardrobe and reached into the back to pull it out.

"Good." Clarissa stood up, took one last look at herself in the mirror, and was amazed when there was a scratching at her door. The footman's voice called out, "The Duke of Drayton has arrived, Miss Ellison."

"Ha! Excellent timing. Tell him I'll be right there."

Annie was just behind her, holding out her blue pelisse, ready for Clarissa to slip her arms into it. She took her parasol, gave one last glance in the mirror, and then headed downstairs.

The duke looked up in surprise when she came down the stairs.

"Goodness, when you said you'd be right down, you meant it."

Clarissa laughed. "Why wouldn't I?"

"Only because when my sister says the same thing, it's usually at least a quarter of an hour before she shows herself," he said, holding out his arm for her to take.

"I didn't know you had a sister, Your Grace." Clarissa took it and allowed him to lead her outside.

"Two," he said affably. "One older and one younger." He handed her up onto his phaeton, making Clarissa remember how superior Miss Ricketts had looked when she'd sat in the exact same spot. Well, she would not do so, she determined. Instead, she looked eagerly about, enjoying the view from so high up.

"You can see quite a distance from here, can't you?" the duke said.

Clarissa gave him a brilliant smile. "You can indeed."

"It is one reason why I bought this phaeton." He clicked to the horses, a beautifully matched pair with silky black coats.

"And the other reason?" Clarissa asked.

"To look good," he admitted with a laugh.

She chuckled. "I'm sure you would look good no matter what you drove." And then, to make the compliment not quite so blatantly referencing his handsome face—which probably got commented on frequently—she added, "You have very light hands at the reins."

He lifted his eyebrows at that one. "And what do you know of driving, Miss Ellison?"

"Quite a bit, actually. My father taught me to drive. Apparently, he used to race before he married and was considered one of the best drivers among the *ton*. Since the Four Horse Club began, he's bemoaned that it was started too late for him to join."

"Really?" The duke looked suitably impressed. "Well, in that case, I accept the compliment from one who knows what they are talking about. Most ladies do not—and sadly—a good number of gentlemen as well."

He pulled the phaeton over to the side of the road as they neared the entrance to Hyde Park.

Rotten Row was crowded, as always, at this time of day.

"Goodness, but there are a lot of people out!" Clarissa exclaimed.

"Which would you prefer, to drive down Rotten Row or perhaps go for a stroll along the Serpentine?" he asked.

She looked at him, considering for a minute. If she chose the drive, then all of society would see her out with the duke. But if she chose the walk, then she would be able to actually converse with him and get to know him better.

Considering she was thinking about marrying the gentleman, she said, "Oh, a walk would be so much nicer, Your Grace. That way we can converse easily—if you don't mind?"

She must have given the right answer because his face immediately lit up. "I don't mind at all."

Another point for Clarissa.

He gave a *click* to start the horses moving and then drove past the entrance. "There's another entrance closer to the Serpentine," he explained.

They turned a corner and drove for a few minutes, neatly avoiding the crowd of those who were out to see and be seen. He pulled over once more and then helped Clarissa down, leaving his equipage in the capable hands of his tiger.

Clarissa once again took his offered arm, and they strolled slowly into the park.

"I gave Miss Ricketts the same option when I took her up in my phaeton the other day," he told her. "We were quite close by and could have stopped." He didn't finish the obvious point.

Clarissa did her best not to smile. "I see," she said,. It was difficult, but she did manage to restrain herself from making any sort of unkind comment regarding the fact that, clearly, Miss Ricketts was much more interested in being *seen* with the duke than actually being with him.

He gave a little chuckle. "Yes, I'm certain that you do."

Score another point for Clarissa, she thought to herself.

CHAPTER TEN

They strolled and talked of inconsequential things, but nonetheless, Clarissa felt as if she was getting to know the duke. He disliked eating at balls, as he found the food too heavy, but enjoyed meeting friends at his club. He and Lord Uxbridge had been friends since their school days at Eton, and his lordship had even bucked his family history of attending Oxford to go to Cambridge with the duke—something he still appreciated.

"Would have had a dev—er, much worse time otherwise," he said.

"Why is that? I'm sure you would have been able to make other friends," she asked.

"Oh, yes, certainly, and I did. Ox and I were not *so* joined at the hip. But it did make things... more comfortable, I should say. For both of us."

Just then, a rather large dog ran right across their path, heading straight for the river.

They paused, watching while the dog jumped into the water.

A boy came running along a moment later, calling out, "Stop, Tiny, stop!"

Clarissa grabbed the child before he could follow the dog into the water. "Oh, no you don't," she said, grabbing him around his waist and lifting the squirming child off the ground.

"Hey, let go!" he screamed.

"Now is not a good time for a swim," she said, holding him tightly.

"But Tiny—" the boy protested.

"Will come right back out when he sees that you have not gone in after him. Just you wait."

She put him down but kept a hand on his shoulder to be sure he stayed put. They watched the dog as he paddled into the middle of the river and then turned to see where his playmate was. When he saw that the boy was still on the bank, Tiny came right back, leaping out of the water and then shaking himself vigorously. The boy and Clarissa were splattered by the water.

"Oh, no! Miss Ellison," His Grace exclaimed. She'd completely forgotten about him but turned around, laughing. Before she could say a word, an older woman came huffing up to them.

"Mas... Master Harry, do... don't you... don't you ever go running... off like that," she panted. She then noticed Clarissa and the duke standing there and turned an even darker shade of red. "Oh, my lord, my lady, I do apologize." She snapped a leash onto the dog's collar and took the boy by the hand. "Master Harold, apologize to these nice people."

"No! She stopped me from going into the river. Tiny could have drowned," he cried.

The woman gave Clarissa an apologetic look. "Oh, God bless you, my lady. I don't know what I would have done if they'd both gone in."

"I do understand, ma'am. I've got three younger brothers who like to get into scrapes as well."

The woman ventured a smile.

"You be good now, Harry," Clarissa said before resuming her place beside the duke.

"Did I hear you say you have *three* younger brothers?" he asked after she took his arm again. Clarissa nodded. "And five sisters."

"Goodness, your parents have been very blessed."

Clarissa stole a glance at him. His eyes were wide and a little worried. "They have indeed. I am the oldest, and my youngest sister is two years old," she told him.

"So, you are well-versed in the antics of little boys." He quickly seemed to be coming to terms with her large family,

"Oh, yes. In fact, I have to admit that I still find myself searching my bed and my shoes for frogs or snails now and then."

He burst out laughing. "Oh, dear. I have to say I was never that naughty, or if I even had the thought, my tutor would have put the idea straight out of my head."

She sighed. "Sadly, my brothers don't have such an attentive tutor." She didn't mention they had no tutor at all beyond a weekly lesson with the vicar and one with their father. Lord Westbury, Clarissa's father, was too miserly to spend money paying someone to do what Clarissa and her next younger sister, Diana, could do very well themselves. Their mother had taught the older children, and then after she died giving birth to the youngest, Clarissa and Diana had taken over. Luckily, all the children enjoyed their studies and did as much to teach themselves as Clarissa did.

"I am sorry about your gown getting wet," the duke commented, looking down at her skirt.

"Oh, it's just water, it will dry quickly." Clarissa gave it a little shake, as much to help it dry as to keep it from sticking to her petticoat which, thankfully, was dry.

Well, one thing was certain, the duke certainly wouldn't forget this outing. She just couldn't tell whether this was a good thing or not. She'd better not award herself a point for this, after all.

It was just twilight as Ox made his way home from his solicitor's office. Normally, the man called on him, but it had been such a lovely day that Ox had told the fellow to stay where he was. Ox had even walked the whole way from Mayfair into the City.

While it had cooled down quite a bit with the setting sun, it looked to be a very pleasant evening. Even better was that Ox had no plans to go out. He was looking forward to a quiet night with a glass of brandy and a good book. Sadly, no amount of candlelight would be enough for him to work on his painting. The work was much too fine and detailed.

A shout suddenly pulled Ox from his pleasant thoughts. The distinct sound of a fist hitting flesh reached his ears. It seemed to be coming from the alleyway just ahead. Ox quickened his steps, even knowing full well that he should not get involved in some spat between ruffians, or whoever it was fighting. Still, he could not help pausing to look.

He reached the alley to see the back of a man holding another in a choke hold while his accomplice punched him in the stomach. A third fellow seemed to be searching through the unfortunate man's pockets. Three against one. That wasn't right. Ox hated it when an innocent man wasn't even offered a fighting chance.

With a sigh, he knew he would have to do something. He slipped into the alley, not making a sound, and then tapped the shoulder of the fellow holding the man being robbed.

As the fellow looked around, Ox planted him a facer, sending him sprawling. The two other men immediately came after Ox.

Now released, their victim threw a punch at the man who'd been going through his pockets. Ox took care of the other. Unfortunately, no sooner had that one gone down than the first fellow was back up on his feet. He tried to get Ox into a hold, putting his arm around Ox's throat, but he wasn't tall enough. Ox was a good four inches taller. With one swift jerk to the man's arm, it was dislocated, and the fellow was howling in pain.

The victim of the attempted robbery was on the ground after the man he was fighting had given him a punch to his gut that doubled him over, then a punch to his face that had him on his knees. The victim pulled himself together and sent a strong blow to the chin of the fellow he was fighting, sending the man down, out cold.

The victim finally turned around to face Ox, his fists in the air, ready to defend himself. Luckily, he stopped at Ox's surprised exclamation. "Welles!"

Ox's friend took a step back and nearly tripped over the man he'd just felled. "Ox! What are you doing here?"

Ox laughed. "Saving your hide, it seems."

"Well, damn my breeches, yes!" Welles looked down at the men, then grabbed Ox's arm. "Let us go before these men come to."

"I'll hail a hackney," Ox said in agreement.

"I, er, I was just on my way to St. Giles with your donation," Welles said, following Ox back toward the main thoroughfare.

"You go on foot? Clearly, that is not safe," Ox commented as he looked up and down the road for a cab.

"It's safer than arriving in style. Even as much as a hack would be noticed."

"Well, I think you're going to have to postpone your trip. You need some medical attention." Ox looked pointedly at his friend's eye, which was already beginning to swell.

Welles touched it gingerly as Ox lifted a hand to hail a passing coach.

The hack stopped, and they both climbed in. "To Colburne?" Ox asked, referring to a well-known viscount who was also one of the most respected physicians among the *ton*.

"No, no," Welles protested. "I'm not that bad off."

Ox agreed. "Then let's get you home." He began to give the address to the driver, but Welles' hand on his arm stopped him.

"If I show up at home looking like this, my wife…"

Ox nodded and changed the address to his own. "You can clean up at my house, but you won't be able to hide that eye."

Welles sat back on the seat. "No, you're right, but maybe I can soften the impact by at least appearing a little more put together."

Ox nodded, and they remained quiet for the duration of the drive.

When they reached his house, he paid off the driver and directed Welles inside.

"A basin of hot water and some raw beef," he told the footman as they entered.

"Of course, my lord, right away." The man went scurrying off.

Ox led Welles upstairs and to a guest bedroom.

"Jonathan, is that you?" his mother asked, popping her head out of the drawing-room door. "Oh, my!"

"Er, Mother, this is Lord Welles. He ran into a bit of trouble on the street," Ox said, pausing by the door.

"So I see," she said, nodding to the bow Welles made to her.

"I am terribly sorry to cause you any trouble, Lady Uxbridge," Welles said.

"Oh, no, no trouble at all." She peered up at his eye. "Let's get you some meat for that and some salve for your cuts and bruises. Uxbridge, you're taking him to the green room?"

"Yes. I've already called for hot water and the meat."

"Good boy," she said, patting his arm. She then went to the top of the stair to await the water and give further instructions.

Ox led Welles to the bedchamber, which had two chairs placed in front of the unlit fireplace. Welles collapsed into one of the chairs with a groan.

"Sorry, my friend, you should probably take off your coat so that it can be brushed," Ox told him. "And I'll get you a fresh cravat."

With a sigh, Welles stood back up and shrugged off his coat. As he did so, Ox went to his own room to get a few cravats and inform his man that his services would be required.

They both returned a few minutes later to find Welles sitting at the edge of the chair with Ox's mother's hand under his chin as she took in the damage to his face.

She *tsked*. "You will have quite a bruise there, my boy. There will be no hiding that. But let's see if we can keep you from the worst of it." Welles, who prided himself on being the most ordinary, unremarkable-looking man with his brown eyes, brown hair, and average height, was now going to stand out with his black eye, scrapes, and cuts. Well, now, Ox supposed, he would still be unremarkable amongst the men of the Rookeries.

She very gently wiped his face with a cloth dipped in the water, paying special attention to a cut on his cheek. She then took the meat off the plate being held by the footman and gently placed it over his eye. "You hold on to that."

He did so, lifting a hand that was scraped and bleeding.

"Oh, dear, no. We can't have that!" Ox's mother exclaimed. "Robert, you hold the meat in place. Give me your hand, my lord."

"It looks like you have things under control, Mother," Ox commented.

She looked up from her task of gently cleaning Welles's hand. "I do. Why don't you have Penley see to you? You are also filthy."

"Thank you, Ox," Welles said, peering at him with one eye.

He just smiled and nodded his head, and Lady Uxbridge *tsked* again, murmuring, "Boys!"

Rebecca looked again at Ox's response to her invitation to join her at Gunter's for ices this afternoon with a laugh. "It would take ten men to keep me away," he'd said.

She had to see that gentleman married and married well—to Miss Ellison if Rebecca had anything to do with it. She was absolutely certain she was the right one for him—Rebecca's tingling hands had told her so, and they were never wrong.

She looked up at the portrait of her dear Brian, taken from this world much too soon. "*You* know my hands are always right," she said to the painting. "Why can I not convince Ox of this? If you were only still here, my love, I know you would have been able to talk some sense into him. He admired you so very much." She swallowed the lump in her throat.

Two years, and she was still missing him terribly.

With a sigh, she put the note down on her desk, picked up her gloves, and headed out.

A quarter of an hour later, she was knocking on the door of Lord Morley's home. A gray-haired butler answered it.

She passed over her card. "Lady Preston to see Miss Ellison if she is at home."

He bowed her into the house and then showed her the way upstairs.

It seemed as if Lady Morley was having an at-home. There were a number of older ladies and gentlemen scattered about the drawing room—and Miss Ellison looking lost and bored in the center of it. Not one person was speaking with her.

"Lady Preston," the butler intoned.

Lady Morley immediately turned from the conversation she was having with Lady Pemberton.

"Lady Preston, what a lovely surprise," she said, coming over to her. She gave a slight curtsy.

Rebecca nodded. "I didn't realize you were occupied this afternoon, my lady. I actually came to see if I might steal away your niece," she said as pleasantly as possible. She wondered if Lady Morley had noted—or cared—that Miss Ellison was being ignored.

"My—oh, of course!"

Had the woman even forgotten the girl was there?

Lady Morley turned and called out, "Clarissa! Clarissa, come here."

Miss Ellison immediately stood. When she saw that Rebecca had arrived, she looked incredibly relieved and happy. She joined them quickly.

Giving Rebecca a deeper curtsy than her aunt had, she said, "Lady Preston, how lovely to see you."

"And you, Miss Ellison." Rebecca turned back to Lady Morley. "Would you mind if Miss Ellison went out with me for a short while? I was heading to

Gunter's for ices and thought she might enjoy the treat."

"Oh, that is exceedingly kind of you, my lady," Lady Morley said. She turned to Miss Ellison. "Go and get changed quickly, now. You don't want to keep Lady Preston waiting."

"Thank you, Aunt. My lady, I will be back in a trice," Miss Ellison said with a little hop of enthusiasm.

Rebecca laughed as she watched the girl go.

"She is such a sweet young woman," Rebecca said, turning back to the girl's aunt.

Lady Morley obviously did her best to put a smile on her lips. "Oh, er, yes. Yes, she is. I am only hoping that she manages to find a husband. This is her only chance, you know. My dear Morley was so very generous as to offer her the opportunity, but of course, he could only do so for this one Season."

"I'm sure it won't be a problem. A girl as nice and attractive as Miss Ellison will certainly receive a number of proposals before the Season is out."

The woman *harrumphed* disbelievingly.

"Especially with your assistance," Rebecca added with a meaningful look.

Lady Morley suddenly turned angelic. "Of course! I have been doing all I can for the girl, naturally."

"I'm sure you have, although I am certain you are aware that the more gentlemen she is introduced to, the sooner she will find a husband."

"It is true," the woman said with a frown, but she then placed a polite smile on her lips. "And, of course, you have done even more than I ever could by introducing her to Lord Uxbridge, who introduced her to the Duke of Drayton." She paused to chuckle. "Of course, now the silly girl thinks she can bring the duke up to scratch."

Rebecca didn't smile. "I'm not certain she is wrong, but I have another gentleman in mind for her."

"Oh?" Lady Morley asked, becoming curious.

"Lord Uxbridge, of course. That is why I introduced them. I am certain they will make a very good match."

"He does not seem to be interested in marriage at all." The woman huffed.

"Ah, but he has changed his mind and has decided to look for a wife, after all. And if I have anything to say about it—and I trust I might, seeing that he is a good friend of mine—I hope he chooses Miss Ellison."

The woman wasn't given the opportunity to reply since the girl in question stole back into the room at that moment wearing a very pretty deep-pink pelisse and a much lighter gown of the same color with embroidery along the hem, matching the pelisse.

"I am ready when you are, my lady," Miss Ellison said, even as she finished putting her hat pin into place to keep a very pretty straw hat with a pink ribbon on her head.

"Excellent," Rebecca said, nodding approvingly. She turned back to Lady Morley. "It was lovely meeting you again."

"And you, my lady."

Rebecca turned and linked her arm through Miss Ellison's, and together they left, heading for Gunter's.

Chapter Eleven

Lord Uxbridge greeted Clarissa and Lady Preston when they arrived at the sweet shop.

"Oh, Lord Uxbridge!" Lady Preston exclaimed upon seeing him. "I am so sorry! I completely forgot it was today we were to meet here. And here I've brought Miss Ellison out for a treat."

His lordship bowed to Clarissa, a smile hovering over his lips.

Clarissa couldn't help it. She outright smiled at Lady Preston's fib even as she curtsied to Lord Uxbridge. She caught his eye and nearly burst out laughing. He could see this was entirely intentional just as well as she.

"Miss Ellison's presence only makes the outing all the sweeter," he said smoothly.

Clarissa could only shake her head and try her best to hold back any further laughter. "You are too kind, my lord."

"Indeed, Ox, too kind. I am so glad there are no hard feelings," Lady Preston said. "And indeed, now we can be a merry three."

Lord Uxbridge inclined his head and then moved to assist the lady to sit at the tiny table he had secured while waiting for them. It was so small, the gentleman nearly looked like an adult trying to sit at a table sized for children. He sat on the tiny metal chair with his knees to one side. Clarissa didn't mind at all that he'd chosen to face her way, rather than toward Lady Preston.

"Have you been to Gunter's before, Miss Ellison?" he asked politely.

"No, I haven't. This is definitely going to be special," she answered, taking the menu offered by a waiter. She looked it over and was surprised at the number of different flavored ices on offer. "Goodness! Chocolate, lavender, maple, Parmesan, Gruyere cheese," she read off the menu.

"I highly recommend the chocolate, but the Parmesan is quite popular too," Lady Preston told her.

"Lord Uxbridge, which is your favorite?" Clarissa asked, as much as to be polite as to assuage her own curiosity. What sort of flavor would a gentleman enjoy?

"I happen to like the maple best, but the cheese-flavored ones do hold their appeal," he said.

"You like sweets of almost any sort," Lady Preston commented.

He gave a little chuckle. "You have discovered my deepest secret, my lady. I beg you will not bandy it about."

She placed a finger to her lips to signal that his secret was safe with her.

"Well, I have to say the chocolate does sound enticing. I've never had chocolate," Clarissa admitted.

"Does your aunt or uncle not drink it in the mornings?" Lady Preston asked, sounding rather surprised.

Clarissa shook her head. "I believe my aunt does. My uncle has coffee, which I find much too bitter."

"It isn't so bad if you add a good quantity of sugar and milk," Lord Uxbridge said.

"Well, we shall definitely have to inaugurate you to the marvels of chocolate," Lady Preston said.

Lord Uxbridge called the waiter back over with a pointed look at the man. He ordered their sweets and then said, "I do hope you've been enjoying your time in London so far, Miss Ellison."

"Oh, indeed I have, my lord," she answered readily. "I have met a great number of fascinating people."

"And some who you might actually like as well?" he asked with a wink.

She laughed. "Indeed, sir. You and His Grace are both extremely kind, and Miss Buttery-Clements looks like she will become a good friend as well."

"I am glad to hear that you are making some good connections," Lady Preston said. "It makes life so much more enjoyable."

"Not just good connections, my lady, but hopefully good friends," Clarissa countered.

"Indeed, but they are both very important. For example, I introduced you to Lord Uxbridge, who, in turn, introduced you to the duke. That was a very good connection to make—if I do say so myself." The lady looked up as their ices were placed before them.

Clarissa couldn't agree more. "You have been so very kind in all that you've done, my lady. Bumping into you at Harrods was certainly the most fortuitous thing that has happened to me since I arrived." She then delved into her ice cream.

"I would warn you, Miss Ellison," Lord Uxbridge said, stopping her before she could place her spoon into her mouth. "You should take small bites, otherwise you will feel the cold intensely."

"Oh! Thank you for the warning." She reduced the amount on her spoon and then placed it into her mouth carefully. Indeed, the cold was rather shocking, but the sweetness of the chocolate filled her with a satisfaction like nothing else. After she had swallowed, she said, "My goodness! This is even better than a fruit tart."

"Is that your favorite dessert?" he asked, after swallowing his own bite.

"It was until now." Clarissa nodded.

"Well, do go slowly," Lady Preston said, echoing his lordship's warning.

"Oh, yes. This is definitely something to be savored," Clarissa agreed.

"And you don't want a headache from the cold," Lady Preston said.

They all enjoyed their ices as slowly as they could, but it wasn't easy, considering how delicious it was.

Once they had finished and had vacated the table so that some other lucky people could enjoy their sweets, they all walked back outside into the warm sunshine.

"I am almost tempted to remove my hat, just to feel the heat after eating such a cold treat," Clarissa told her companions.

Lady Preston laughed. "I know exactly what you mean. And the sun is lovely after all the rain we've had recently." She paused and then added, "In fact, I believe I shall take advantage of this fine weather and do a little shopping." She turned toward Lord Uxbridge. "Ox, might I impose upon you to see Miss Ellison home?"

"I would be delighted," he said with a bow.

"Wonderful. Then I shall see you soon, I hope." She then headed off in the direction Clarissa thought must be toward Bond Street.

Lord Uxbridge offered her his arm, and they headed back toward her home.

"I do hope my presence wasn't too much of a surprise," she said as they walked around Berkeley Square.

"It was a most pleasant surprise," he told her.

"How clever of Lady Preston to arrange for us to meet in this way."

"I suppose you could call it that."

She looked up at him. "What would you call it?"

"Oh, clever indeed, but perhaps also a little conniving. She has been after me to marry for some time, and now that I have decided to search for a wife, I have a feeling she would like to be the one to choose her for me," he explained. "She fancies herself a bit of a matchmaker, you see."

"I didn't realize that." That did explain why the lady had been so insistent on introducing them.

"She believes that one can tell who would suit by using astrology."

"Oh, she was telling me something of that the first time we met. She told me what astrological sign I was born under..." She thought for a moment. "Aries, that was it."

He nodded. "I was born under Gemini. She believes that we would make an excellent match because of this."

"I'm afraid I don't understand the significance," Clarissa admitted.

"I can't say I do either, but Lady Preston clearly does and is convinced of it."

"How very unusual." Clarissa did like Lord Uxbridge, but she had already decided that the Duke of Drayton would be the man for her. He was, after all, the most eligible and sought after gentleman of the *ton*. Clarissa *was* going to win—the man and the Season. She never gave up and never lost.

"Indeed. I am sorry to have put this upon you, but I did feel that you should be aware," he told her.

"I do appreciate your honesty, my lord. I assume you feel as I do, however, that no matter what Lady Preston says, we would each like to choose who we will."

"Yes. Thank you, Miss Ellison. And let me say that despite Lady Preston's efforts—or perhaps because of them—I am happy to call you friend."

"I appreciate that and am honored by it," she told him honestly.

He smiled down at her, clearly in accord.

"Indeed, you have already shown your friendship just by introducing me to the duke."

"Oh, yes. How is that going?"

"Very well, I believe. I'm sure you've noticed that we have danced a number of times."

Ox chuckled. "He told me that you rescued him from a crowd of hopefuls and their mamas. You certainly gained his gratitude for that. Well done!"

"Thank you." Clarissa bowed her head in acknowledgment. "He's also taken me for a walk by the Serpentine."

"Has he, indeed? Well, you *are* doing well, aren't you?"

"Yes," she said, drawing out the word hesitantly.

He lowered his eyebrows over his beautiful, deep-set green eyes. "Did something go wrong?"

"I'm not certain. I mentioned that I had a large family, and he didn't look particularly happy about that. I jollied him out of his worried expression, but he did not seem pleased," she admitted.

Lord Uxbridge was thoughtful for a moment. "I honestly don't know his feelings about family. He's on good terms with both of his sisters, so I can't imagine why he would take exception to yours."

"Perhaps it is the size of it," Clarissa said, knowing full well that was the issue precisely.

"How big is it?"

"I have eight siblings, all younger."

A smile played on his lips. "You are very lucky, I'd say. But, well, the Queen had fifteen children."

"And many people have large families," Clarissa agreed.

"That is not always so with the aristocracy, but that's frequently because people marry for position or wealth and don't particularly like their spouses. They have the required heir and a second son, if possible, and that's all."

"Were your parents like that?"

"No. They liked each other well enough. I was such a big baby, however, that the doctors told my mother she probably wouldn't survive a second birth."

"Oh, I am sorry!"

He gave a little shrug. "She managed not to have another, but I've always wished for a younger sibling or two."

"I'd be more than happy to give you one of mine—maybe even two or three," she said with a laugh.

He smiled at her. "You are too kind."

Clarissa thought about not having her brothers and sisters and simply couldn't imagine it. They were everything to her, and she'd devoted her life to their happiness and well-being. "Actually, now that I think about it, I would probably be devastated if I didn't have my siblings. I love them all with every bit of my heart."

"As I say, you are very blessed."

"Yes. Yes, I am."

They had reached her home. Lord Uxbridge mounted the steps and knocked upon the door for her. It was opened almost immediately by the footman on duty.

His lordship descended the steps so that she could go up, but before she did, he bowed graciously over her hand. "Thank you for a very pleasant afternoon, my lord," she said as he did so.

"The pleasure was all mine."

Ox, sitting in his study on the ground floor a few days later, heard a knock on the door of the house. He glanced at the watch in his pocket. One o'clock precisely. He smiled. You could always count on Dray to be exactly on time.

A moment later, there was a scratch on the door, and the butler came in to announce His Grace.

"Thank you, Andrews," Ox said, getting up from behind his desk.

Dray came in, plopped down into one of the wingback chairs near the fireplace, and leaned his head back so that he was staring at the ceiling.

"So that's how it's going, is it?" Ox said with a chuckle. He poured out two glasses of brandy.

"I didn't know you had cherubs on your ceiling," Dray commented.

Ox glanced up. "My grandmother had it painted. I try to forget they're there."

Dray squinted. "What *are* they doing?"

"I have no idea. I've always imagined they were playing blind man's bluff." He put Dray's drink down on the table next to him.

"Oh, yes... one of them does appear to be blindfolded." He lifted his head and then picked up his drink. "Here's to cherubs and the hope that we aren't blind men others are trying to bluff."

Ox laughed and then saluted with his glass. "I hope you don't feel that way."

"I bloody well do. So many young ladies all vying for my attention." He shook his head.

"Well, better that than my situation, which consists of so many young ladies shrinking back in fear whenever I'm introduced," Ox said into his drink. At that thought, he emptied the glass in one go.

"No!" Dray protested.

"Well, not all, but a good many," Ox conceded.

His friend just shook his head in dismay. "You are the gentlest of men—"

"He is indeed, but he is also quite large. You cannot deny that," a woman's voice came from near the door.

Both men jumped to their feet.

"Mother!" Ox wondered how long she'd been standing there. At least neither had said anything they wouldn't have wanted her to hear.

She gave a slight curtsy but couldn't go deeper. "How do you do, Your Grace?"

"Very well, my lady. And yourself?"

She gave a little shrug. "My knees, you know."

"Yes, Ox has mentioned you've had a hard time getting around. I am sorry to hear it."

"Getting old is not for the weak-willed," she said with a smile.

"Er, is there something we can help you with, Mother?" Ox asked.

"Why, how good of you to ask, dearest. There is. And I am very glad—or rather Andrews will be very glad—that Drayton is here as well," she said.

A slight feeling of foreboding sank in Ox's stomach. "Oh?"

"Yes. I need some furniture moved. Come along," she said on her way out the door.

That didn't leave them any possibility of arguing, even if they'd thought of doing so. Clever woman.

Dray just chuckled. "If I'd known there would be manual labor involved in this visit, I might have reconsidered your invitation." He put down his drink and followed Ox's mother.

"This was not anticipated. I can assure you," Ox told him, hard on Dray's heels.

He passed his friend in order to assist his mother up the stairs. He feared it wouldn't be too long before she wouldn't be able to manage them at all on her own. He would have to hire a strong footman or two to carry her—and she wasn't a small woman. Ox hadn't inherited his size solely from his father.

In the drawing room, Lady Uxbridge pointed to a card table near the inside wall. "I'd like that next to the window, which means you'll need to shift the sofa, chairs, and center table over."

"But then they won't be in front of the fireplace," Ox told her.

"Yes. Perhaps we can open up the arrangement a little more to allow for a few people to sit closer to the fire," his mother said, putting her hand to her chin.

"And why do you need the table by the window?" Ox asked. "What's wrong with it right where it is?"

She frowned at him. "Two reasons, my lord. First, because when we play cards, the light will be better by the window if we are playing during the day. And second, because I think I may begin taking some of my meals here, so I do not have to traverse the stairs any more than necessary. Does that meet with your approval?" She lifted one eyebrow as if daring him to disagree with her.

"Er, yes. That makes perfect sense," he answered. He gave Dray an apologetic look. "If you want to wait in my study, I'm sure Andrews and I—"

"No, no, don't even think of it. I'll be happy to help," Dray said, taking off his coat for easier movement.

Chapter Twelve

Ox thought that an excellent idea and did the same. It took them half an hour of grunting from Dray and exclamations of "Don't scratch the floor!" from his mother, but they managed to rearrange the furniture to her liking. While Ox was certainly strong enough to move each piece by himself, the sofa, especially, was a two-man job.

Dray put his hands on his hips after they'd finished and looked around the room. "Now, tell me why you didn't ask your footmen to do this for you?"

"This is their half-day," Ox told him. "Only the butler is here."

"Ah, and this couldn't have waited until tomorrow?" Dray asked.

"No, it could not," Lady Uxbridge stated in such a way that no gentleman would argue with her. "Besides, a little exercise is good for you boys," she added in a softer tone.

Dray chuckled. "I haven't been called a boy since..."

"Since you were one?" Ox asked.

"Yes, as a matter of fact," he said.

"Well, I have known you since then, and you and Uxbridge will always be boys in my eyes," Ox's mother said.

It was true. Dray had been friends with Ox since they were twelve.

"Are you certain, my lady, that you want the furniture like this?" Dray asked, looking around the room. "It doesn't look as nice as it did before if you'll excuse my saying so."

Ox's mother surveyed the room. "No, you are right. However, the arrangement of furniture does not need to be beautiful or perfect, so long as it is practical and comfortable. The same is true of a great many things in life. It's always better to decide upon what feels right, rather than external beauty.

"Now, put your clothes back on, and I will promise not to bother you again. Oh, and I'll have the housekeeper bring you up some tea and biscuits. Cook made some very nice ones with icing," Lady Uxbridge said, patting Dray's arm.

The men put their coats on and then went back to Ox's study to await their treat.

"She does manage to make me feel like a child again," Dray said, picking up his brandy. "Biscuits with icing."

Ox could only laugh and agree.

Dray picked up his brandy and took a sip. "You don't think that whole exercise was some sort of lesson, do you? I mean, all that talk about it being more important to be comfortable."

Ox didn't need to think about it for even a moment. "I wouldn't put it past her."

Dray nodded. "She's a sly one, your mother."

"Well," Ox said, "let me make you feel more like the man you are. Tell me who you are considering for the esteemed position as Duchess of Drayton."

"Ah, yes. I can assure you that is something I never considered when I was twelve. Just the thought would have had me climbing the nearest tree." He paused while the biscuits and tea were brought in.

"May I pour, my lord?" Mrs. Andrews asked.

Ox nodded, and she poured out a cup for Dray and then him.

Dray took the cup and then looked at his nearly empty brandy glass. With a little shrug, he took two biscuits and settled back with his tea.

"The biscuits go better with tea than brandy," Ox commented after the woman had left.

"Mmm, much," Dray said around a mouthful. "Spiced biscuits are my favorite." He swallowed, took a sip of tea, and then said, "Did you know that Miss Ellison has eight brothers and sisters?"

Ox lifted his eyebrows. "Yes, she did mention it the other day. Said she was worried you'd be put off by it."

"Oh, goodness, I don't know. Eight siblings!" Dray said. "I can barely manage my two."

"But yours are sisters," Ox pointed out.

"Miss Ellison said she has three brothers and five sisters."

"Yes?" Ox thought it was wonderful and envied her. Clearly Miss Ellison had been right about Dray's feelings on the matter.

"No wonder she needs to marry. Probably expects her husband to pay to launch all those girls," Dray said before biting into his second biscuit.

Ox nodded, his own mouth full. What Dray said was probably right. Miss Ellison's uncle and aunt were sponsoring her. Surely she would sponsor her own sisters when they were of age. The thought didn't disturb Ox at all. He had the blunt, and would have more when he married, thanks to Great-Aunt Agnes. He'd always wished for a brother. Ox rather thought he would have been happy with a sister, but perhaps not as much. "Three brothers?"

"Yes. Miss Pemberton, on the other hand, has only one brother, and he's at Oxford. Miss Buttery-Clements has an older brother."

"An older sister, too, from what I understand. What about Miss Ricketts?" Ox asked with a lift of his eyebrows.

Dray shook his head. "I don't know and don't really care."

Ox could only smile. It didn't take too long to get that girl's measure. "Well, Miss Pemberton is a very pleasant young lady." Was that a feeling of relief in his stomach or just the biscuits settling? He did not like spiced biscuits, although the icing did make them tolerable.

After her visit to the park with the duke, Clarissa could not stop thinking about her family—she'd even dreamed of them the previous night. Holding on to that little boy, Harry, had reminded her so forcefully of her little brothers, Kenneth and Michael. They were seven and four, and such a handful. Clarissa hoped that Frederick, who was fourteen, was helping Diana and Eleanor watch them.

Clarissa had left the two older girls in charge. Diana, who was seventeen, was taking over the running of the house—something Clarissa had done for the past two years. And Eleanor was in charge of the schoolroom. At fifteen, she was probably better educated than most of the young ladies Clarissa had met here in Town. She not only could read and speak French, Italian, and German, but she could play the pianoforte and had a lovely singing voice. While Diana was the undisputed beauty of the family, Eleanor was most certainly the brightest so far. Both Isabelle, ten, and Kenneth—when you could get him to sit down— were quickly catching up. And Clarissa couldn't help but swallow the lump in her throat when she thought of the baby, two-year-old Naomi. Clarissa expected she was more than a handful, as she'd gone directly from crawling to running.

No, she couldn't stand it any longer. The embroidery her aunt was insisting she do could wait. She jumped to her feet, went straight to her aunt's escritoire, and sat down. She was pulling a piece of paper from the drawer and uncapping the ink when her aunt said, "And just what do you think you're doing, young lady?"

Clarissa half-turned in the chair to face her aunt. "I'm writing to my family."

"I thought I'd told you to work on your stitching," her aunt reminded her.

"You did, ma'am, but I am missing them so much. I have written only one letter since I arrived, and that was simply to inform them that I was safe and sound."

"That should be enough," her aunt started to say.

"No, ma'am, I'm very sorry, but it's not. I've already received four letters from Diana and two from Eleanor, but you have not allowed me the time to write back to them. I truly must or they will begin to think—"

"Your uncle is writing your father, informing him of your progress. That is enough."

Clarissa ground her teeth together. Why was this woman keeping her from writing to her sisters? Clarissa stopped to think about that before she said anything she would later regret.

"Aunt Lily, do you have any siblings?"

"I have a brother. We are not on speaking terms," she informed Clarissa.

Ah. That explained it.

"I am very sorry to hear that. My siblings and I are all very close. We share everything. We study together, play together—and I'm certain they would like to hear directly from me how I'm getting on. Please, allow me to maintain my relationship with them," she said gently.

Lady Morley turned back to her own embroidery. "Do what you will."

Clarissa let go a silent breath of relief and turned back to the desk.

My dearest Diana, she began and then stopped. What and how much did she want to tell her sister of what she'd been doing and with whom? She was certain that whatever she wrote would be shared with the entire family. Dare she get their hopes up concerning the duke? Even she didn't quite know how she was faring in that game. Oh, she supposed she'd tallied up more points yesterday with that walk in the park, but she and Miss Ricketts weren't the only ones playing.

She'd seen the duke dancing with a number of other young ladies, and even though she and her aunt hadn't been invited to Lady St. Vincent's picnic at Kensington Gardens, they'd heard that he'd gone for a walk with Miss Buttery-Clements, Lord Uxbridge, and Miss Pemberton, with the gentlemen exchanging partners for the walk back.

No, she definitely could not state that she had an edge over the other girls in this game, not yet. She could, however, be completely honest and at least tell them of her standing and that, while it was uncertain, she thought she was well on her way to winning this match.

Clarissa dipped the pen into the ink and began to write all she'd just thought about and more. She told them of Lord Uxbridge, Lady Preston, and their outing to Gunter's. The one thing she did not tell them, however, was anything concerning the treatment she was receiving from Aunt Lily. She had nothing nice to say about that, and her mother had always told her that if she had nothing nice to say, it was better not to say anything at all. Besides, she didn't want to worry her sister. And finally, she begged for a detailed accounting of how they were doing there. Goodness, but she missed them terribly.

When she finished, she waved the second page dry and then carefully folded them together into a puzzle, since she was reluctant to use her aunt's wax and seal.

She felt so much better for getting all her thoughts down on paper. Now, she could return to her stitching with a light heart—as soon as she'd seen the letter into the footman's hands to go into the morning post.

Ox was in his usual place by the wall, Rebecca noticed, as she came into Lady Buton's ball. Whoever had said that wallflowers were only young ladies had clearly never met the Earl of Uxbridge. She turned and headed in his direction. That man truly needed to branch out more. It wasn't that he was shy, either. If she managed to pry him from the wall, he could be very charming.

"Lady Preston, what a delight to see you this evening," the earl said, encountering her before she could him.

"And you, my lord." She gave him a slight curtsy, which he returned with a bow.

"My lord, is it? Have I done something to incur your wrath?" he asked, widening his eyes pathetically and putting a hand to his heart.

She chuckled. "Wrath? No. I am distressed, however, to see you here against the wall as always. I thought you had decided to look for a wife?"

"I have. There is no better place to stand and observe than here. You see those three young ladies just there?" He nodded toward the ordinary wallflowers who were standing nearby, one of them wringing her hands with worry. "And I can see the door from here as well, so I know exactly who has come and who is yet to show."

"Are you waiting for someone in particular? Miss Ellison, perhaps?" She lifted one eyebrow.

He smiled but shook his head. "She has already arrived and has danced with Lord Easton already."

"Well then, why is she not dancing with you?"

His face lost all its good humor. "You know very well that I do not dance."

"Remind me again why this is."

"I fear injuring some unlucky young lady," he said quietly.

"How so? I cannot imagine you would be, er, overenthusiastic."

"No, of course not. But should I miss my footing and step on her accidentally, I'm certain bones would be broken."

Rebecca considered that and could not disagree. "Perhaps, then, what you need is some practice."

Ox looked very dubious.

"I don't suppose I could convince you to make an attempt?" she asked.

"No," he answered with a brevity that made her understand the topic was not open for debate.

Rebecca pursed her lips together. Unusual for a Gemini to be so stubborn—they were infamously fickle.

"I will, however, be happy to promenade with a young lady if there is someone you wished to introduce to me," he said, softening a little.

She appreciated his efforts. "I am glad to hear that. Perhaps you might ask Miss Ellison?"

He chuckled. "You do not give up easily, do you, Lady Preston?"

She couldn't help but match his smile. "Now, why would I do that when I know I am right? Did you not enjoy yourself the other day when we went for ices?"

"I cannot lie. I did. Miss Ellison is a lovely young lady."

"She is clever and charming," Rebecca added.

He inclined his head in agreement. "And we have decided to maintain a cordial friendship."

"Friendship? Oh, no, Ox," Rebecca said with dismay.

"And what is wrong with being friends?"

"Well, there is nothing wrong, precisely, but you know—"

"I know you believe we would suit. We have agreed we would both prefer not to make any premature decisions."

Rebecca *harrumphed.* Premature decisions. She wasn't asking him to propose to Miss Ellison, merely for them to get better acquainted. "You are a very difficult man, Lord Uxbridge."

His smile grew broader. "I do apologize for being so, but truly, if you were in my position, would you not want to be absolutely certain that the person you chose was the right one for you? Marriage is for life, my lady. I would like mine to be as joyful as possible."

Ox could not know how his words, so gently spoken, were like a knife plunged into her heart. Marriage was for life, but life had a terrible tendency to be taken away from those too young and vibrant to lose it. Her Brian was... No, she sighed, she would not allow her mind to go down that path.

Ox must have realized where her thoughts had gone. He put a hand on her shoulder. "I do beg your pardon, Lady Preston. Of course, you know well what it is to be married, to pledge your life to someone."

She swallowed back the tears that had threatened for a moment. "I do, Ox, which is why I am encouraging you to get to know Miss Ellison better."

His hand dropped. "My lady…"

"Very well, I will not pester you any further this evening," she said, understanding that furthering her arguments would be pointless.

"Thank you. Now, if you will excuse me, Miss Buttery-Clements has just entered the ballroom, and I would like to greet her."

"Of course." Rebecca would stand down for today, but she was not even close to giving up.

CHAPTER THIRTEEN

Ox hadn't even made it halfway across the ballroom when he saw Dray approach Miss Buttery-Clements. Within moments, he was bowing over her hand and then leading her onto the dance floor for the next set of country dances about to begin.

Ox stopped. What was Dray up to? He knew Ox was interested in the girl.

Even as he watched, Dray bent closer to Miss Buttery-Clements to say something to her. She laughed and then stepped away with the movements of the dance, but her eyes stayed on the duke.

A moment of ice, quickly followed by intense heat, rushed through Ox's blood. But what could he do? He hadn't officially established that he was courting the girl. Hell, he didn't even know if he wanted to—saying as much would be as good as declaring that he wanted to marry her. He wasn't sure...

"Good evening, Lord Uxbridge," a quiet voice said from just next to him. He snapped his head to the right to find Miss Ellison there. She wasn't looking at him, but at the couples on the dance floor. "I see you are watching the duke and Miss Buttery-Clements as well," she said.

"Yes."

At that, she did turn to look at him. "I think a point goes to both the duke and Miss Buttery-Clements. What do you think?"

He looked down at her again, but this time his frown was gone, replaced with something closer to a smile. "I beg your pardon?" He leaned down slightly so he could hear her better.

"Points. One for each, the Duke of Drayton and Miss Buttery-Clements," she repeated a little louder but still not quite loud enough to be heard by anyone standing too close.

"That's what I thought you said," he replied, matching her volume.

She nodded and turned back to watching the much-too-happy couple, now turning about each other while staring into each other's eyes. His frown returned.

"You keep points, do you?" he asked unnecessarily, just to keep his mind off his friend's duplicity.

"Of course. This *is* a competition, after all. Don't you always keep track of points when you play cricket or battledore?"

"Yes, of course. And since this is, in your view, a game... I suppose it does make sense that you are keeping score," he conceded. She truly was the most unusual woman he'd ever met! "Er, so, what's the score at present?"

"Miss Ricketts, one; I have three; and Miss Buttery-Clements has two."

He laughed. "Well, it sounds like you are winning."

She gave a little shrug. "I was until Miss Buttery-Clements joined the competition. Now, my lead is being threatened."

"Hmm, yes." Ox turned back to face the dancers. Clearly, he wasn't the only one who was feeling threatened by the couple now giggling together as they promenaded up the line. And then something she said struck him. He turned back to her. "You said they *each* got another point? What is Dray's point for?"

Miss Ellison cocked her head a little. "For attracting Miss Buttery-Clements's interest, of course. Are you not also vying for her hand?"

He nodded slowly. "I am."

"Well then, the duke just gained a point over you."

"Ah. Except I haven't been keeping score," he commented. How was he enjoying this ridiculous conversation so much? Honestly, he should be appalled at how callously she was treating the delicate matter of finding a spouse. He truly must be a terrible person not to dismiss her out of hand. But goodness, he was having fun.

"You might consider it, or at least consider thinking about it that way. You need to know who your competition is, analyze their strengths as compared to yours, determine any advantages they have, or disadvantages, naturally. You might even create a strategy to win Miss Buttery-Clements. Although, I have to admit, I haven't fully developed mine yet. I'm still figuring out the rules—what is allowed and what would be frowned upon as unsportsmanlike or, in this case, unacceptable behavior for a young lady of society."

She paused to think about this. "I suppose, since you are a man, it will be easier for you to take control of the game. As a woman, I am reliant upon my wiles to tease out an invitation to dance or for a drive. You can visit Miss Buttery-Clements in her home when she and her mother are receiving visitors. I have to simply let it be known that we will be receiving and then hope the duke comes calling."

"Yes, you're right. You are at a disadvantage here. But then again, so are all the young ladies vying for Dray's hand. So, at least you are on equal footing," he pointed out.

"That is true and does make me feel a bit better," she said, giving him a warm look.

Somehow, he could feel that look all the way to his toes. It made him warm, happy, and as if he always wanted to be the one to put such an expression on her face. No. What was he thinking? He was going to marry Miss Buttery-Clements or someone like her. Miss Ellison was for Dray.

He turned back toward the dance floor and found that the dance had ended. He lifted a hand to get Dray's attention. A moment later, his friend and Miss

Buttery-Clements were headed their way. Before they arrived, however, he leaned down to say quietly to Miss Ellison, "I will make sure you are the next lady to dance with Dray, and if you are accepting visitors, you only need let me know, and Dray and I will be there."

She smiled up at him. "Thank you."

"Another point for you, I believe," he added.

She was still giggling when the duke and Miss Buttery-Clements joined them.

After Clarissa's dance with the duke, she stood by the wall, wondering whether she should find her aunt or perhaps just get herself a refreshment. She had nearly come to the conclusion that Aunt Lily wouldn't appreciate the annoyance Clarissa's presence would cause and was going to seek out some lemonade when Lady Buton, their hostess, approached her, a gentleman in tow. He wasn't one of the most handsome men in the room, but he was pleasant enough to look at. His dark blond hair was carefully styled a la Brutus, and his brown eyes looked friendly.

"Miss Ellison, Mr. Saunders has requested an introduction," Lady Buton said.

Clarissa put on her best polite smile. "I am honored."

"Excellent. Mr. George Saunders, may I present Miss Clarissa Ellison?" the lady said, looking from one to the other.

Clarissa curtsied as Mr. Saunders bowed over her hand, placing a kiss in the air just above it.

"How do you do, Miss Ellison?" he asked politely.

"Very well, sir, I thank you."

"I am so happy to hear it. And are you enjoying your evening? I do believe I saw you dancing with the Duke of Drayton just now, did I not?"

"You did. He was so kind as to ask me for a country dance," she told him.

"I'm afraid I'm not much of a dancer, but—"

"Oh, then, would you mind very much escorting me to the refreshments? I was just about to get myself a glass of lemonade," she said.

He paused, a little nonplussed at being interrupted, but then smiled and nodded his head. "I would be delighted."

Oh dear, had she been imperious? She was too used to telling others what to do.

He held out his arm, and Clarissa gently placed her hand on it and allowed him to lead her toward the small room off the ballroom where the refreshments were located.

He asked her all the usual polite questions, and she answered in equal measure as they traversed the ballroom. After she had quenched her thirst and Mr. Saunders had had some lemonade as well, he turned to her. "I hear you are quite the competitor, Miss Ellison."

It was a good thing she wasn't drinking anything when he'd spoken, or she might have spewed lemonade all over him. As it was, she widened her eyes and gave him a hesitant smile. "And where did you hear that, sir?"

He waved a negligent hand. "Oh, you know, one hears such things. The reason I am mentioning this, however, is because I know that Lady Broughton is hosting a card party later this week, and I was wondering if you might be interested in allowing me to escort you there—and your chaperone, of course."

Clarissa could feel her heart begin to pound. How... who could possibly have been putting it about that she played cards? And a card *party*? She wondered what sort of woman this Lady Broughton was to be hosting such a gathering. She put down her lemonade glass before it fell from her hand. Taking in a deep breath, she straightened her back. "Thank you, Mr. Saunders, it is very kind of you to make such an offer. However, I'm afraid I must refuse. I do not play cards."

He lowered his eyebrows in confusion. "Not at all?"

"Well, I know how to play, but I do not make a habit of it," she conceded.

"Oh, I see. Well, if you change your mind, Lady Broughton's party is a weekly affair, and I would be honored to escort you." With that, he bowed and walked off.

Who was spreading such horrid gossip about her? Miss Ricketts? Would she? *Well, yes, of course she would*, Clarissa immediately answered herself. But did she know of Clarissa's love of competition? The only way she could, would be if Lord Uxbridge had told the duke and then he had told her. Clarissa crossed her arms and started tapping a finger on her arm as she thought. It wasn't impossible. In fact, it was quite likely. But she had never mentioned cards. Who else would want to hurt her by dangling something as enticing as a card party in front of her?

But if Clarissa had learned nothing else from her father, it was the dangers of playing cards.

Ox found Dray sitting with Lord Aston at Powell's later that evening. He joined the men, ordering his usual glass of rum.

"I'm rather surprised to see you here, Dray," he said, taking a seat to his friend's left.

"Oh? I'm frequently here of an evening," Dray commented.

"I thought you'd still be at the ball dancing with all the lovely young ladies there," Ox said with a broad smile.

Dray gave a weak chuckle and a shake of his head. "My feet needed a break, and Miss Ricketts was after me again. I thought it most prudent to simply make a hasty exit."

"Miss Ricketts?" Aston asked. He was already married, so he must not be keeping up on all the eligible young ladies, despite the fact that his sister was one of them.

"She's a blonde girl, blue eyes, good form," Dray told him.

"She's a schemer who is trying to marry as high up the social scale as possible. I believe her father is a baron?" Ox asked, turning to Dray who would know better than he.

"Baronet," he supplied. He turned back to Aston. "She's been after me, but I'm not interested in a girl who is only attracted to my title."

Aston looked amused. "Does she at least come with a good dowry?"

Dray thought about that for a minute. "You know, I don't think I ever asked."

"Really? I thought that was the first question when considering a girl," Aston said.

"Was that your first question regarding Lady Aston before you married?" Ox asked, a little surprised.

"I didn't need to. Her mother volunteered the information soon after we met," he told them. "Poor Marianne was incredibly embarrassed. It was quite adorable, actually." The smile on his face told them that he clearly had softer feelings for his wife—not all men did. "By the way, Ox," he said, leaning forward, "Katherine's got a very nice dowry. My father made sure of it before he passed on."

"Ah, very good," Ox said, not quite knowing what else to say. He wasn't particularly in need, especially since he'd be getting thirty thousand from his great-aunt just for marrying—so long as he did so within the year.

"So, how *is* your courtship of my sister?" Aston asked.

Ox's glass was still half full. He finished it in one gulp before answering, "Not really courting her, you know."

"Well, yes," Aston said with a wave of his hand. "Don't need to ask me for permission, anyway. You have it."

"Er, thank you. I haven't asked her either," Ox pointed out.

Aston frowned. "So, it's not going well? That's disappointing."

"Oh, no! I didn't say that. No, not at all. She's a lovely girl, just as you said. I find her company extremely enjoyable—she's got a sly wit," he said.

Aston chuckled. "She does at that."

"I have asked her to go driving with me the day after tomorrow," Ox added. At least, he'd meant to ask her. He'd better write her a quick note to be sent over first thing tomorrow morning.

"Excellent!" Aston approved enthusiastically.

"I enjoyed my dance with her this evening a great deal," Dray said quietly in a rather offhand way.

"Ah, yes. I did see you," Aston said, turning his attention to Dray.

"She's very charming," Dray added.

"She is," her brother agreed. He turned back to Ox. "Going to take her up in your phaeton? You've got a nice pair there."

"Thank you. They're not nearly as nice as Dray's, but I like them," Ox said. He wasn't quite finished with the topic of young ladies, though. He turned to Dray. "You also danced with Miss Ellison, I noticed."

"I did," Dray agreed.

"She's also quite charming and intelligent," Ox said, watching Dray's face. It was oddly passive.

"Indeed," he said. Damn, he'd spoken with more enthusiasm about Miss Buttery-Clements than he had about Miss Ellison. That wasn't what Ox wanted to hear.

"And she is quite lovely," Ox added.

"Very tall, isn't she?" Aston asked.

"Yes, very," Dray agreed. "A little taller than your sister, but reed-thin. Hardly a curve on the girl." He paused and then turned back to Ox. "I'm afraid she's just not..."

"Not what? She's beautiful, intelligent, charming. What more could you want?" Ox asked, beginning to get annoyed with his friend's attitude toward the girl. All right, she was slender, but she had curves. They were just in proportion to the rest of her.

"And she has eight brothers and sisters and almost no dowry to speak of." He turned back toward Aston and added, "Her uncle volunteered that information while trying to talk the girl up to me."

Aston looked confused. "Did he think that was an advantage?"

"I don't think so, but at least he was honest about it." He then turned back to Ox with a rather apologetic look. "I know you think we would suit, Ox, but I'm not so sure."

"Well, you're wrong. You don't need a girl with a large dowry, and you won't need to worry about her family either," Ox said, pretty certain that he wasn't telling the truth.

Clearly, Dray didn't believe him either. He scoffed and said, "I think I'll explore other options."

"You really should give her another try," Ox pushed.

"Why?" Dray asked, looking at him suspiciously.

Hmm, maybe he'd pushed too hard. He gave a negligent lift of one shoulder. "Because she's a nice girl. I think she'd make you a good wife."

"And you're not interested in her?" Aston asked.

"Goodness, no!" Ox said quickly. "Much too, er, fragile for me."

"Fragile? In what way?" Aston finished his own drink and lifted a hand to catch a waiter's attention.

"Thin. Easily breakable," Ox explained. "Your sister is a much better fit for a fellow my size."

"Ah." Aston gave a little laugh. "Yes, she is, er, sturdy. We all are in my family—big bones."

"Yes. That's the sort of girl for me," Ox agreed. He may not like it very much, but he couldn't risk anything else.

Chapter Fourteen

Clarissa waited until after breakfast to open the letters from her family that had come with the morning's post. Although she was eager to read them, she was reluctant to do so in front of her aunt and uncle.

In the privacy of her room, Clarissa finally opened the first letter. It was from her oldest brother, Frederick. She quickly scanned the letter to be sure there were no emergencies or immediate questions that would need her attention, but words kept popping out at her. School. Tuition. Uncle. She stopped and read the letter carefully from the beginning.

Dear Clarissa,

I have heard from Diana that you are doing well in London. I am exceedingly glad to hear it. You know that both Diana and Eleanor are looking to you to provide both an example and the means for their own

Seasons. They talk about this incessantly. It's getting rather annoying, but I can see why they are so excited. The prospect of going to London is enticing. I cannot deny it.

It is not something I wish to do, however—although I will if it comes to that.

What in the... why would he come to London?

I was wondering if I might prevail upon you to ask our uncle, since he has been so kind and generous as to give you a Season, if he might be as generous with me. In other words, would you ask him if he could pay my tuition to Eton? I am desperate to go!

Oh dear, not this again. It happened every time their neighbor's son returned to school after a holiday.

While Vicar Smithson's lessons are enlightening, and he has done an excellent job of teaching me Latin and Greek, he simply doesn't have the breadth of knowledge I am craving. Father tries to make up for his deficiencies, but he has very little time to sit with me, and when he does, it is mostly farming techniques and—ugh!—animal husbandry which he talks about. Truly, if I have to hear one more time about a stallion covering a mare or the necessity of keeping the male sheep apart from the female sheep unless we want to increase our flock, I might just go mad.

Please, dearest sister, please ask if Uncle Lawrence might do this for me?

Yours as ever,

Frederick

A smile teased Clarissa's lips. Animal husbandry! What could Papa be thinking to teach such a thing to a fourteen-year-old boy?

On the other hand, the idea of asking their uncle—who had been so very generous and not grudged a penny of what was certainly an enormous expenditure—to spend so much more for Frederick's tuition... Just the thought sent a shiver of apprehension down her spine. She couldn't. She just couldn't do that. He'd already given them so much more than they'd ever expected.

Of course, it was out of the question that their father might part with even a farthing if he didn't have to, and clearly, he thought Frederick and the other boys were getting a good enough education from him and the vicar. But was it good enough? Clarissa truly had no idea. She was aware that a great many of the gentlemen she had met—including Lord Uxbridge and the Duke of Drayton—had formed their closest friendships at school. So, it would be to Frederick's advantage to go to Eton and not just for the education, although that was certainly important, too.

But Frederick had Lord Tyne, the Marquess of Winbourne's son. He and Frederick were of an age and fast friends. They did everything together, and being close with the son of a marquess, well, he could hardly do better.

Clarissa sighed. She was certain Frederick wanted more than just one friend. She knew he was eager for an excellent education, beyond agriculture and animal husbandry, although he would need to know those as well, being Papa's heir. But to ask Uncle... No, Frederick would simply have to be patient and wait until she was married and could convince her husband to pay for his tuition.

Before she wrote her response to her brother, Clarissa opened the letter from Diana. A quick read-through of this letter had Clarissa giggling at the antics of her younger siblings and nodding at the clever associations Helena was making between history and today. She was a clever little puss. Clarissa could only hope she didn't have a hard time finding a husband who would respect that.

When Clarissa flipped the page to continue reading, she found the insight to Frederick's letter she'd been hoping for.

"Frederick, I am sorry to say, has been moping about for the past week ever since his friend, Tyne, returned to school at the end of the Easter Holidays.

Exactly as Clarissa had suspected.

He's been short-tempered with the little ones and not putting much effort into helping Papa with the running of the estate as he had been doing. Clarissa, I just don't know what to do for the boy. I know he wants to go to Eton with his friend—he's even mentioned it to Papa!—but no one has either the money or the willingness to spend it despite that it's for a good cause.

Clarissa lowered the letter into her lap. It *was* a good cause. There is no reason why an intelligent, enterprising young man like Frederick should be denied a proper education. But their father simply wasn't willing to make the expenditure. Everything he earned went straight back into the estate or was invested in safe projects that were certain to earn money. Surely their father could be convinced that Frederick was such a project. That investing in his education would be to Papa and the estate's advantage.

Clarissa had made such arguments before to her father, but he'd dismissed her as being too naïve to know what she was talking about. Well, now she was more knowledgeable, had met more people, and experienced more of the world. Surely he would listen to her now.

She pulled out a piece of paper and began to write.

Ox was admitted to Dray's house by a very stately looking butler. His black suit contrasted sharply with his white hair and blue eyes. He wished his butler looked so intimidating.

"I am here to see the duke," Ox told the man.

"From what I understand, my lord, you are here to see Lady Edgerton?" the man corrected him politely.

"Er, well, yes, but also His Grace," Ox reiterated.

"I'm afraid His Grace is otherwise occupied. He did say, however, that when you arrived, I was to take you straight to her ladyship in the breakfast room."

"Oh, very well."

He followed the man as he glided toward the back of the house. How did the fellow walk that way? And without making a sound, too. No, really, Andrews needed to take some lessons from this fellow.

Lady Edgerton stood at his entrance. They'd met a few times before, but Ox didn't know Dray's older sister very well. She was only one, perhaps two years older than Dray and himself. She was very much a female version of her brother—dark brown hair, green eyes, a little on the tall side—but she was also quite shapely, the soft round mounds of her breasts rising above the low neckline of her gown.

Ox stopped and bowed. "Good afternoon, my lady."

She looked pleased to see him—which was always a good thing—and gave him a slight curtsy. "It is lovely to see you again, Lord Uxbridge."

"Please, call me Ox. All my friends do," he said, coming forward.

She nodded. "Thank you." She paused and then continued, "I can't tell you how pleased I am that you are willing to paint this miniature. It was a lovely surprise when Dray told me what he'd planned on giving Edgerton before he leaves for the Continent. It isn't very often, but my brother can be very thoughtful."

"It must be very difficult for you to see your husband go."

Her brows drew down as her gaze dropped to the floor. "It is. I'm still quite annoyed with him for choosing to do this, but he feels he owes it to his country."

"And his father isn't upset that his heir is risking his life in this way?"

"Oh, he is absolutely furious! He said if Edgerton didn't have a younger brother, he would have forbidden him to go."

"That can't have been very comforting for you."

She sighed. "Not at all." She looked up at him. "But we are not here to discuss my nincompoop of a husband. Where do you want me to sit? Have you brought your paints? That is a very small satchel you have. I mean, I know this is a miniature, but…"

Ox laughed. "No, I will not paint the portrait today. I merely want to take a few sketches if you don't mind. And I'll make some notes as to your hair color and eyes. I'll then do the actual painting in my studio."

"Really? You can do that from just a few sketches?"

He nodded. "I have an excellent memory for colors." He then moved forward to pull out a chair from the table where she'd been sitting. The light in the room was excellent. "If you wouldn't mind sitting here, my lady, I'll be able to get a better idea of the colors I'll need and be able to make a good likeness."

She did as was asked, seating herself at a very pretty angle. Ox pulled out another chair for himself and then retrieved his sketchbook and pencils.

They sat in silence for a little while as Ox sketched her likeness, making notes of the colors he would use to capture the lovely blend of the rich brown of her hair. It had highlights of lighter brown and even some red blended in, which would be great fun to paint.

"Drayton tells me you are now looking for a wife as well," Lady Edgerton commented.

Ox glanced up at her, then nodded. "Yes."

"He said you've been spending a great deal of time with a young lady by the name of Miss Ellison? Do I have that right?"

He smiled. "Miss Ellison is the young lady I would like to see your brother marry. She is merely a friend to me."

"Really? You feel they would suit?"

"I do."

"Why is that?" she asked, tilting her head slightly.

"I'm sorry, my lady, could you tilt your head back the way it was?" he asked.

"Oh, sorry." She did so.

"Miss Ellison is all that is kind. She is charming and intelligent. I can easily see her as the Duchess of Drayton as well. She has poise and a grace about her."

"Goodness, she does sound to be quite a paragon. And what of this other young lady? Miss Buttery?"

Ox nodded. "Miss Buttery-Clements. She is the one who I have my eye on, to be honest. She is also quite lovely, with a clever wit and a good eye for people."

"How so?"

He gave a little shrug as he smudged the pencil marks on his page to create the shadows along her jawline. "She has an uncanny ability to see the truth of a person even behind the facade they show the world. She can size up people very well and does so in a most amusing manner."

"She sounds fascinating. I am definitely going to have to meet both of these young ladies."

He nodded. "That would be a good idea. Then, perhaps, you can convince Dray that Miss Ellison is the right one for him."

She gave a slight nod. "If that is the case, I will most wholeheartedly support you in that endeavor."

Rebecca looked at the invitation from Lady Malton with dismay. She was sitting at her breakfast going through her diary, and she had slipped this into the book, as she did with all the invitations she'd accepted, so she wouldn't forget.

Connor, the butler, came up next to her to refill her teacup. "Is there something wrong, my lady?"

Rebecca sighed. "I just can't recall why I accepted this invitation. Lady Malton is constantly trying to convince me to return to Ireland. I'm almost certain the new Lord Preston has put her up to it."

He looked at her quizzically. "For what purpose, my lady?"

She shook her head. "I have a feeling he'd like to sell this house."

"But is it not yours? I'd thought his lordship, your late husband—"

"He bought it and gave me the right to live here for as long as I wished, which is why his cousin cannot sell it while I am here, but it is still part of his estate," she explained.

"Oh, I see." He looked a little concerned.

"Would you prefer that we return home? You have family there, do you not?"

He gave a brief nod. "My sister, but we have never been on very close terms."

"So, you don't mind staying in London?"

"Not in the least, my lady. Besides which, I would never abandon my duties to you. So long as you will have me, my lady, it is my honor to serve you. Wherever you go, there go I."

She smiled up at him. "I am truly blessed to have you, Connor."

His cheeks turned a slight pink even as he bowed. "You are too kind, my lady." When he straightened, he nodded toward the invitation still in her hand. "Still, if you might accept a word of advice, I believe it would be best for you to attend Lady Malton's gathering. If only to show her which way your thinking lies in the matter of your return."

She frowned at the invitation. "Yes, I believe you are right, though I am reluctant to agree with you. I prefer London to either Dublin or the quiet of the country. I shall go and ensure she knows that I have no intention of returning to Ireland anytime soon. And she may pass the information on to Lord Preston."

If only Rebecca liked the woman better. If only she wasn't constantly being pestered by her husband's cousin. If only horses had wings and could fly.

A little after three that afternoon, Rebecca presented herself in Lady Malton's drawing room. She was pleasantly surprised to find a number of other ladies of her acquaintance—all wives of the Irish representatives to Parliament—in attendance.

"Lady Preston," Lady Malton said with a little too much enthusiasm as she came to welcome her. "How wonderful to see you. I was just thrilled that you accepted my invitation."

"Thank you, Lady Malton. And I was delighted to receive it. What a wonderful idea it was for you to invite us all here today."

Lady Malton gave a little laugh. "Well, we Irishwomen must stick together, don't you think?"

Rebecca held her tongue and merely smiled.

Her hostess took this for agreement and so turned to lead Rebecca farther into the room, where there were already four other ladies chatting and sipping tea.

"I'm certain no introductions are necessary?" Lady Malton asked, looking around. One of the other ladies Rebecca had known for years merely nodded. A younger woman rose to curtsy. The other two also nodded to Rebecca.

"We were just discussing the lack of good beef to be found here in London," Lady Thomond said. She had been in London nearly as long as Rebecca had.

"It is nothing like it is in Dublin, now is it?" Lady Seaforth agreed. "And not just the beef, but the vegetables as well. They are simply not as good as what we get in Ireland."

Rebecca accepted a cup of tea from Lady Malton. "Perhaps your cook doesn't know which vendors to frequent," Rebecca suggested. "Mine goes to the market every few days herself and chooses the freshest produce. I have never heard her complain."

"Well, perhaps your cook should speak with mine," Lady Thomond conceded.

"What I cannot abide is the air," Lady Seaforth commented.

The other women were agreeing to this, which Rebecca thought was ridiculous. You couldn't possibly compare the air in the city to that of the countryside.

Happily, Lady Carbury joined them just then, so Rebecca didn't have to hide her expression, which was probably showing her feelings on the matter. Lady Carbury was quickly followed by Ladies Keith and Ongley, and soon people began to split off into smaller groups of two or three.

Lady Carbury, who had also come to London at the same time as Rebecca, joined her on the settee.

"I don't believe I saw you at Lady Sorrell's soirée the other night," she said by way of greeting.

"No, I decided to attend Lady Buton's ball instead," she told her friend.

"Oh? You wouldn't be thinking of remarrying?" Lady Carbury asked, lowering her voice and leaning a little closer.

Rebecca didn't hold back her laughter. "Oh, goodness, no!"

Lady Carbury tilted her head curiously. "Then, perhaps, helping another enter into marital bliss?"

Rebecca had always liked Lady Carbury. She wondered why she didn't see her more often. "I must admit I have considered that."

"Oh-ho! And who is the lucky couple?"

"I'm afraid I can't say yet. They haven't quite realized I am right when I tell them that they were meant to be together. They are pursuing others at the moment."

"But surely you've told them—"

"Oh, yes. A number of different times and in different ways."

"Ah, but they'll not be listening to you now, I suppose?"

Rebecca could only shake her head sadly.

"Then they've danced together? You can always tell from a dance."

Rebecca's shoulders drooped for a moment before she righted herself. "The gentleman says he doesn't dance."

"That, then, is the problem. He's got to dance with the young lady," Lady Carbury said with certainty.

Rebecca frowned, wondering how she could convince Ox that he would not harm a lady should he dance with her. An idea came to mind. It was a wonderful, clever idea, and it would be just the thing.

"Surely this can't be right," Clarissa said as she lowered the invitation from Lady Preston.

"What's that m'dear?" her uncle asked from behind his newspaper.

Clarissa pulled his empty plate away before he accidentally dipped the newspaper in the egg yolk pooled on his plate.

"Lady Preston has asked if I would assist a shy gentleman with a dancing lesson," she told him.

"That's very nice. What is not right about it?" Uncle Lawrence asked, lowering a corner of the paper so he could see her.

"She told me to wear my sturdiest boots," Clarissa said, looking back at the note.

Uncle Lawrence laughed, then ducked back behind the paper. "Sounds like an excellent idea should the gentleman prove to be a bit clumsy. Wouldn't want to hurt your toes, now, would you?"

Clarissa smiled. "I understand now. She is a clever lady, isn't she?"

Ox couldn't believe what he was doing when he showed up at Lady Preston's home the following day. Why did he agree to this? He didn't need dancing lessons. He knew very well how to dance. He'd been taught all the steps by an excellent dancing master when he was younger.

It had to be her persistence. That woman was incredibly stubborn. So absolutely certain she was right that he and Miss Ellison would suit, she simply was not going to give up this bone until it had been thoroughly chewed.

And so here he was, being shown into the lady's drawing room by her butler. Ox had his white gloves and was wearing his dancing shoes. He simply hoped there would be no broken bones by the end of the day.

"Ox, thank you for indulging me," Lady Preston said, rising from a chair that had been pushed off to the side to make room for the dancing lesson.

He gave her a short bow. "My lady. You call and I am there."

She laughed and reached out her hands to him. "Thank you. Truly, I don't think I could find a better friend."

"And so you feel you should repay me in this way?" he asked, allowing a smile to play on his lips.

She squeezed his hands before letting go. "Yes. I want to see you happy, Ox."

"I..." He stopped and shook his head, deciding to keep to the topic at hand. "I am certain you are aware that I *do* know how to dance but simply choose not to, yes?"

"Yes. But I'm hoping this lesson will revive your rusty skills and show you that should you ask a young lady to dance, you will not break her."

There was a brief scratch at the door, and the butler entered, announcing, "Miss Ellison, my lady."

Ox turned to bow to the young lady, not at all surprised that she would be his dancing partner this afternoon. In fact, he would have been a great deal more surprised if she hadn't been.

"Ah, Miss Ellison, thank you for coming," Lady Preston said as the girl curtsied.

"Thank you for the invitation, my lady," she said. Ox had not missed the girl's efforts at controlling her smile when she saw him standing there. So far, she was doing an admirable job at keeping her composure. He was impressed.

"Yes, thank you, Miss Ellison," Ox added.

"Of course." Their eyes met. Her lovely blue eyes were filled with laughter, which made it difficult to keep his own chuckles under control. "And I have done as Lady Preston asked and worn my riding boots. I'm certain I'm going to be a great deal more clumsy attempting to dance in them, but should you accidentally step on my toes, they should be safe." She lifted the hem of her gown a little so he could see her boots.

At that, he did burst out laughing. "My hat off to you, my lady. That was an excellent suggestion."

Lady Preston gave a graceful nod of her head before clapping her hands together. "All right. Let us begin, shall we?"

CHAPTER FIFTEEN

Clarissa took up her place opposite Lord Uxbridge as Lady Preston sat down at the pianoforte. It was so good of the lady to arrange this for her friend. Clearly, she'd gone to some trouble, having her drawing room furniture all moved off to the side to give them the space to dance.

"I think we'll start with something simple, a country dance," Lady Preston told them.

"But, my lady, there are only two of us," Clarissa protested.

"We'll just go through the figures, Miss Ellison," the lady explained.

"Oh, yes, of course."

Lord Uxbridge cocked his head a little. "Is that not how you learned to dance, Miss Ellison?"

"Well, yes, but there were always four of us learning together so we could form a square," she explained.

"Did you learn at school?" Lady Preston asked.

"No, my lady. I have a good many siblings, and we're not all so far apart in age."

"Oh, how fortunate you are," the lady said. "Today, we will simply have to make do." With that, she turned toward the pianoforte and played the opening notes of "The Isle of Skye."

Clarissa turned toward her partner and curtsied as he bowed.

They set out with the beginning steps. Clarissa was surprised to discover that, despite his size, his lordship was very graceful and light on his feet. He only miss-stepped once, which resulted in Clarissa stepping on his toes.

"Oh, I do beg your pardon!" she exclaimed.

"No, no, that was my fault," he said. His face took on a more serious expression as he paid closer attention to the steps.

They skipped and hopped their way down the room before coming together side by side. Clarissa put one hand behind her back and, with her other, took hold of Lord Uxbridge's hand behind his back. As he grasped her hands, she looked up into his handsome face with his strong chin and intense green eyes. At the same moment, he looked down at her. When their eyes met, a strange thing happened that Clarissa was never able to explain, much to her sisters' annoyance. It was as if kindling had been lit in a dark room. There was a spark, an intake of breath, and a knowing—all within one tick of the clock.

Lord Uxbridge's hand was warm, even through his gloves. It held Clarissa's with a strength that made her feel secure, protected. And yet he held her as if she were the most precious, fragile piece of glass that might break at any moment.

They turned about, her pale, delicate shoulder just a breath away from his strong arm and broad chest. He was so muscular he could probably break a cricket bat with little effort, and yet he was so gentle with her.

Clarissa felt a pang of disappointment when they separated, each skipping to the opposite ends of the space. Happily, they came together again, this time spinning in the other direction.

He had flecks of gold in his eyes and the palest eyelashes. But there was something else in his eyes—a warmth, a joy. It sent heat through her and made her heart beat as fast as if she'd just run a race.

With a jolt, reality hit her in the gut when she realized the music had stopped. She turned away the moment he'd let go of her hands. Putting a hand to her cheek, she could feel the heat of it through her own gloves and knew she had to be blushing. She only hoped neither Lord Uxbridge nor Lady Preston had noticed.

"Shall we take a break? You both look a little flushed," Lady Preston said.

Lud, she *had* noticed!

On the other hand, he was as flushed as she? She stole a peek. He was!

Even as he stammered his assent to Lady Preston's suggestion, Clarissa could see the color in his cheeks begin to fade.

"It's been so long since I've danced," he said to explain away his color.

"Of course," Lady Preston said, giving the bell a pull. "I've got some cider and ale that will cool you both right down."

"Thank you." Clarissa joined the lady at her sofa against the wall. "You dance very well, Lord Uxbridge. I can't imagine why you don't do so more often."

He settled himself into a nearby chair. "Thank you, but please, we are friends. Won't you call me Ox like everyone else does?"

Something constricted within Clarissa's throat. Friends. Yes, that's what they were, and she'd be wise to remember it.

She looked over at him with some slight embarrassment. "It is obvious why you are called that. I'm sure it is said without any malice at all, but I just couldn't call you that, my lord."

"Would you prefer to use my Christian name?"

"I... I couldn't," she admitted and then quickly added, "It is extremely kind of you to offer. I truly appreciate it, but it wouldn't be right." She could feel her face heating with embarrassment. She didn't call anyone but her immediate family by their given names, not even people she'd known her entire life.

"I understand your reluctance. I beg your pardon. I should not have asked."

"No, no, it was extremely generous. It's just that…"

"You are a proper young lady who does not want to appear forward," Lady Preston said with approval laced through her words.

Clarissa looked at her gratefully. "I only call my younger siblings by their given names, no one else. It was how I was taught."

"Of course," the lady nodded. "Although, you may have noticed I call Lord Uxbridge by his nickname while he still addresses me by my title."

"Yes! I noticed this," Clarissa said.

"It is for precisely the same reason. He invited me to call him Ox, but when I invited him to use my given name, he declined just as you are doing now. Is that not right, my lord?" She turned to include him in their conversation.

"It is, my lady. I felt exactly as I imagine you do now, Miss Ellison—an odd mix of embarrassment and horror of overstepping the bounds of propriety."

"Yes! But that is it, precisely," Clarissa said, amazed that he understood her so perfectly and had even felt the same.

"Have no fear. I am not at all insulted." He paused and then added, "I'm actually rather honored that you hold me in such esteem."

"I… I do, my lord." If only he knew how much esteem she held for him. Esteem and, well… oh, dear, so much more. Even she hadn't yet deciphered the extent of her feelings for him. She would have to mull it over later. For now, however, she would allow him to think what he would.

"Does anyone call you by your given name, Ox?" Lady Preston asked, much to Clarissa's relief. What a very awkward topic, indeed!

A maid entered with their refreshments and then paused awkwardly, clearly uncertain as to where to put her tray down since the furniture was all pushed against the wall.

Lord Uxbridge jumped up and moved a table to a more convenient spot, where they would all be able to reach their drinks.

"Thank you, my lord," the maid said as she placed the tray down.

He resumed his seat and returned his attention to Lady Preston. "My mother, on occasion, but that is all." He turned to Clarissa. "It would be nice to hear my name spoken without having to wonder what I'm about to be scolded for. I do hope that, at some point, you will feel comfortable enough to do so."

She nodded, allowing a small smile to play on her lips while inside heat sent tingles through her. She was so grateful when Ox turned his attention to the refreshments and offered to pour her a glass of cider from the pitcher there.

"Yes, thank you," Clarissa said and then accepted the glass from him. How she wished their fingers had touched when she did, but sadly, they had not done so. She rather longed to feel the warmth of them. Holding his hands earlier had been the most wonderful thing she'd ever experienced with a man. Perhaps… someday…

"Well, Ox," Lady Preston said, interrupting Clarissa's wayward thoughts. "I fully expect to see you dancing at the next gathering we attend together."

"Have you been invited to the dinner being hosted by Lady Ayers?" He sat back in his chair with his own glass of ale after having served Lady Preston some cider.

"Yes, of course. Lord Ayers is Irish, you know," she said,

"Yes, of course. I had forgotten." He turned to Clarissa. "Were you invited, Miss Ellison?"

She had never met either Lord or Lady Ayers and was certain her aunt and uncle had no connections within such exalted circles. "Lady Ayers is a member of the Ladies' Wagering Whist Society, isn't she? I've heard talk of them, but only with notes of awe," Clarissa admitted.

"Lady Ayers was one of the founders," Lady Preston told her. "But she is truly the most kind and generous person." She turned back to Lord Uxbridge. "How do you know her, Ox?"

"Lord Welles is a friend, and we've, er, done some business together," he told them.

Lady Preston nodded and said with a big smile, "Yes, if you know one member of the Wagering Whist Society, you quickly get to know them all."

His lordship turned back to Clarissa. "I would be very happy to escort you to this dinner, Miss Ellison.

I'm certain Lady Ayers has room for two more—I'm sure your aunt would accompany you?"

Clarissa just nodded, rather dumbfounded. Wouldn't Aunt Lily be shocked to receive such an invitation! "Thank you so much, my lord. That is incredibly kind."

He waved it away with a wave of his hand. "Lord Welles owes me a favor. I, er, helped him get out of a tight spot not too long ago."

Lady Ayers' dinner party. Clarissa could hardly believe Lord Uxbridge had actually managed to get Clarissa, her aunt, and her uncle invited.

The members of the Wagering Whist Society were the queens of the beau monde, nearly surpassing the prestige of the Lady Patronesses of Almack's.

Almack's, naturally, was closed to Clarissa because of a dislike one of the patronesses had taken to Lady Morley, but an invitation to a party hosted by one of the founders of the Ladies' Waging Whist Society... It still baffled Clarissa that such a thing had come about.

Her aunt had been running around all morning, ensuring Clarissa's new gown was perfect and that her own was impeccable. She'd even discussed what Uncle Lawrence would be wearing with his valet.

Thank goodness the lady was now in her bath in preparation for the evening. Clarissa had bathed earlier that morning, and she thought Aunt Lily might have even convinced Uncle Lawrence to bathe as well—despite the fact that he didn't believe it healthy to do so more than once a fortnight, and he'd bathed the previous week after church.

Clarissa ran her hairbrush through her still-damp hair, attempting to both dry and straighten it so it would be easier for her maid to pin up later.

Lady Ayers' dinner party!

And there was to be dancing. This was a good thing. Clarissa sincerely hoped Lord Uxbridge would ask her to dance. If he did, she thought, she would be able to determine if what she'd felt at Lady Preston's was just a touch of transient madness or if it was real. Was it a trick of the moment or... Clarissa got up and moved farther away from the fire. She was getting much too warm.

A knock on the door happily interrupted her thoughts. A maid came in, bearing a small silver tray.

"I beg your pardon, miss, but this came with the post this morning. It accidentally got mixed in with his lordship's mail."

"Oh, thank you." Clarissa took the letter and then sighed. It was from Frederick.

She had done nothing about her brother's request that she speak to Uncle Lawrence about paying for Frederick to go to Eton. That pang of guilt nagged at her as she opened his letter. It was brief.

Clarissa,

I have not heard back from you regarding my request that you speak with our uncle on my behalf. I, therefore, must assume that you have not done so.

I know you tend to avoid unpleasant tasks in the hopes that they will just disappear. This one won't.

However, if you do not—or cannot—speak with him, you may be sure that I will. In person. This is not something that can be done via post—I've been trying that for years to no avail. No, if you won't speak with him for me, I will have no choice but to come to London to speak with him myself.

I expect to hear back from you forthwith.

<I>F</I>

Clarissa dropped her head against the back of the chair. What was she to do? She couldn't ask Uncle Lawrence, not when he was currently spending so much money on her so she could make a good match.

No, Frederick would just have to wait until she married. And, truly, she didn't believe he would actually come to London—would he?

Lady Ayers' concept of a small, private dinner party was twenty people, including the host and hostess. Ox knew it wouldn't be a problem for two more people to be added to the guest list, but still, he was pleased to overhear Lady Ayers greet Miss Ellison and her aunt and uncle. "How delightful to make your acquaintance. I cannot tell you how greatly I appreciate you being able to help us balance our numbers on such short notice."

"Oh, my dear Lady Ayers," Lady Morley enthused, "it is we who were so honored with your invitation."

Ox moved away, satisfied. He made his way over to where Lord Aston and his sister were speaking with Lord and Lady Welles. His friend's wife was a delicate little thing with deep brown hair and brilliant green eyes. And speaking of eyes, there was still a slight discoloration around his friend's eye, but it was looking much better than the last time Ox had seen him.

"Looking good, my friend," Ox said, giving Welles a pat on his back. "Good evening, Aston, Miss Buttery-Clements," he added, giving them a bow.

"Evening, Ox," Lord Aston said at the same time as his sister curtsied.

"We were just commenting on what a lovely evening this was shaping up to be," Welles said.

"Oh, truly," Miss Buttery-Clements agreed. "Byron—I beg your pardon, Aston—and I were talking about it on our way here. I'm certain you are used to such things, Lord Welles, but for my brother and I this is a rare treat."

"Indeed, it was most kind of Colborne to pass his invitation to us," Aston said. He then quickly added, "With Lady Ayers' permission, of course."

"Well, I am very glad to see some new faces here. I see the women of the Ladies' Wagering Whist Society every week, so it's wonderful to have the opportunity to mix with others in a more private setting," Lady Welles agreed.

"I'm especially happy to be here because the Ayers have an excellent cook," Lord Welles said with a wink to Ox.

They all laughed, and his wife gave him a playful swat on his arm.

"Did I hear correctly that there is going to be dancing after dinner?" Miss Buttery-Clements asked.

"Oh, yes. That's why Lady Ayers was so anxious to have an equal number of gentlemen and ladies," Lady Welles told them.

Ox found this to be his cue. He turned to Miss Buttery-Clements and said, "I do hope you'll save a dance for me, Miss Buttery-Clements."

She looked at him curiously. "I thought you didn't dance, my lord."

He inclined his head slightly. "I have been convinced by a friend that it would be in my best interest to begin to do so."

She blinked at him. "I'm surprised His Grace managed to do that."

"Oh, it wasn't Dray, but Lady Preston who was the successful one. She even invited me to her home for a little practice the other day to make sure I remembered the steps."

"That was very kind of her," Aston commented.

Ox was about to agree when dinner was announced. Lady Ayers clapped her hands together to get everyone's attention.

Chapter Sixteen

"My lords and ladies, if you will indulge in an old woman's fancies, instead of going to dinner by rank—indeed, it would be most confusing since we have two dukes with us—I have decided we shall go in with our dinner partner. And no, married couples will *not* be together."

There was some chuckling at this, but Lady Ayers recalled everyone's attention and began calling off people.

"His Grace, the Duke of Warwick shall escort Lady Preston. His Grace, the Duke of Drayton will escort Miss Buttery-Clements. the Marquess of Sorrell will escort Lady Morley..." She continued down the list going in order of the gentleman's rank. Ox, as an earl, was pretty much in the middle and assigned to escort the Duchess of Warwick. He didn't know the woman but knew that she and the duke hadn't been married for more than a few years. He'd heard that she'd been a seamstress before that, but he was certain it was simply an exaggeration of whatever the truth was. Perhaps he'd be able to find out without asking directly.

He wasn't at all happy that Dray had been assigned to Miss Buttery-Clements. At least he'd already secured a dance with her, although he wasn't entirely certain that she'd accepted. Well, he would ask again later.

As he searched out the duchess, he noticed Miss Ellison speaking with Lord Wickford. He supposed she had been paired with the owner of Powell's Club for Gentlemen. Ox didn't know the man well, but he'd heard that, with his West Indian heritage, he was considered intriguing. The fact that the man had gone to school here in England and probably had lived most of his life here didn't seem to be taken into consideration.

It turned out that the duchess had, in fact, been a modiste before she'd married, and Welles was absolutely right, the food was excellent. Ox ate so well that he was grateful for the time the gentlemen were allotted to have some port afterward. However, precisely half an hour after the ladies had left, Lord Ayers looked at his watch and declared that Lady Ayers would be most upset if they didn't make their way immediately to the drawing room for dancing.

As they were climbing the stairs, Dray came up alongside Ox. "A little mouse has whispered in my ear that *you* are going to dance this evening."

"Hmm, well, your little mouse is quite correct. At least, I will dance one or two sets, but that is all. I don't want to make a complete fool of myself nor tempt fate too many times."

Dray just laughed and went on ahead to catch a word with the Duke of Warwick, who had been sitting across the table from him at dinner.

Ox found Miss Buttery-Clements chatting with Lady Wickford on the far side of the room, close to where a violinist was tuning his instrument. There seemed to be only two musicians, the violinist and a gentleman sitting at the pianoforte.

"Ladies, I do hope you enjoyed your dinner?" he asked, joining them. Lady Wickford was as beautiful as he remembered from two seasons ago when she'd made her debut into society. Her blonde hair was pulled up becomingly, and there was a lovely glow to her soft, creamy complexion.

"Indeed," Lady Wickford said immediately.

"Lord Welles was absolutely correct. The cook is brilliant," Miss Buttery-Clements said.

"He is quite good," Lady Wickford agreed, "but have you eaten at my club? We have a French chef—"

"My darling," Lord Wickford said, joining them, "you should not be speaking of your club in such a setting." He tapped a finger under her chin and looked like he wanted to kiss her, but then remembered where they were.

She just shook her head. "We were discussing dinner."

"Still…" He looked at her meaningfully.

Miss Buttery-Clements giggled. "I would love to visit your club, my lady, but my brother feels it might not be proper for an unmarried young lady to go without a proper chaperone."

"He may be right, I'm afraid," the lady agreed reluctantly.

"Must we stand directly next to the musicians?" Lord Wickford asked, frowning at the violinist, who was now running his bow across the strings of his instrument.

"Well, I would like to dance," Lady Wickford said, looking pointedly at her husband.

"And I would like to ask Miss Buttery-Clements if she would do me the honor of the first dance," Ox put in, giving the young lady a slight bow.

"I would be honored, my lord," the young lady said with a curtsy.

"And I would be most grateful if you would honor me with this dance, my lady," Lord Wickford said, bowing to his wife.

She nodded and then turned with a sly little smile to Miss Buttery-Clements. "Smart husband," she said in a loud whisper. "You should get yourself one." She then turned and smiled at Ox.

He was delighted to see Miss Buttery-Clements flush prettily. "Well, luckily for me, a good number of intelligent gentlemen here this evening."

That wasn't exactly the response Ox had been hoping for. There was nothing for it but to hold out his hand to the lady as couples were already taking their places in the center of the room. They were followed by the Wickfords, and the four of them formed a square with two other couples forming a second.

Ox didn't know if it was fortunate or just a matter of coincidence, but they began to play the same dance Lady Preston had ended with the other day at her home. He vividly remembered looking into Miss Ellison's eyes as they'd danced and feeling as if the world had somehow been off-kilter, but when they'd gazed at each other, it had been righted. He was certain it was because he wasn't used to dancing that his heart pounded so.

Forcibly pulling himself from his daydream, he concentrated on the steps to ensure he didn't accidentally tread on a lady's foot. None of the women here were wearing riding boots as Miss Ellison had the other day. The thought brought a smile to his lips. Luckily, it coincided with the part of the dance where he grasped Miss Buttery-Clements's hands as they turned shoulder to shoulder.

He looked down at her, hoping to feel the same or, if it was at all possible, something even more profound. She, however, was looking elsewhere. They moved apart and then came back together for the same turning, only going in the other direction. This time, she did look up into his eyes.

Hers were such an incredible shade of blue, almost turquoise, but they didn't shine. They didn't have that inner light and joy as Miss Ellison's had. And they didn't right the world. No, it simply wasn't the same.

Clarissa simply couldn't take her eyes from Lord Uxbridge and Miss Buttery-Clements as they turned in the center of the room, looking deeply into each other's eyes. She could feel the pinprick of tears in the back of her throat, but she would not, could not, allow her unhappiness to show.

It wasn't that she was jealous. Nor was she upset that his lordship had asked Miss Buttery-Clements to dance and not her. No, it was... *What was it, then?* she growled at herself. What was the problem?

She gave a quick shake of her head. There was none. No—

"Really, my dear, if you are going to stare at him, at least make it less obvious." Aunt Lily hissed in her ear.

Clarissa closed her eyes for a moment to clear them. When she opened them again, it was with strength and, if she must admit it, a touch of annoyance that she turned toward her aunt. "I was only admiring how well they look together," she lied.

Her aunt clearly didn't believe her. Her lip curled up. "Of course. You were not looking longingly at Lord Uxbridge at all."

Clarissa was terrified for a moment that someone else might have seen her looking as such, but she schooled her expression into one of indifference. "I was not."

Aunt Lily lowered her chin. "Yes, well, while you were standing here *not* looking at Lord Uxbridge—who you have absolutely no reason to look at, after all—the

Duke of Drayton is standing on the other side of the room nursing a glass of brandy entirely alone, also watching the dancers. I thought you'd said you were going to bring the man up to scratch? Have you given up on that ridiculous dream already?"

"It is not ridiculous, and no, I have not. The last time I looked, he'd been speaking with Lady Ayers. I hadn't realized he was now alone. If you will excuse me, I shall seek him out." She swept past her aunt, whose gaze Clarissa could feel on her back even as she walked away.

Inside, Clarissa berated herself. Not only had she been caught mooning over the wrong man, but it had been her aunt who had been the one to catch her. And to make matters even worse, she'd been absolutely right. Oh, yes, Clarissa hated that more than anything. Very well. She could manage this. She was an adult and could take some cutting words, and she could do what she must to achieve her goal—to win this game.

Score one point for Clarissa. While Miss Buttery-Clements was very obviously enjoying her dance with Lord Uxbridge, Clarissa would have the duke all to herself.

"They make a rather lovely couple, do they not?" she asked, coming up alongside the duke.

He started, nearly spilling his drink. "I... I beg your pardon, Miss Ellison?"

"I said they make a very nice couple. Well matched, I believe."

"Oh, er, Miss Buttery-Clements and Ox? Well, er, I suppose so," he hedged. It was more than obvious that he did not think so, which was quite interesting in itself. Clarissa wondered if she needed to award a point to Miss Buttery-Clements after all.

"And how are you enjoying your evening so far?" Clarissa asked, taking refuge in the ordinary.

He smiled at her. "Very well. And you?"

"It is wonderful to be among such excellent company," Clarissa said, smiling up at him.

His face relaxed as he returned her smile. "I'm afraid I didn't notice. Who were you partnered with at dinner?"

"Lord Wickford. He's a fascinating gentleman. Did you know that he's from the West Indies and owns a sugar plantation there?"

"I did, as a matter of fact. You do know that he owns Powell's Club for Gentlemen?"

"Yes, he was telling me. He said it's very well-known for the rum, which is of his own making, of course."

"Indeed. I can attest to its excellence."

"You are a member of Powell's?" she asked.

"I am." He glanced around the room. "I believe most of the men here this evening are."

Clarissa noticed her uncle speaking with Lord Ayers. "I don't know if my uncle is or not."

His Grace frowned a moment in Lord Morley's direction. "I don't know either. I don't believe I've seen him there. It's a rather exclusive club. Lord Wickford probably denies as many applications for admission as he accepts."

"My goodness. I didn't realize."

He nodded and then gave her a little smile. "It's what makes having a membership so much more desirable."

"I'm certain you are right. Everyone would want to be a part of an organization that might not accept them," she said with a little laugh. "How very clever." When he didn't say anything to that, she added, "I wonder if Lord Wickford would accept an application from my uncle now that he's met him here?"

"Quite likely. You might suggest he apply."

Clarissa nodded. "And what is it that you gentlemen do at such a club, aside from drinking exclusive rum, if I may ask? Or is it a secret?" She gave a lift of her eyebrows.

His Grace chuckled. "Oh, it is very secret, but I shall tell you if you promise not to share it with anyone," he said, leaning down toward her so he could speak more softly.

She widened her eyes at him. "I swear not to tell a soul," she said and moved closer to him as well. Oh, this was going so much better than she could have hoped. Another point for her, no doubt.

"We talk," he told her in a loud whisper.

She opened her mouth to show surprise when, in truth, she simply wanted to laugh. "About?"

He put a finger to his lips, signaling that he couldn't say.

"And that is all?" she asked.

He gave a little shrug. "Some men gamble as well. There is a gaming room."

A slice of cold ran up her spine. "Oh. But you do not?"

"Not often."

She nodded. "Good. Gambling is a horrible pastime," she said with more feeling than necessary.

He looked at her curiously but said nothing.

Clarissa quickly fished for another topic of conversation. This one was coming too close to the bone. She was saved by Lady Ayers, who'd come to see if they were enjoying themselves and tell them of some cakes and tea that had been set out.

Saved by the tea!

CHAPTER SEVENTEEN

Ox returned Miss Buttery-Clements to her brother after the dance. Normally, he would have eagerly gone in search of Dray, but he'd seen his good friend while dancing. How could he possibly not have noticed?

Ox still didn't quite know how he'd managed to finish the dance rather than stalking over to Dray and rearranging his face as he so desperately wanted to do. Somehow, Ox had managed to finish the dance without Miss Buttery-Clements even remotely aware of the murderous, bloody thoughts coursing through him.

Ox had turned his eyes away from Dray and Miss Ellison, even as the two of them had stepped even closer together. No, Ox had very deliberately turned away and began to name all the colors he could find in Miss Buttery-Clements's hair. There was brown, of course, but also burnt umber, a few touches of orange, perhaps a bit of black, or just a very deep shade of brown.

When Miss Buttery-Clements had looked up at him as they'd turned about for the last time, she found him staring at her and had flushed. That was good, thought Ox. He could choose the colors of her cheeks because he would not be looking back at Dray and Miss Ellison.

"You look very deep in thought," a light voice said just next to him.

He turned toward Lady Preston. "I was just thinking what a lovely couple Dray and Miss Ellison make."

She gave a little laugh. "Liar." And walked away.

Ox opened his mouth to protest but found he couldn't—because she was right.

"You and my sister do make an excellent couple," Lord Aston said, joining him a few minutes later. Ox had only left Miss Buttery-Clements with the man not ten minutes earlier, but she was nowhere to be seen. Aston must have noticed Ox looking around because he said, "Gone to, ah, take care of something personal."

Ox nodded.

"Saw you were looking over at the duke and Miss Ellison," Aston commented.

"Er, yes."

"Looks like your efforts at putting them together is paying off."

They both watched as Dray gave Miss Ellison a slight bow and then headed off toward the door of the drawing room.

"Suppose he's got personal things to take care of as well. I might follow before too long," Aston said. He then looked back at Miss Ellison, standing there alone. "She will make an excellent duchess."

"Yes. Yes, she will." Ox forced himself to look away. "I said as much to Lady Preston not too long ago."

"I don't believe I know her," Aston said, drawing his brows down.

Ox looked at him a moment before asking, "You are married, are you not?"

Aston nodded. "We're expecting the arrival of my heir early this summer. Lady Aston has gone to her mother to await the happy event."

"Congratulations," Ox said. "In that case, I'll introduce you to Lady Preston."

Clarissa received a most welcome invitation the following day while at breakfast.

"What is that?" Aunt Lily asked with an oddly accusing tone, as if Clarissa was planning a secret assignation.

She looked up at her aunt with a tilt to her head. "It is an invitation to walk in Hyde Park," she began.

"Ahh, with the duke?" her uncle asked. Clarissa smiled at him as he peered around his newspaper at her. "Sadly, no. It is from Miss Buttery-Clements."

"Her brother is a viscount, is he not?" Aunt Lily asked.

"He is, and I hear he and his wife are expecting a happy event soon," Clarissa added so that her aunt wouldn't get any funny ideas.

"Oh, yes, so I've heard," she said, disappointment laced through her words.

"But his sister is lovely. If you don't mind, Aunt Lily, I shall accept her invitation."

Her aunt waved a careless hand. "Do what you like, just so long as I do not need to accompany you."

"No, I shall take my maid," Clarissa confirmed.

That afternoon, a little after three, Miss Buttery-Clements picked up Clarissa. They walked out together arm in arm, their maids trailing behind.

"You could not have chosen a more lovely day for such a walk," Clarissa said as they made their way toward the park.

"I know. Apparently, it is going to rain tomorrow," she answered, clearly in excellent spirits.

Clarissa gave her a quizzical look. "How do you know that? It's so bright and sunny today."

Miss Buttery-Clements giggled. "My brother's wrist aches whenever it is going to rain. I think it has something to do with the fact that he broke it as a child."

"How fascinating! I have heard of such things but never knew anyone who had such premonitions."

They reached the park and found it as busy as ever at this time of the afternoon. Rotten Row was filled with equipages driven by well-dressed gentlemen, usually in the company of pretty ladies.

A barouche passed them, and Miss Buttery-Clements exclaimed, "There are Lady Jersey and Mrs. Drummond-Burrell."

Clarissa watched the two lady patronesses of Almack's go by.

"Have you received vouchers?" Clarissa asked.

Miss Buttery-Clements nodded. "I attended a few times last year, but it was so dreadfully dull and proper that I didn't go back."

Clarissa laughed. "Well, I don't feel so bad for not receiving any, in that case."

"No, do not. And what they say about the lemonade is absolutely true."

They continued their stroll, watching and being watched.

As they approached the Serpentine, a handsome woman with deep-brown hair and a lovely poke bonnet approached them. "I do beg your pardon, but you wouldn't happen to be Miss Buttery-Clements, would you?"

They stopped. "Yes, I am," Clarissa's friend responded.

"Ha! I'd hoped that was the case. I've heard quite a lot about you from my brother."

At Miss Buttery-Clements and Clarissa's confused expression, the lady chuckled. "I am Lady Edgerton. The Duke of Drayton is my younger brother," she explained.

"Oh!" Miss Buttery-Clements exclaimed, dropping into a curtsy.

Clarissa did likewise as her friend introduced her. "This is Miss Clarissa Ellison," she told Lady Edgerton.

"How lovely to meet you both. I have heard quite a lot about you, as well, Miss Ellison," the lady told them.

"The pleasure is mine," Clarissa murmured. She didn't know why, but the lady made her feel rather nervous.

"I have heard your brother is doing an excellent job of introducing you around this Season," Lady Edgerton said, turning back to Miss Buttery-Clements. "But this is your second Season, is it not?"

"It is, my lady. Last year, a cousin of mine sponsored my debut, but she knew few people, so we did not have so many invitations," Miss Buttery-Clements explained. "This year my brother has taken over, and we are able to go to so many more parties."

"Why did he not do so last year?" the lady asked.

"He had recently married himself, and so he spent the Season with his new wife in the country."

"Oh, I see. But your sister-in-law...?

"Is in her confinement," Miss Buttery-Clements explained.

"How wonderful." The lady turned to Clarissa. "And you are being sponsored by your aunt, Lady Morley?"

"That's right, my lady," Clarissa said.

"Dray tells me you have an enormous family," Lady Edgerton added.

"Er, yes, my lady. I have eight brothers and sisters."

"My goodness. They must be quite a handful for your mother," the lady said with a laugh.

Clarissa looked down at her hands clasped in front of her. "I'm afraid my mother did not survive the birth of my youngest sister."

"Oh, dear. I am sorry," the woman said.

"We have managed. I have two sisters after me, and between the three of us, there is always someone to watch the baby—well, she is two years old now," Clarissa amended.

"Goodness, children that age can be quite a handful."

Clarissa smiled at that. "It does take all of us to ensure she doesn't get into trouble."

"And I suppose you will be counting on whoever you marry to help with your sisters' debuts?"

Clarissa could feel her chest tighten with embarrassment.

"Yes, of course," the lady said before Clarissa could figure out how to respond. Lady Edgerton then turned to Miss Buttery-Clements. "And your family, Miss Buttery-Clements?"

"I have one brother, my lady and a sister who is already married," Miss Buttery-Clements answered quickly. "And while my mother has also died, it was four years ago, and she ensured that I was well trained in everything I would need to know to be a nobleman's wife."

Lady Edgerton seemed very happy with this, but Clarissa wondered why her friend had even pointed it out—unless she truly was interested in the duke.

Hmm... score one point for Miss Buttery-Clements.

And none for herself, Clarissa thought ruefully.

Lady Bunbury's soirée was only slightly more tolerable than all the other parties Ox had been to lately. In its favor was that there was no dancing. Sadly, he also saw very few new faces. Despite the fact that Ox had been making a concerted effort to attend more parties, in the hope that familiarity would reduce the stares leveled at him and the young ladies from shrinking from him, he had yet to see evidence of it.

He heaved a sigh as he resisted the urge to lean back against the wall.

"Well, that was not a satisfied nor even remotely happy sound."

His head swung to his left. Miss Ellison was looking up at him with a vaguely worried expression on her face.

He couldn't help the smile that came to his lips upon seeing her. "I'm afraid you caught me, Miss Ellison."

"At what, my lord? Surely you can't be unhappy in your courtship of Miss Buttery-Clements. She seemed to be quite smitten when you danced at Lady Ayers' last night."

"I wonder if smitten is too strong a word. She looks to be very happy right now in Dray's company." He nodded over to where the two of them were chatting with Lady Welles.

"Hmm... yes." Miss Ellison's lovely demeanor did not look happy at all.

"What is it?" he asked, watching her. She continued to stare off in the direction of Dray and Miss Buttery-Clements. Ox had the suspicion she was no longer seeing them but instead was lost in her own thoughts.

She suddenly snapped back to the present and turned to him. "I was walking in the park yesterday with Miss Buttery-Clements," she began, but then seemed hesitant to continue. She was quite possibly waging a war inside herself whether to tell him what was on her mind.

"Oh? Did you meet by accident or was it a planned outing?" he asked, trying to encourage her to share whatever it was.

"Planned. She invited me that morning. But while at the park, we met Lady Edgerton. "

"She's a very nice woman, Dray's sister."

"Yes, well, she asked a number of questions of both of us. I could tell she was rather more pleased by Miss Buttery-Clements's answers than mine. I'm certain there is nothing to it. I can't imagine the duke would appreciate marital advice from his older sister, but..."

"You fear she gained a point over you?" he asked, referring to her odd way of gauging a gentleman's interest.

She smiled at him. "Precisely."

"I wouldn't be too worried. Dray is an intelligent fellow. I'm certain he is just biding his time before he requests your uncle's permission to ask you for your hand."

She didn't look so certain. With a tiny shake of her head, she asked, "And you? When are you planning to ask Lord Aston for the hand of Miss Buttery-Clements?"

He gave a little chuckle. "When I'm certain my suit would not be dismissed. I'm afraid I am not at all certain of a positive outcome should I broach the matter now."

"Oh, come now," she protested. "No woman in her right mind would turn down a proposal from you. You are handsome, kind, and thoughtful, not to mention gentle and very generous."

Ox wondered if his face had turned pink at such praise. His disobedient thoughts also silently had him jumping for joy, not to mention wanting so very badly to pull Miss Ellison into his arms and swing her about in his happiness that she saw him this way. His baser thoughts had plans of their own, but he quickly shoved them aside. All this, however, was entirely inappropriate because she wanted to marry Dray, and he wanted... well, he supposed he *should* want to marry Miss Buttery-Clements. She was his best option at the moment—if she was, in fact, an option.

"You are too kind, Miss Ellison," he finally said.

"And too outspoken," she added. Her own face had also gone pink.

"You are a good friend," he corrected her. "I only wish others saw what you claim to be true—not that I'm saying it is, but I cannot help but wish others were as befuddled as you."

She laughed and shook her head. "Miss Buttery-Clements would be blind not to see it, and I think her sight is excellent. If only she wasn't currently looking at the duke." She turned to look back at the couple who had lost the company of Lady Welles.

"Come, let us set those two right, shall we?" He offered her his arm. When she took it, he realized he was feeling so much better now that he had spoken to Miss Ellison—but then, he always did.

Ɏ

CHAPTER EIGHTEEN

There was no dancing! Clarissa didn't know whether to be happy or upset at this. She'd spotted Lord Uxbridge the moment she'd entered the party. Her aunt had gone off immediately to find her friends. Uncle Lawrence had headed straight away to find a card room or, failing that, some other gentleman also wishing there were.

Poor Lord Uxbridge. The man had looked so forlorn and had been sighing so heavily when she'd approached him. Perhaps—no, most certainly—she had been too bold in voicing all that she admired about him, but she'd felt he'd needed to hear it.

And now they were listening to Miss Buttery-Clements tell them about her latest visit to the British Museum, but all Clarissa could see was the rapt attention of two gentlemen. She didn't know how Miss Buttery-Clements had done it, but somehow, she'd managed to win both men for herself. Of course, she could have only one. Clarissa looked for clues in the girl's posture, trying to determine which man she was leaning toward—emotionally and physically.

For both her and Lord Uxbridge's sake, she sincerely hoped Miss Buttery-Clements preferred Lord Uxbridge over the duke.

The men both broke out into laughter. Oh darn! She'd missed something. Clarissa pulled her lips up into a smile, pretending she knew what had been said.

"Oh, dear," Miss Buttery-Clements said as the laughter died away. "It looks as if my brother is motioning for me. I am so sorry, but you must excuse me."

Both men bowed as she walked away. "I'm afraid I must see what Warwick is dipping his fingers into now," the duke said.

"Might it be something I'll be seeing on the floor of Parliament?" Lord Uxbridge asked.

"Oh, most certainly," His Grace answered.

"And I believe I see my aunt," Clarissa said quickly before it could become awkward. She gave the gentlemen a quick curtsy and then went to see if she could find her uncle, as she preferred his company to his wife's.

Unfortunately, her aunt was the one who found her first. "Well, Clarissa. It seems as if you cannot keep—"

Whatever nastiness was about to come from her was abruptly cut off by the arrival of Mr. Saunders, who she had met at Lady Buton's ball. "Good evening, Miss Ellison," he said, joining them. He looked as ordinary as she remembered, although she now wondered whether he curled his hair so that it remained so perfectly disheveled.

"Good evening, sir," Clarissa responded, trying not to sound too relieved. Her aunt caught her eye as she was rising from her curtsy. "May I make you known to my aunt?" she asked quickly.

"Yes, please," Mr. Saunders said, turning his attention to Aunt Lily.

When the introduction was completed, and the pleasantries dealt with, Mr. Saunders turned to Clarissa. "We certainly missed you the other night at Lady Broughton's gathering."

"What is this, Clarissa? Did you receive an invitation and not tell me?" her aunt asked.

"Er, no, I mean, yes," Clarissa answered, suddenly put off-balance. "Mr. Saunders invited me to join him at this gathering, but I believe we already had plans for the evening, and it completely slipped my mind."

"I'm afraid that is partially my fault," Mr. Saunders added. "I should have approached you first, my lady. Miss Ellison did the right thing in putting me off."

Lady Morley drew herself up. "Indeed, you should have, young man. Is your father not the Earl of Holberth?"

He lowered his eyes in acknowledgement.

"Then you truly should have known better," Aunt Lily finished.

"May I make amends by extending the same invitation again? It is a weekly gathering hosted by Lady Broughton," he said.

Aunt Lily frowned. "What sort of gathering? Is it a political discussion or something of a literary nature? You can be certain Miss Ellison is no bluestocking."

"Oh, no, my lady. It is a card party. We get together to play whist for very reasonable stakes," he explained.

Aunt Lily's initial reaction was to frown, but then an odd transformation occurred, and she ended with a broad smile. "Oh, indeed? Well, there can be no harm in that. We would certainly be happy to come."

Clarissa wanted to allow her jaw to drop but instead ground her teeth together. Why was her aunt accepting this horrid invitation? "I do beg your pardon, Aunt, but I do not—"

"*Tsch*!" Lady Morley interrupted her. "Do not be ridiculous, Clarissa. I'm certain you know how to play whist."

"I do, but—"

"Then, there is no problem," her aunt said, cutting her off again. She turned back to Mr. Saunders, all smiles. "If you wouldn't mind having Lady Broughton send us an invitation, we would be most happy to accept."

Mr. Saunders bowed. "I most certainly will, my lady. Thank you." And with that, he took himself off.

"Now, he is a very nice young man, Clarissa, and much more appropriate for you—the younger son of an earl. I'm certain he has a good income and would make you a fine husband. You've been reaching far above your station with this duke. No wonder you are failing miserably at trying to get him up to scratch. He knows who you are and what sort of young lady he should marry, and it is not you!" Having put Clarissa in her place, the woman turned on her heel and walked away.

Clarissa wanted to stamp her foot and scream after her. She was the eldest daughter of a viscount! Marrying a duke was absolutely not beyond her reach. What ridiculousness. She knew—as well as any young lady in the room—how to be a duchess, how to manage a household. She'd been managing her father's for the past two years.

But her aunt's opinion of her wasn't even the worst part of this invitation. It was the card playing, the gambling. Aunt Lily knew of her family's history with such things. Why would she deliberately put Clarissa in such a situation?

Well, now that she thought about it, it *was* possible Uncle Lawrence had not told her exactly how her family had fallen into such dire financial straits. Clarissa couldn't blame her aunt for her ignorance.

Clarissa should not have been surprised by her aunt's animosity, and yet it still hurt. She realized, when someone bumped into her, that she was just standing to one side of the room—not moving, not speaking to anyone. No, but somehow her eyes had unconsciously found Lord Uxbridge.

He was back to standing against the wall, but this time he looked to be watching someone or something in particular. It was clear that he didn't like what he saw.

Clarissa followed his gaze and found the Duke of Drayton. He was now speaking with Lord Ayers as well as the Duke of Warwick. The only thing was, he didn't seem to be paying much attention to the conversation. He was staring over the shoulder of Lord Ayers.

For a moment, Clarissa thought him to be looking at her—his head was generally pointed in that direction. But since she wasn't making eye contact with him, Clarissa turned to see what he was looking at.

Of course, it was Miss Buttery-Clements. Completely oblivious to all this, she was happily chatting with some gentleman Clarissa didn't know.

Clarissa looked back at the duke watching Miss Buttery-Clements, and then to Lord Uxbridge watching the duke. It was all she could do not to burst out laughing.

And there she was in the middle of it all, not knowing which way to turn. The playing field had expanded, and each team was biding their time before the next engagement. Strategizing, she wondered?

She supposed *she* should be since Miss Buttery-Clements had clearly gained the upper hand. But what could Clarissa do? She had an undeniable handicap that was her family, and what man wanted to marry a girl with very little dowry and eight siblings who were sure to be a drain on his finances?

The Duke of Drayton had pretty much made it clear that it wouldn't be him.

A bubble of sadness rose in her throat. She was going to lose. Clarissa Ellison had never lost, but here she was standing among the highest of society, and she was beginning to have doubts as to whether she was going to be able to win any husband at all.

No! Clarissa was not going to give up, not without a fight. She wondered how good the duke was at debate. Could he, for example, possibly convince her father to part with some of his recovered fortune to pay for Frederick's schooling and Diana's debut in two years?

Perhaps now would be a good time to find out, and at the very least, she would go down swinging—or in this case, being charming and amusing. She needed to be sure the Duke of Drayton knew exactly what he would be losing if he chose not to propose to her.

Sadly, Ox's good mood did not last long after he and Miss Ellison joined Dray and Miss Buttery-Clements. The lady had been called away by her brother. Miss Ellison's presence, too, had been requested by her aunt.

Once the two ladies had left the gentlemen, Ox had attempted to truthfully gauge his friend's interest in Miss Ellison. He'd been put off by Dray asking instead about the miniature Ox was painting of Lady Edgerton and then had gone off to speak with the Duke of Warwick about a bill in Parliament. Ox was left feeling deeply unsatisfied. Then, to make matters worse, he'd been unable to even get close to Miss Buttery-Clements, as the lady her brother had introduced her to was parading her about the room, meeting any number of other gentlemen. No, Ox was not happy at all. He finally got so fed up, he left the party altogether.

What he needed, he decided, was a good walk to clear his head. With that in mind, he dismissed his coach and set off for home on foot.

His path happened to pass by the Morleys' home, and it was there that he saw an unusual sight. A boy, no older than fourteen or fifteen, was loitering near the steps to the Morleys' front door.

As Ox watched, he went up the first two steps, then down again. He paced back and forth a few times, only to go up and down once more. It was the oddest thing!

Ox crossed the road and approached the boy. "May I help you?" he asked.

The boy started and then stared up at Ox, clearly taking in his size. The child wasn't very much shorter, perhaps nearly Miss Ellison's height. Surely when he hit his growth spurt, he would end up as tall as Ox if not even taller.

"I, er, I…" the boy hesitated.

"Let me introduce myself if I may?"

At the boy's nod, he said, "I am the Earl of Uxbridge and well-known by the occupants of this house."

"*You* are Lord Uxbridge? Clarissa mentioned you in her letters," the boy blurted out.

Ox's lips twitched. Well, that would explain the boy's height and coloring, so similar to Miss Ellison's.

"I beg your pardon," the boy said quickly. He bowed and then said, "I am Frederick Ellison."

"I figured you were one of the Ellison siblings from your last statement," Ox told him. "So why are you hesitating at your uncle's door?"

"Er, well, two reasons, actually," Mr. Ellison answered a little reluctantly. "First, I don't want to disturb my aunt and uncle so late at night. And secondly..." He paused and scratched his head under the soft cap he wore. "Well, they're not expecting me, and Clarissa will be particularly angry at me for being here. But I just couldn't leave it up to her! She won't do it. I just know she would never get up the gumption to do so. And if she won't, well then, it's up to me to do so, right? I mean, I'm certain you would if you—" His words stopped abruptly when he clearly recalled who he was speaking to. "I, er, I do beg your pardon, my lord. I got carried away."

Ox laughed. "Yes. Well, as to your first concern, Lord and Lady Morley and your sister would not be disturbed if you were to knock on the door because they are not at home. I just left them at Lady Bunbury's soirée."

The boy's mouth dropped open. "In the middle of the night? "

Ox pulled out his watch and tilted it to catch a bit of moonlight. "It is only... a quarter past midnight. They probably won't be home for another hour or so." That had Ox frowning as something occurred to him. "How is it that you have only just arrived? Surely it is too late for... How did you get here?"

"I took the mail," the boy offered. "It was delayed due to a broken wheel, and then I didn't want to land up without having eaten, and then I, well, I got rather lost walking here."

"So, you've had quite an adventure," Ox commented.

Mr. Ellison nodded sadly.

"Well, in that case, and, er, seeing as how you are not expected, may I offer you a bed for the night? Tomorrow we will discuss your other problem. "

Once again, the boy's mouth opened, and this time shocked eyes were added to the expression of awe. "Oh, sir, er, my lord, I-I couldn't!"

Ox put his hand on the boy's shoulder. "You can and you will. I assure you that my mother will be thrilled to have another mouth to feed."

Mr. Ellison bent to pick up a carpetbag near the fence in front of the Morleys' house. "Your... your mother?" he squeaked.

"You will like her. I'm certain. And she will love you."

CHAPTER NINETEEN

Much to Clarissa's chagrin, Lady Broughton did, in fact, send an invitation to her card party the day after Lady's Bunbury's soirée. Now Clarissa had no choice but to put on a nice gown and a smile and go.

She wondered if she could watch instead of actually playing cards. Goodness, she hoped so because she had no idea what would happen if she picked up a hand of cards. The last time she had done so she had won Frederick's horse—until their father absolutely refused to allow her to take possession of it. After that, he had reminded her of the story of her grandmother and banned cards from the house.

That had been three years ago when she'd been sixteen and Frederick eleven. They'd both been old enough to know better. And Clarissa hadn't touched a card since. Now she was going to a party centered around them.

Mr. Saunders picked them up a little after 8:30—a little early for a normal party, but the invitation had actually said eight, so she supposed they'd be arriving at the right time.

Lady Broughton greeted them at the door to her game room. There must have been a hidden wall that had been opened to combine two rooms, as the space was large enough to hold a dance party comfortably. But there certainly wouldn't be dancing this evening. Tables were scattered throughout the room, and its usual furnishings pushed against the wall. Most of the tables were already filled with people playing cards.

"It is such a pleasure to welcome you to my little gathering," Lady Broughton said, holding out her arm to indicate that they enter.

"Thank you for your gracious invitation," Aunt Lily said after bobbing a curtsy to the woman.

Lady Broughton was a middle-aged woman with silvery-blonde hair and an impressive bosom. Her gown was cut rather low, clearly so that no one could possibly miss her charms.

"Please come in and let me introduce you," Lady Broughton said.

She went over to a table where only two people sat, a man and a woman facing each other from opposite sides of the table. They rose, putting down the cards in their hands as they did so.

"Lady Shipton, Lord Thandler, may I present Lady Morley and her niece, Miss Ellison?"

Everyone bowed and curtsied, and then Lady Broughton added, "And, of course, you know Mr. Saunders."

Lady Shipton curtsied again, and Lord Thandler reached out and shook his hand.

"It's a little odd with five, but—" Lady Broughton started.

Clarissa immediately jumped in. "Oh, I am not going to play. I am merely here to watch—and for the excellent company, naturally." She smiled at Mr. Saunders. Her aunt had frowned at the beginning of her statement but seemed mollified by her smile.

"Do, please, say that you will play at least one game," Mr. Saunders said. "I understand if you'd prefer to watch to start, but perhaps after you've grown more comfortable?"

"Of course she will play," Aunt Lily said. "It would be rude of her not to," she added with a pointed look at Clarissa.

With no choice in the matter, Clarissa nodded. "Of course, but as you say, Mr. Saunders, a little later."

Her aunt seemed satisfied with that, and an extra chair was pulled up to the table for Clarissa.

She watched her aunt, partnered with Mr. Saunders, play the first hand. The stakes were very reasonable—a penny a point—just as the gentleman had said. Clarissa did have to admit it looked rather fun, even though her aunt was a terrible player.

Finally, Clarissa couldn't stand it any longer. She'd been positioned so she could see Lady Morley's hand.

The woman was about to play a three when she had the queen right there.

"No!" Clarissa burst out. When everyone turned toward her, including her aunt, she flushed and said, "I do beg your pardon, but Aunt Lily you should play that card instead." She pointed to the queen.

"Oh, yes," her aunt said, giving Clarissa a little smile. "I forgot I had that. Thank you, my dear."

For the next hand, her aunt began to consult Clarissa on nearly every move she made. She and Mr. Saunders won that hand.

When Clarissa was about to do the same thing for the next hand, her aunt stood up, laying her cards face down on the table. "Why don't you and I switch places? You are so much better at this than I am."

Clarissa did so eagerly. There was nothing worse than watching a game being played badly, especially when she was so good at it.

She and Mr. Saunders paired well and played off each other's strengths and weaknesses. He, of course, was an excellent player.

At the end of the game, points were tallied, and she and Mr. Saunders lost by a tuppence.

"Well, shall we go again?" Lord Thandler asked after they had all refreshed themselves with a glass of ratafia for the ladies and brandy for the gentleman.

Mr. Saunders gave Clarissa a questioning look, as if silently asking if she'd like to.

"That sounds lovely," Clarissa agreed, and then remembered her aunt. "If that's all right with you, Aunt?"

"Oh, absolutely. I feel as if I'm learning so much just watching you play."

Clarissa nodded, and they all sat down again.

"Shall we double the stakes? Tuppence a point?" Lady Shipton suggested.

Clarissa was about to protest when her aunt said, "What a wonderful idea!"

Once again, Clarissa had no choice. Well, it wasn't her money, as her aunt had readily put in the coins for the last game.

"Excellent," Mr. Saunders said, clapping his hands together. "Now we'll get a chance to win back our money—with interest."

They all laughed and play began. It turned out that they did win, and Clarissa's aunt happily dropped the winnings into her reticule and then said, "Shall we double it again for the next game?"

Clarissa just looked at her in shock. Now they were beginning to get into real money.

"Indeed," Lady Shipton agreed. "And this time, we'll tally points at the end of each hand, rather than each game," she suggested.

Clarissa looked at her quizzically. She smiled, clearly seeing the confusion. "It's easier to lose a shilling than a crown," she explained.

"But you'll eventually lose the crown anyway," Clarissa pointed out.

"Oh, most definitely, but it doesn't hurt as much when it goes in smaller amounts." The lady gave a trilling laugh.

Clarissa didn't like this, though. She completely understood the woman's reasoning. It was easier to lose money little by little, but she would still be losing—or winning—a significant amount of money. With sudden clarity, she realized how her grandmother had so easily lost a fortune. If they played for a pound a point or even more—Clarissa swallowed.

No. She couldn't do this.

"I'm so sorry, but I don't think—" she started.

"Clarissa, don't be a goose. You are not your grandmother. You won't lose everything," her aunt said from behind her.

Clarissa jumped to her feet and spun around. "You know? You know about my grandmother, and yet you encouraged me to come to this party and play, anyway?"

For a moment, Lady Morley looked like she was having difficulty keeping the smile from her face, but then she too stood. "You will not speak to me thus, young lady." And then added in a whisper, "And especially not in public!"

"I wish to leave. Now." Clarissa turned toward Mr. Saunders, who had brought them there in his coach. "Sir, I am terribly sorry to inconvenience you, but would you...?"

"Are you certain, Miss Ellison? It truly isn't—"

"I am absolutely certain, sir. Thank you." Without waiting for a response, she headed toward the door to collect her wrap.

Mr. Saunders kept up a polite prattle all the way home. Aunt Lily had absolutely no problem chatting with him.

She knew she was being rude, but Clarissa simply couldn't bring herself to participate in such inanity. She still couldn't believe that, knowing precisely how her grandmother had lost the family fortune, Lady Morley had still encouraged Clarissa to play cards. Was it possible that she didn't know—?

No, her aunt had specifically said 'you're not your grandmother. You won't lose everything.' So, she had to know. She had to know that it was while playing whist that her grandmother had lost the family fortune—something that had killed Clarissa's grandfather and her grandmother soon after. Something that the entire family felt the effects of every single day and was the reason why Clarissa absolutely had to make a good match.

When they finally stopped in front of the Morley's home, Mr. Saunders descended from the coach first in order to help the ladies out.

Clarissa paused before following her aunt up the steps to the house. "Please accept my apologies for the way the evening ended."

"Oh, no worries. No worries at all," he said with much more good cheer than Clarissa had expected.

"You are very kind. I do hope we will see each other again."

"Of that, there is no doubt," he said with a bow.

Clarissa was grateful when the butler informed her that Lady Morley had retired straight away. She simply didn't have the energy to deal with her and her spite.

The following morning, Ox was baffled by the sound of laughter coming from the dining room. And then he remembered—Frederick Ellison. Well, clearly, he and Lady Uxbridge were getting on well, just as he'd predicted.

"Oh, Uxbridge, you have just missed the most amusing story from Frederick's journey here," his mother exclaimed as he came through the door.

Mr. Ellison jumped to his feet and bowed. Ox waved him back to his breakfast. "Good morning, Mother, Mr. Ellison." He turned to fill a plate with eggs, ham, and potatoes. "I knew the two of you would get on well."

"Oh, indeed. I am so glad you convinced this dear boy to stay with us rather than his aunt and uncle."

"Ah yes, concerning that..." Ox sat down at the head of the table between his mother and Mr. Ellison. He paused while the footman poured his tea. "You *do* plan on making your presence in Town known to your relations?"

Mr. Ellison played with the food on his plate for a moment.

"Why would he not, Jonathan?" his mother asked.

"It seems that young Mr. Ellison, here, came to London without notice or permission."

"Oh, no!" Lady Uxbridge turned to Mr. Ellison. "Is that true, my dear?"

"Yes, my lady," the boy mumbled.

"But your parents, they must be worried not knowing your whereabouts. Or… you didn't run away from school, now, did you?"

"No, my lady," Mr. Ellison answered, not lifting his eyes. "But I did leave a note for Diana—my sister. I didn't tell her exactly where I was going, only that she shouldn't worry."

"Which means, for certain, that she will," Ox pointed out.

"Indeed! You must write to them at once, Frederick," Ox's mother said.

"If you don't, I'm certain Miss Ellison will," Ox added.

At that, the boy's eyes did lift. "I… I suppose I *will* need to go see her—and my uncle. It is, after all, why I am here."

He sat straighter as he remembered exactly why he'd come to London.

"Would it be out of line for you to tell us why it was so important that you come to speak with them in person?" Lady Uxbridge asked.

"Oh no, my lady," Mr. Ellison answered immediately. He then seemed to deflate a touch. "It's just, well, it's rather embarrassing, and I am certain I should not be spilling such personal details concerning my family."

Lady Uxbridge looked about the dining room and then made a shooing motion to the footman. When he had closed the door behind him, she said, "There, now, it is just you, me, and Lord Uxbridge—and you can be absolutely certain we will not speak of this to anyone. On my husband's name do I so swear it, may he rest in peace," she finished.

Ox was rather shocked at this, but if this was what it took to get the truth from the boy... "And I, too, swear not to tell a soul," Ox added.

The boy looked satisfied. "Well, it is just this—my father is refusing to pay for me to go to school like my closest friend, the Earl of Tyne." He turned toward Ox and added, "His father is a marquess and bestowed his lesser title on my friend."

"Understood," Ox said, trying his best not to laugh at the boy's earnest explanation of something so common among the nobility.

"Tyne goes to Eton and has told me all about it. It sounds like heaven on earth. Classes, sports, and other boys my age. But my father..." Mr. Ellison paused, clearly upset. "He reinvests a good proportion of his profits back into the estate. He thinks I shall get a sufficient education between the tutoring he gives me and what I get from the vicar. But I have already surpassed the vicar in my knowledge of history and mathematics, and my father rarely has the time to sit with me."

Ox frowned. "So, you have never been to school?"

Mr. Ellison shook his head. "And I would so love to go. I thought that since my uncle was so generous as to pay for Clarissa to come out in society, that I might be able to convince him to pay for a year at Eton. After that, well, perhaps I can find some kind of sponsor or Clarissa—"

"She is hoping to marry a gentleman willing to undertake such expenses," Ox put in.

The boy's cheeks turned pink. Perhaps he knew that Ox and his sister were friends and thought there might be more between them. That Ox's feelings were, in fact, so engaged that neither Miss Ellison nor her brother would ever know.

Ox's mother nodded. "That does seem to be the best course of action, Frederick. Wait for your sister to marry and then apply to her husband."

"But that might not happen for months," the child protested.

"You were honestly thinking that you could start school immediately?" Ox asked.

"Well, yes. The Easter half term has just begun and—"

"Mr. Ellison, schools do not allow students to come in midyear. No matter what, you will have to wait for the next term to start," Ox told him. This was clearly news to the boy, for his mouth dropped open, and then he slumped back against his chair. "So, this was all for nothing? Whether my uncle agrees to pay or Clarissa's husband, I can't go until the autumn?"

"I'm afraid so," Ox told him.

"However, the trip doesn't have to be a complete loss. You are welcome to stay here with us for a few days," Lady Uxbridge offered.

"Indeed, I would be very happy to show you around London. There is Astley's Amphitheatre—"

"I heard that was for children," Mr. Ellison objected.

Ox attempted to hold back a laugh and managed to disguise it as a cough. "Actually, a great many adults enjoy the entertainment there as well. However, we could go to the British Museum, if you prefer, and perhaps a visit to Tattersalls?"

Mr. Ellison's eyes immediately lit up. "Oh, yes, sir! Yes to both!"

"Excellent, we shall begin straightaway," Ox told him. But an idea was forming in his mind. This child had traveled half the length of Britain to go after what he wanted. Surely Ox could travel across Mayfair.

He stood up decisively. "We had better get going. I have a call I need to make this afternoon." He paused and turned back to his mother. Their daily routine of reading through the post—

"Go on, I shall have Robert leave your mail on your desk," she said, waving him away.

He came around the table to give her a quick buss on the cheek, then ran off to call for his phaeton.

Chapter Twenty

Ox was pleasantly surprised by how enjoyable it was to view London through a boy's eyes. Frederick exclaimed over just about everything once he stopped being so self-conscious.

He and Ox had only had time to visit the museum and have ices at Gunter's before Ox needed to return home to actually get some work done, so he would be free to call on Miss Buttery-Clements that afternoon.

It was already three by the time he'd gone through the post and read up enough to be able to have an opinion on Warwick's latest legislative proposals to Parliament.

He ordered his phaeton to be readied, then ran to his room to change his cravat, don a more fashionable waistcoat, and run a brush through his hair. Both he and his equipage arrived at the front of the house at the same time.

Lord Aston's home wasn't too far, but Ox didn't want to arrive sweaty, and he knew that it was quite warm from his excursion with Frederick.

He was bowed into the house after presenting his card to the footman who answered the door.

"The Earl of Uxbridge to see you, miss," the footman said after he'd scratched at the partially open drawing-room door.

Ox stepped in just in time to see Dray jump to his feet. It looked as if he'd been sitting next to Miss Buttery-Clements on the settee. It looked as if he'd been sitting very close to her on the settee.

"Ox!" his friend exclaimed. "What are you doing here?"

Ox narrowed his eyes at the duke but did not miss the young lady's flaming red cheeks. As casually as he could, Ox sauntered into the room. He bowed to Miss Buttery-Clements and ignored Dray and his idiotic question.

"Good afternoon, Miss Buttery-Clements," he said.

She stood and curtsied. "Good afternoon, my lord. What a... a surprise it is to see you here."

He noticed the missing word—lovely, perhaps? Pleasant would have worked as well. But, no, it was merely a surprise.

"Yes, I was hoping we might—"

"Excuse us, Katherine," Dray said, cutting Ox off.

He also noted Dray's use of her given name as he dragged Ox back to the door. "What, in the name of all that's good, are you doing here?" his friend whispered urgently.

"In the name of all that's good? Really?" Ox had never heard Dray use that phrase before. Usually, he simply took the Lord's name in vain and thought nothing of it.

"Ox!" Dray's jaw was clenched.

Ox casually crossed his arms over his chest. "I might ask the same of you. I might also ask why you were obviously sitting so very close to Miss—oh, no, wait, it is Katherine now, isn't it?"

Dray had the grace to flush. "Listen, we were just, ah, talking," he began. He then seemed to recall himself and added, "Not that it's any of your concern."

"Not my—"

"No, it is not," Dray interrupted him. "You have never asked Aston if you may court his sister, nor asked her if she would like to be courted by you. So, no, it is not," he said again, this time with more emphasis.

Ox was about to throw his words right back into his face and point out that Dray had not done those things either when Miss Buttery-Clements walked over.

"My lord," she said, giving Ox a sweet smile, "His Grace and I were about to go out for a drive. Perhaps the two of you could continue your conversation at a later time?"

Ox could hear Dray release a breath of relief. "Yes, old man, we'll talk about this later." Dray patted Ox's shoulder.

It wasn't so much the false friendliness as the pleading look in Dray's eyes that made him relent.

Ox nodded. "Very well. Perhaps I'll see you this evening at Powell's," he said to Dray.

The duke nodded. "Perhaps."

Ox was faced with his phaeton the moment he stepped out the door. He had no desire to drive. No, what he needed was a good long walk. Luckily, he'd brought his groom with him, thinking the man would need to walk the horses as he visited with Miss Buttery-Clements. Now, he just told the groom to return the vehicle to the mews.

What in the hell was Dray up to?

Clarissa managed to avoid spending time with her aunt by asking to go to the bookshop. Aunt Lily had no use for books and, therefore, book shops.

Clarissa was happily browsing through the newly released fiction when she heard her name. She turned and found a middle-aged lady approaching her. Brown ringlets dangled by her powdered cheeks and sharp green eyes seemed to analyze everything they fell upon.

"Miss Ellison, how lovely to meet you again."

Clarissa gave the older woman a curtsy as she scoured her mind for who she was. Perhaps she was one of her aunt's friends? But that didn't seem right. Hopefully, it would come to her as they spoke.

"How do you do, my lady?" Clarissa said, certain the woman was a lady and not a Mrs.

"Very well. I do hope you've recovered from whatever it was that drove you from the card table so precipitously?"

The card table? Oh no, this was the lady she'd played cards with at Lady Broughton's, of course! Clarissa could feel her face heat with embarrassment over her rude behavior that evening. "I do beg your pardon for my outburst. My aunt made me very upset when she mentioned my grandmother."

"Yes, I did notice that. Well, think nothing of it. In fact, if you'd like to join us, I am hosting a card party this evening."

"Oh, I don't know—" Clarissa began, already feeling that horrible sensation in the pit of her stomach.

"Well, you don't need to decide immediately. Here is my address. If you would like to join us, just come." The lady handed over her calling card and then strolled away.

Clarissa looked down at the card—Baroness Isabel Shipton. The address was not far from the Morleys' house, but Clarissa was certain she would not attend. She dropped the card into her reticule. When she turned back toward the novels, she found she was no longer interested. She left the shop and decided to go for a walk.

She'd been out so few times on her own, she rather thought she would take advantage of the opportunity.

As she walked past the street that led to her aunt and uncle's home, Annie hopped up next to her. "Miss Ellison, you missed the turn," the girl said.

"No, Annie, I have decided to go for a walk. I've been wanting some exercise, and today is such a lovely day for it."

The girl didn't say anything. She just fell back a step or two to where she had been walking before.

After a little bit, Clarissa just randomly turned down a street in generally the same direction as her uncle's home.

As she walked, admiring the houses, she noticed a large traveling coach standing in the street. Two footmen were carrying a trunk out of the house nearby, and she watched as they strapped it onto the back of the coach on top of another one.

Well, someone was leaving Town before the end of the Season. How odd. But then a gentleman, followed by a lady, came out of the house. There was a second man as well, and Clarissa was shocked to recognize the Duke of Drayton.

A closer look at the first man revealed him to be Lord Aston, which meant that the lady with them, whose face Clarissa couldn't see because of her bonnet, must be Miss Buttery-Clements.

Clarissa started to hurry forward to greet her friends when Miss Buttery-Clements turned and gave her brother a hug. The duke took her hand and helped her up into the coach. He paused to shake hands with Lord Aston, then followed after her. A footman closed the door, and the coach drew away from the house, moving away from Clarissa.

As Lord Aston turned to go back into his home, he caught sight of Clarissa and paused. She could see his hesitation as he decided whether to greet her or pretend he hadn't seen her. Clearly, his gentlemanly manners won out, and he strolled toward her as she approached him.

"Miss Ellison, this is a surprise," he said, bowing to her.

She curtsied. "Indeed. I was just out for a walk with my maid. I didn't realize this was where you lived," she said, trying her hardest not to think about what she just saw.

He glanced back at the house. It wasn't the largest one on the street, but it was a nice brick house with a black door that had a very pretty fanlight window above it. "Er, yes."

No, she couldn't avoid it, no matter how much she wanted to. "Was that your sister and the Duke of Drayton—"

"Please, Miss Ellison," Lord Aston said, cutting her off. "I beg of you not to tell a soul what you just witnessed." He sounded almost desperate.

She knew full well why. It was clear the couple was leaving Town—together. She felt oddly detached. "I assume there will be an announcement in the paper soon?"

He looked a little relieved. "Yes. They just wanted a small, private wedding, that's all. They're heading to Drayton."

She nodded and even managed to pull her lips up into a smile. "How lovely. I wish them all the happiness in the world."

He relaxed even further. "Thank you."

She nodded. "I won't say a thing until a public announcement is made."

"You are very kind and understanding."

"It is nothing at all. I should be going, however. If I'm not home before long, my uncle might worry."

"Of course." He bowed. "It was lovely to see you and, once again, thank you for your discretion."

She curtsied and then continued on her way. She glanced back and saw him have a quick word with her maid and, if she wasn't mistaken, slip her a coin.

Clarissa waited for Annie to catch up to her and then continued in what she hoped was a homeward direction.

CHAPTER TWENTY-ONE

Miss Buttery-Clements and the duke. The duke and Miss Buttery-Clements. She swallowed and somehow was beginning to find it difficult to breathe.

Well, she supposed she shouldn't be too surprised, considering how he'd been looking at her the other night. Clarissa had, of course, spoken to him after that. She'd even had him laughing and looking at her with what she'd thought at the time was approval, possibly even interest. Clearly, she'd been mistaken.

Clarissa turned down another street and was surprised to find herself back at her uncle's home. She wasn't entirely certain how she'd found it. She hadn't even been paying much attention to where she was going.

The footman let her in at her knock, and she headed straight up to her room. Unfortunately, as she passed the drawing room, her aunt called out to her. Clarissa had no choice but to go in.

"No books?" the woman asked.

"No. There were none that interested me."

"We have no plans for this evening," her aunt told her. "I suppose you will think it a shame since you will not have the opportunity to, once again, throw yourself at the Duke of Drayton. How goes that, by the by?" Her aunt's eyes glittered with malice. "Have you embarrassed yourself or will be you continuing—"

Clarissa opened her mouth to protest her aunt's cruelty but found she couldn't. Instead, she was suddenly caught off guard by a sob and found herself nearly doubled over, crying for all she was worth. She didn't know how that came on or why now, but she could no more control herself than... than... control who the duke married.

The thought and the tears sent her running for her room.

She dropped down onto the floor in front of the unlit fireplace and cried until there were no more tears left in her. A handkerchief was put into her hand. After mopping her face and blowing her nose, she looked up and found Annie looking at her in distress.

"You had a fondness for the duke, didn't you?" the girl asked.

Clarissa nodded.

"I heard you talkin' about him to your aunt," Annie explained. "And your aunt talkin' to your uncle about it."

Clarissa didn't even want to hear what they had said, but Annie told her anyway.

"She told him that she couldn't believe how you thought you were good enough for him. She didn't think you'd be able to land 'im." Annie paused and then added, "I thought you could. You're so beautiful and kind. Any man would be a fool not to want to marry you."

The tears came again, but Clarissa pulled Annie into a hug. "You are too good to me, Annie," she said when she could.

"Oh, no, Miss Ellison. It is you who are good to me. You brought me here to London with you and have been so patient while I learned to be a lady's maid."

"And you have learned! You have become a wonderful lady's maid."

The girl blushed. "Thank you. I am glad you're pleased with my work. But-but what are you goin' to do now? You still need to find someone to marry."

"I know." Clarissa sat back down on her bottom. "I just don't know who—"

"What about that big fella? Lord Ox?"

Clarissa gave a sad little smile. "Lord Uxbridge," she corrected. "His friends call him Ox, but I never would."

"Well, whatever you call 'im, what about him?"

Clarissa fiddled with the handkerchief in her hands. "I... I don't know. I don't think he likes me. He had wanted to marry Miss Buttery-Clements—the girl who got into the coach with the duke."

"Oh. So, he was interested in her? Well, now he's got no one either. Are you sure he wouldn't want to marry you?"

Clarissa could only shake her head. "I'm pretty certain. He and I are just friends."

"Are you sure?" Annie persisted.

Clarissa closed her eyes to stop the tears from falling again as she nodded. "I... I..."

"You have feelin's for him!" Annie exclaimed.

Clarissa covered her face.

"Why don't you tell him? Maybe he does too—for you, I mean."

"No, I couldn't." Clarissa took a shaky breath but managed to fend off another bout of tears. "We-we agreed to just be friends, nothing more. And since then, he has shown no more interest in me."

"I can't believe it to be the case, miss."

Clarissa nodded. "You know, thinking about it," she said, searching through her muddled feelings, "it's not that I'm upset about the duke and Miss Buttcry-Clements getting married."

"You're not?" Annie asked in surprise.

"No. I-I truly do wish them happy. It's just that..." This was hard to explain, and she wondered if Annie would think less of her for it. She ventured forth anyway. "Do you remember at home whenever my brothers and sisters and I would play a game?"

Annie laughed. "You all got really competitive."

"Exactly," Clarissa said. "And I always won. Always. No matter what we played. No matter what we were doing. I always won—and not just because I'm the eldest."

"No. Master Frederick is probably stronger than you, and even paired up with the other boys and even some of the girls, they could never best you."

"Exactly. Well, this, with the duke, is the same thing. He was the one everyone wanted, but I said I was going to win him."

"Oh," Annie said, understanding. "But you didn't. You lost."

Clarissa nodded because her throat had tightened up again.

Annie put a hand on Clarissa's back. "But you didn't even like him—well, not as much as you like Lord Uxbridge, right?"

With a sniff, she agreed. "That isn't the point, though."

"Right. The point is that you had to win."

Clarissa looked up at her maid. "Now that I think about it, I'm... I'm rather ashamed. Lord Uxbridge once pointed out to me that this really isn't a game. It's marriage. It's for life."

Annie smiled. "He's right."

"But I've still lost. I've got no suitors. No one who might marry me." The tears threatened again. "Not only that, but Frederick wanted me to ask Uncle if I would petition him to pay for his schooling, but I... I just can't!" She wiped away her tears. "He's paying for me to have this Season. I couldn't possibly ask him to pay for Frederick's school as well. So... it's not just that I've lost at the marriage game. I've also failed my brother, who deserves so much more."

Annie sighed. "I do understand now. And there's nothin' you can do?"

Clarissa began to shake her head when suddenly a thought popped into her mind. She looked around the floor.

"What is it?" Annie asked.

"My reticule."

Annie turned around and plucked it off the chair behind her and handed it to Clarissa.

"Thank you!" She opened it and found Lady Shipton's card. Swallowing hard, she said, "This. This may be my answer."

"What's that?"

"The card Lady Shipton gave me today at the bookshop. She said she was hosting a card party and invited me to come."

"Oh."

"I just..." Clarissa thought about asking her aunt if she would accompany her, but it just gave her such a bad taste in her mouth. She didn't want her aunt there. But she needed someone. "Annie. Would you go with me?"

"Me? I, er, of course, Miss Ellison."

"Good! We will sneak out of the house after dinner and go to this party. You will just need to sit nearby while I play."

"All right. I can do that."

Clarissa gave her maid a quick hug. This was going to work out. She knew it would. She was still devastated at losing the Season. This was the first time in her life she'd lost. But she would not lose Frederick. She would not, could not, disappoint him. And for herself, well, she would simply have to find another way to win. Was it possible, she wondered, for her to come in second place?

Clarissa's determination began to flag a few minutes after she and Annie left her uncle's house that evening. They'd sneaked out from the garden, both of them wearing long cloaks with their hoods pulled up.

What would she do if she was caught? Well, she was certain to be sent home in disgrace. That would be all right, so long as her father never learned of the reason. If he ever found out that she'd been gambling, he'd disown her and throw her out of the house for certain.

Her footsteps slowed at that thought. On the other hand, there was Frederick to think of. Yes, she must think of him and only of him, or she would never get through this night.

"Miss Ellison, how lovely to see you," Lady Shipton greeted her. Clarissa was once again struck by how calculating the woman looked as she took in Clarissa's hair, lack of jewelry, and gown, which was deliberately one of her plainest evening dresses. "I honestly didn't think you would come. Well, aren't you just full of surprises?" The lady laughed, but Clarissa didn't know what was so amusing, so she just smiled.

"Thank you for the invitation, my lady," Clarissa said.

"Of course. Do come in." She leaned in closer to Clarissa before leading her toward the tables set up on the far side of her large drawing room. "Are you using your name this evening?" she asked quietly.

Clarissa didn't understand what this meant. "I beg your pardon?"

"Are you using your real name, or would you prefer that I introduce you as Miss Smith?"

"Oh! You mean so no one knows who I am?"

"Yes. And everyone here understands that Miss Smith must never be recognized outside of this room. So should you run into, say, Lord Ralston at a party, he will pretend to have never been introduced to you That would, literally, be true," Lady Shipton explained.

"But that's... that's an excellent idea, my lady," Clarissa said, stopping herself from saying it was dishonest. It was, but it was also clever and would allow her to hide her identity—not that very many knew her, but still it was a good thing.

Lady Shipton nodded and then led her over to a table where two women and a man were sitting playing a children's game—probably just to pass the time until a fourth joined them so they could play properly.

"And here you are," she said, coming up to the table. "I told you that you wouldn't have to wait long." She looked around the table saying, "Lady B, Lady P, and Lord Ralston, may I present Miss Smith?"

So there really was a Lord Ralston present. The gentleman rose and bowed while the two ladies—both about ten years older than Clarissa and dressed very fashionably—nodded from their seats.

"Miss Smith, would you like to partner with Lady P?" Lady Shipton asked.

"Yes, thank you." Clarissa took the fourth chair and smiled at her new partner.

"I do hope you are good," the woman drawled. Clarissa frowned. "I believe I am, but you will have to decide for yourself, my lady."

Lady B burst out laughing. "She got you there, Matilda."

Lady P gave her friend a scathing look before turning back to the gentleman who had the cards in his hand. "Deal, would you, Ralston?"

Lady P was a good player, Clarissa quickly learned, but so were Lady B and Lord Ralston. At the end of the first rubber, Lord Ralston tallied up the points and found that, as a team, she and Lady P had won by just two points. Individually, the lady had won overall, which meant that she won all the money wagered.

They had begun at a tuppence a point, but with the understanding that it would go up from there. Clarissa had brought all the money she had—everything she'd saved and brought with her from home as well as the pin money her uncle had given her—but she wasn't sure it would be enough.

Lord Ralston won the second rubber, and Lady P won the third. Clarissa heaved a sigh of relief when she won the fourth.

They played another two hands, and Clarissa lost them both. She had to win the next, or else she would have lost everything. She thought furiously of Frederick. She had to win for Frederick.

When Lord Ralston tallied the points once again, he informed Clarissa how much she owed to Lady B, who had won the rubber. She just stared at him blankly for a moment. "Wh-what? How could that be?"

"The wager was increased from the last game," he explained patiently. He turned the book where he tallied the score around, so she could check his calculations.

"You do have the money, do you not, Miss Smith?" Lady P asked with a lift of one eyebrow.

"I, er, I..." Clarissa thought hard and fast. She, in fact, did *not* have the money, nor could she write an IOU because then her uncle would surely hear about it.

"Those are lovely earrings you have on," Lady B commented.

Clarissa put a hand to her ear. She was wearing her mother's diamond earrings.

They were the only jewelry she had inherited when her mother had died, the rest of the family jewels being set aside for Frederick's wife.

With a trembling hand, she passed one of her earrings over to the woman.

"Well, that will more than pay what she owes," Lord Ralston said, peering at the earring still in her other ear.

"Let us play," Clarissa said in a strained voice.

Her hands trembled, but Clarissa began to count the cards, paying even closer attention to which cards were played and even *how* they were played. She won the next rubber.

"Well done," Lady B said, handing her back her earring.

Clarissa accepted it with a sigh of relief. She won the hand after that and, in fact, two more.

Finally, Lady P exclaimed, "How is this that you are suddenly winning every hand?"

Clarissa just shrugged. "I've just been dealt very good cards, my lady." She looked over at the dwindling pile of coins in front of the others.

"Well, if you do it again, I'm going to have to give you *my* earrings," she said. Clarissa looked at the large emeralds dangling from her ears.

"I would not ask that of you," Clarissa told the woman, remembering how it had felt when she had done so. "Instead, I will ask that you excuse me. I believe it is time I returned home."

Lord Ralston chuckled. "Clever girl, quit when you're ahead."

She gave him a little smile and then slid her winnings into her reticule. The thing had to weigh over five pounds, filled with so many guineas and other coins.

She got up, curtsied, and then went to thank Lady Shipton for an enjoyable evening.

CHAPTER TWENTY-TWO

Ox's question concerning Dray and Miss Buttery-Clements was answered the following morning when a note was delivered to him before he'd even finished dressing for the day.

He recognized Dray's handwriting and dismissed his valet despite the fact that his cravat was untied and he had only one boot on.

He sat down at the edge of his bed and opened the note. A quick scan of it made him drop his head into his hands.

Eloped! Dray and Miss Buttery-Clements had eloped! They had been just waiting for her bag to be packed when he'd come in. Dray's traveling coach had been waiting just out of sight to whisk them out of London and to start their journey.

Ox looked at the letter once more. There really wasn't very much to it. Apologies... love... more apologies...

Ox sighed and let the letter fall from his hand onto the floor. What was he—wait, when had they left? He sat up. It sounded as if they'd left yesterday afternoon. If that was the case, Aston must be out on the road after them, even as Ox sat bemoaning his lost opportunity.

He wondered if he should go after Aston. If Ox could catch up, perhaps they could convince Dray and Miss Buttery-Clements of the mistake they were making.

Ox was putting his other boot on when a footman knocked. "Well?" Ox called out.

The man opened the door and took a step into the room. "Er, my lord, I was asked to tell you this a quarter of an hour after I delivered the note," he began nervously.

Ox stood and started tying his cravat. A simple knot would have to do. "Tell me what?" he asked.

"Er, that Lord Aston is waiting for you in your study."

That made Ox's head snap toward the man. "He's in my study?"

"Yes, my lord. He was the one who delivered the note. He then told me—"

"Not to tell me for a quarter of an hour. Yes, I got that." It was probably to give him time to read the note and digest the information, although news like that could hardly be said to have been thought through in such a short amount of time.

Ox frowned and finished tying his cravat. "Tell him I will be down... no, forget it. I'll just go."

"I do apologize..."

"Not your fault, Robert. You were following orders—not mine, but orders, nonetheless."

"Thank you, my lord," the man answered with obvious relief in his voice.

Aston looked very comfortable sitting in a chair in Ox's study when he arrived. He had a cup of tea in front of him and was happily nibbling on a biscuit.

"Ah, Ox, good morning. Terribly sorry to disturb your morning routine and all that," Aston said, not getting up.

Ox seated himself across from him and poured himself a cup of tea. "Well, clearly, as you are here, I am assuming that you did not, in fact, go haring after your sister and Drayton?"

"Er, no. Actually waved them goodbye, good travels, and all that," the man admitted.

Ox lifted his eyebrows at that. "So, you knew and approved of the ruining of your sister?"

"Not ruining. Just, er, getting married elsewhere."

"Elsewhere? You call running off to Gretna Green marrying elsewhere?"

"Oh, they're not going to Scotland. They're headed for Dray's estate in Yorkshire. They'll be married by the special license he acquired yesterday."

Ox just blinked at the man, his mind oddly blank. "Why?" he finally asked.

Aston shrugged. "Didn't want to have to deal with a whole big fuss and whatnot. Thought it would be much better if they just went off and got leg-shackled on their own." He reached for another biscuit. "Don't blame them at all. Lady Aston and I had an enormous party—a ball, actually, in addition to the wedding breakfast for fifty of our nearest and dearest. You know, the whole thing. Katherine didn't want any of that. Neither did Dray." He bit into the biscuit and munched happily.

There was nothing Ox could do. Dray was his own man. Miss Buttery-Clements had the blessing of her brother. And Ox was left with... nothing. No wife, no prospects for a wife, just a looming deadline after which he would lose thirty thousand pounds.

Honestly, now that he thought about it, it had been ridiculous of his great-aunt to think he would be able to find a wife within the year. Him! Ox. The man proper young ladies shied from if he came within five feet.

Oh, all right. He supposed that was a slight exaggeration. Two feet. If he attempted to speak with them.

With a sigh, Ox raised his teacup. "To Dray and his bride."

That evening after dinner, Ox retired to his study to be alone. He'd once again spent the morning with Frederick and the afternoon at work, but he hadn't been there, not really. He'd been distracted by imaginings of Dray and Miss Buttery-Clements. Of Miss Ellison. Even of what Lady Preston would say to all this.

He couldn't even bring himself to go out to his club. He was certain all he would receive would be the pitying looks from other men, and he wouldn't be able to deal with that without breaking some bones.

He'd just settled into his favorite chair when there was a light knock on the door. "Come," he called.

"I'm sorry, my lord, but may I have a word?" Frederick asked, coming hesitantly into the room.

"Of course! Come in, sit down. I'd, er, offer you a drink, but I think you're a little young yet."

Frederick laughed. "That's all right. I don't need one." The boy fidgeted for a minute, clearly trying to put his thoughts into words.

"Just spit it out, Frederick," Ox said after watching the boy struggle. "Whatever it is, I will understand."

Frederick looked at him a little nervously, but then said, "I just... I noticed that you've been rather preoccupied today, and I was wondering if there was anything I could do to help. I know I don't have a lot of experience and don't know much, but I'm a good listener and, well, I do have five sisters."

Ox chuckled. "That obvious, am I?"

"Well... yes," Frederick admitted with a sheepish little grin. He sat down at the edge of the other chair as if he wasn't sure he was allowed.

Ox sighed and took another sip of his drink. "The, er, young lady who I was thinking of proposing to ran off with my closest friend yesterday." God, it hurt to put it so bluntly.

Frederick nearly jumped from the chair. "What? But that's horrid! No wonder you've been out of sorts all day!"

Ox waved to the boy to calm down. "It's not as bad as all that, in a sense," he reassured Frederick. "I didn't love her. I just thought we would suit. Clearly, Drayton *did* love her, and she him. I'm happy for them, honestly. It's just... well, I suppose it came as a shock, that's all."

"Oh," Frederick said, sitting back. "Yes, I can imagine it would. And it wasn't very nice of your friend—Drayton?—not to even give you any warning."

"Yes! That is it precisely," Ox said. "You've just hit it in one. That is exactly why I'm annoyed. It's because Dray, who I've known since we were boys at school together, didn't even tell me. He didn't say a word! And he knew that I was thinking of proposing to Miss Buttery-Clements. He knew—and he said not one word about his own attraction to the girl. If I'd even had an inkling that he was interested, I would have backed off. I would have left the field wide open for him. But he didn't say a word."

Frederick just shook his head. "Well, I suppose there's nothing you can do about it now."

"No. I've just got to go on searching for a wife," Ox agreed.

"What was it about Miss Buttery-Clements that you liked? That made you think you would suit?" Frederick asked.

"She was not delicate," Ox told him. That was really the gist of it. "She was also funny and sweet."

"Not delicate?" That seemed to perplex the boy.

"I'm a rather, er, large person," he said, pointing out the obvious. "I'm afraid that if I even touch a woman too firmly, she'd break."

Frederick burst out laughing. He laughed for nearly a minute before he realized that Ox wasn't laughing. Wasn't joking. "Oh! Wait. You're serious? You're afraid of breaking a girl?"

Ox just frowned at him. "I've broken people before. I'm a lot stronger than I look."

"Really? How? Who?"

"When I was a little older than you. We were playing cricket, and I was the wicketkeeper. The batter came running at me, and I grabbed him to stop him from getting to the wicket. His arm broke."

"But he was running. He had all the momentum of that, his weight, and the sudden force of you stopping him," Frederick argued. Ox was impressed. He clearly understood science and the physical world.

"And then there was the time some fellows were fooling around and shaking hands as hard as they could—deliberately, you know how it is. Someone shook my hand, and I broke one of his fingers and injured the others."

"You squeezed too hard?"

Ox nodded. "The boy couldn't use that hand the rest of the term. I felt awful."

"Sounds like he asked for it," Frederick said with a huff.

Ox chuckled. "He was a nasty fellow. There were some who congratulated me on breaking his hand. But it still wasn't right."

Frederick smiled. "Well, I can tell you, girls are not at all fragile, no matter what they look like. Take Clarissa, for example. You wouldn't believe what she can do. She once hit a cricket ball so far it went through a window—on the second story! She's outrun me any number of times. And can climb a tree faster than you would believe!"

Ox was delighted. He couldn't help it. Just thinking of the beautiful, proper young lady doing any of those things tickled him.

"And once—I'm not proud of this, mind you—I grabbed her arm to pull her around a corner while Eleanor was holding on to her, pulling the other way."

"You were both pulling at her?" Ox asked, a little horrified.

"I was pulling around a sharp corner. If she'd been the least bit fragile, her arm could have easily broken. It didn't." He shrugged. "She was fine, if angry."

"Huh." Ox sat back and thought about that.

"And with all the sports we've played? We don't play gently or necessarily proper. Diana broke her leg once ice skating on the pond—well, not so much skating, since we didn't have blades to attach to our boots, but sliding on the ice."

"And Miss Ellison has never hurt herself?"

He shook his head. "She's tough! A real right one, too. Never shies away from any challenge."

Ox held back a laugh. "That I knew. The moment she heard Dray was the catch of the Season, she set her cap at him and did everything she could think of to win him." Now, he did laugh, just thinking about it. "She even kept score!"

Frederick just smiled. "Sounds like Clarissa." They were both quiet for a moment, then Frederick picked up on what he'd been saying earlier. "The thing is, you don't need to worry about hurting a girl, honestly. They're a lot tougher than you'd expect." The clock in the hall struck the hour. Frederick stopped and listened, counting out the chimes. "Goodness! Ten. I should go to sleep." He stood up to go.

"Thank you, Frederick. You've made me feel a lot better and gave me something to think on," Ox told him.

The boy shrugged. "Of course." He stopped at the door and turned around. "I also really think you should court my sister. She's tip-top." He paused, lowering his gaze to the floor, and added more softly, "And then we'd be brothers." He fled out the door.

Brothers. Ox would like that. He'd like that very much!

CHAPTER TWENTY-THREE

Clarissa awoke the following morning wondering if the card party had just been a bad dream. She jumped out of bed and reached into the back of her wardrobe. Her fingers closed around the reticule, still holding her winnings.

No such luck.

"Miss Ellison, what are you doin' on the floor?" Annie asked. She was carrying Clarissa's tea and toast. It was an indulgence Clarissa took advantage of since she would never have it at home—not with eight younger siblings, many of whom needed attention or assistance getting dressed and eating their breakfast.

Clarissa got up and climbed back into bed so Annie could place the tray on her lap. "Just checking to see if last night really happened."

The girl giggled. "It sure did! You won a huge purse full of money." Annie stepped back so Clarissa could drink her tea. "Have you counted it yet?"

"No, and I don't think I want to. Oh, Annie, what I did was wrong." Clarissa dropped her face into her hands. "I feel sick."

"Take a bite of toast. It will settle your stomach," the maid advised. Clarissa knew she was right, but just the thought made her stomach cramp.

"And I don't know why you think you don't deserve that money. You won it fair and square."

"I don't know. I just... I swore to my father I would never gamble. My grandmother lost thousands of pounds that way, and I nearly lost my mother's earrings."

Annie became serious. "I did notice that," she admitted.

"Why didn't you say something?"

"I was thinking of doin' so, but I thought it wasn't my place. I thought I would, though, if you lost the other one. But then you started winnin'. How did you do that?"

Clarissa shook her head. "Desperation. I had to get that earring back."

"Well, whatever it was, it worked. And then you had the good sense to stop. I was never so proud."

"Well, I am not. It is... tainted money. It's not mine."

"No, you said you were goin' to give it to your brother for his schoolin'."

"I can't. It wouldn't be right." An idea came to her. "I am going to visit Lady Shipton this morning and see if I can't learn the names of the people I played with. I am going to return the money."

But Lady Shipton just burst out laughing when Clarissa told her of her idea later that day. "You are too amusing, Miss Ellison," the lady said when she caught her breath.

"I don't mean to be, my lady. I just…"

Lady Shipton lost her smile and began to look a little concerned. "Please do not be offended by what I'm about to say, but you didn't cheat, did you?"

Clarissa was horrified. "No! Absolutely not!"

The woman narrowed her eyes at Clarissa. "Lord Ralston did say that you were having a remarkable streak of good luck just before you left."

Clarissa nodded. "I had lost a number of hands to Lady B and was forced to give her one of my diamond earrings," she explained. "Those are the only things I have of my mother's—she died two years ago."

"I see."

"I just couldn't lose her earrings," Clarissa explained.

"So, what did you do?"

"I began paying closer attention to the cards that were played and how the other players moved their hands when they pulled out a card to play. I was able to guess whether they had better cards that they were holding for later or if they had a bad hand from their expression."

One side of Lady Shipton's lips quirked up. "That was very clever. However, paying close attention to your fellow players is not cheating. You deserved to win that money. It is yours to do what you want with it." She paused and then asked, "Just how much did you win?"

"I don't know. I haven't been able to bring myself to count it, but my reticule was very heavy, and Lord Ralston had to write an IOU."

Lady Shipton chuckled. "I doubt he'll be able to pay that before next quarter day."

"But I don't—"

"This has been highly amusing, Miss Ellison, but I do have other things to do today. Whether you want the money or not, it is yours. You cannot return it to the people you won it from. If they couldn't afford to lose it, they shouldn't have been playing."

The woman stood up, forcing Clarissa to do the same.

"Thank you, my lady. I do appreciate your time," Clarissa said as she curtsied.

They should not have wagered if they couldn't afford it, Lady Shipton had said. If only that had been the case with her grandmother. Clarissa tried to swallow down the lump in her throat as she made her way home, but it seemed to be stuck.

This was going to be awkward, Ox thought to himself as he knocked on the Edgertons' door. He was bowed into the house by a footman, who immediately showed Ox up to the drawing room.

"Oh, Lord Uxbridge, how delightful to see you again," Lady Edgerton said before the footman could even announce him.

Ox bowed and heard the click of the door behind him.

Lady Edgerton gave him a conspiratorial grin. "I have told no one, not even the servants, that we are having this portrait done. It is going to be such a wonderful surprise for my dear Edgerton."

Ox pulled out the half-finished canvas from the case he'd brought. He came forward as he carefully unwrapped it from its cloth. "What do you think?" he asked, showing it to her.

"My word! It's so small, and yet perfectly detailed," she exclaimed, peering at the miniature portrait. "And it is an excellent likeness. Oh, my lord, it is wonderful. Such talent you have."

"I am happy you are pleased. Now, is that what you'd like me to paint for your gown? Of course, not much of it will be seen," he reminded her.

"Yes, of course, but I do believe the neckline of this dress is just right." She turned, so she was slightly turned away from him, just as she was in the painting.

It was clear why she liked the dress. It was cut so low the tops of her breasts showed as enticing little mounds.

Ox pretended not to notice, gave a nod, and then asked, "Where will you sit? There won't be any background, but I do need the right light."

"It is such a shame Drayton has gone out of Town, so I couldn't sit in his morning room once again." She paused and then widened her eyes. "Oh, dear, you *do* know that he—" She left her words hanging.

"Yes, I do. Aston was kind enough to come tell me in person," Ox told her.

She sat down in a chair by the window, and he pulled up another so he could sit as well.

"Did you know about it right away?" Ox asked.

"No," she said with a frown. "Lord Aston came and told me as well, the day after they'd left. I think it perfectly horrid of my brother to deny us the joy of planning his wedding. I've written to him and told him that there will be a ball whether he likes it or not. I don't care if it is this Season or next, but we *will* have one."

Ox just chuckled, feeling bad for Dray and Miss— the duchess. They didn't want a fuss, but it looked like they couldn't escape it.

"I must say it was such a relief to me to hear that he'd run off with Miss Buttery-Clements. It's not that Miss Ellison isn't a perfectly nice girl, I'm sure, but that family. How many siblings did she say she had? Twelve?"

"Eight," Ox corrected, although he wouldn't have minded twelve any more than he did the eight.

Frederick's comment the evening before, that they would be brothers if Ox married Clarissa, struck his heart. He hadn't been able to look away from the closed door for a good five minutes.

Of course, her family wasn't the only reason why he would want to marry Clarissa. There was, of course, her wit, beauty, and discernment. She saw things in a way that was completely new and different for Ox. He loved that about her.

That thought stopped him. His pencil hung in midair for a moment.

"Is something wrong?" Lady Edgerton asked.

"What? Oh, no, I, er, just thought of something, that's all." He went back to his sketching.

He not only loved that Clarissa had a large family, but he loved Clarissa. And she? How did she feel about him?

He heaved a sigh. They were friends. Nothing more.

"Now something is truly wrong," Lady Edgerton said. "Never have I heard such a forlorn sigh."

Ox quickly applied himself to his work. "No, no," he insisted. "I'm just trying to ensure I get the color of your gown just right."

"Oh, yes, please do. This color especially suits me. I think it complements the green of my eyes."

"Yes, that it does." Ox agreed. He had to stop thinking of Clarissa. His feelings were unrequited, and he truly wanted to keep to a minimum the inevitable pain he would feel when she found another.

Speaking with Lady Shipton had not helped Clarissa at all. She still had no idea what she was going to do. She couldn't ask her aunt or uncle. She couldn't ask Diana, who would be sympathetic but unhelpful, nor Eleanor, who might be helpful but not sympathetic, and would probably accidentally share the information with Diana in front of the little ones who would—no, it was too horrible to even contemplate.

But who else could help her?

Clarissa jumped from the sofa where she'd been sitting with her embroidery.

"What in the world?" her aunt exclaimed.

"I do beg your pardon. I just remembered Lady Preston had requested I call upon her today," Clarissa lied.

"Oh, well, it would not do to ignore such a summons," her aunt admitted.

"No, indeed. I shall take Annie. You need not concern yourself," Clarissa said, when she saw her aunt begin to set aside her own stitching.

"Very well. In that case, do enjoy yourself."

That was too easy, Clarissa thought as she went for her bonnet and pelisse.

Chapter Twenty-Four

Not much later, she was knocking on Lady Preston's door. It was answered by her butler, who Clarissa had met once before when she'd come for Lord Uxbridge's dance lesson.

"I was wondering if Lady Preston was at home to callers?" she asked hesitantly. "I am Miss Clarissa Ellison."

"Good afternoon, Miss. If you would step inside, I shall inquire," he said in his unusual Irish accent.

Clarissa did as asked, grateful not to be left on the doorstep while he went down the long hall leading to the back of the house.

A few minutes later, he returned and showed Clarissa up to the drawing room.

"Lady Preston will be with you shortly," he told her.

Clarissa thanked him. The room had been put back to a more normal arrangement than the last time she'd been here.

She had just taken a seat on the settee when Lady Preston came in.

"Miss Ellison, what a lovely surprise."

Clarissa jumped to her feet and curtsied. As she did so, she began to wonder if this had been a good idea after all. How could she even think of admitting to such a horrid, embarrassing thing to an elegant and kind woman as Lady Preston?

"I am so sorry, my lady," Clarissa said. "I should not have disturbed you."

"Nonsense, I'm certain Connor, my butler, was very grateful you did." She came over and sat on the chair nearest the sofa, indicating for Clarissa to resume her seat. She then smiled and leaned forward as if divulging a great confidence. "I have a tendency to lose myself in my work and completely forget about everything else. I don't believe I've even had anything to eat since breakfast."

As if on cue, a maid came in, bearing a tea tray with little sandwiches as well as biscuits.

"What is it that keeps you so distracted, my lady? If you don't mind me asking."

Lady Preston poured them both a cup of tea. "My studies into astrology. I believe I told you about it once before."

"Oh, yes, the, er, stars?" Clarissa asked.

"That's right." Lady Preston offered the plate of sandwiches.

"No, thank you."

The lady nodded and proceeded to place quite a few on her own plate. She picked one up, but before taking a bite asked, "But you did not come to hear about my work, did you?"

"Er, no, my lady," Clarissa admitted. "But I…" She wasn't quite sure how to go on.

"You? Perhaps you were looking for some advice?"

Clarissa put down her teacup and knotted her hands together. "Well, yes, but I don't know…"

Lady Preston reached out and put a hand on top of Clarissa's. "Miss Ellison, we are friends, are we not? When I needed help with Lord Uxbridge, I called upon you. I do hope you would not hesitate to do the same."

Clarissa could not argue with such logic and kindness. "It's just a little embarrassing," she admitted.

"I am certain you know I would never share a confidence."

"Yes, of course!" Clarissa said quickly. She took in a deep breath and proceeded to tell the lady about her grandmother's downfall, and then how she, herself, had behaved in the same atrocious way. Tears pricked her eyes as she said, "I am just like her. I have the same addiction."

"Oh, my dear Miss Ellison, one evening of cards does not an addiction make," Lady Preston said with a kind smile.

"But it wasn't just one—my aunt took me to a card game before this one. That is where I met Lady Shipton."

Lady Preston sighed. "I do not understand her reasoning for doing so. I must admit. Does she not know of your grandmother's story?"

"She-she does," Clarissa admitted.

"Then it was very wrong of her to tempt you in that way. However, considering how you feel after having won this money, I have no fear that you will fall into such a bad way."

"But it was still wrong. And when I went to Lady Shipton this morning to try to return the money, she just laughed at me."

Lady Preston's lips twitched as if she too were suppressing laughter. "But you won the money fairly, did you not?"

"I did. Lady Shipton asked the same question," Clarissa admitted.

"And she was satisfied with your answer?"

Clarissa just nodded.

"And yet you still feel guilty for having won." It was a statement, not a question. Lady Preston ate another sandwich as she thought about this. She then turned back to Clarissa. "The only resolution I can think of is to give the money to Lady Welles to give to those who need it."

"Charity, you mean?"

Lady Preston nodded as she'd just taken another bite.

"But that's a brilliant idea," Clarissa exclaimed. "That would solve my dilemma over what to do with the money and help others!"

"And you must determine not to gamble again," Lady Preston added.

"Oh, no! Never. I have learned my lesson," Clarissa agreed.

"Excellent. Now, tell me something else," the lady began. She paused to take a sip of tea. "Why do you not like Lord Uxbridge?"

Clarissa would most certainly have choked if she had been drinking her tea at that moment. "I... I don't dislike him. We are friends," she said when she could find her voice again.

Clarissa absolutely could not admit to Lady Preston that she wouldn't dare allow herself to consider Lord Uxbridge for her husband. The man had been so besotted with Miss Buttery-Clements he would be heartbroken when he discovered his friend's duplicity. She wondered if the duke had told Lord Uxbridge what he'd been planning. It would have been the kind thing to do.

But, no, she could not even dare to consider that his lordship felt anything beyond friendship for her. That she had fallen in love with him was a secret she would not, could not share—and especially not with Lady Preston, who was such a close friend of his.

Clarissa knew the lady had tried on numerous occasions to throw her and Lord Uxbridge together, and his lordship had ignored them all—because he was not interested. Clarissa was grateful he'd accepted their friendship. She could not hope for more.

"I understand, and a friendship with the earl is truly wonderful, but you have been pursuing the Duke of Drayton. While he is both a very nice man and a duke, I don't believe he is the right one for you. You don't seem the type to want a man merely for his title."

"No! Goodness, no," Clarissa said quickly. Clearly Lady Preston had not yet heard of the duke's elopement with Miss Buttery-Clements, nor was it her place to inform her. Instead, she admitted to the truth of the matter concerning the duke. "I was only pursuing him so I could win the Season."

Lady Preston frowned. "Win the Season?"

"Yes. He was the most sought-after gentleman. Clearly, whoever married him would win the Season," Clarissa explained.

As understanding dawned, Lady Preston first allowed her mouth to drop open and then burst out laughing.

Clarissa could only smile and wait.

After a minute, Lady Preston wiped a stray tear from her eye and said, "My goodness, but you most definitely are an Aries, aren't you? It's all a game. A competition which you must win."

Clarissa was confused. "Well, yes. Is it not?"

That sobered Lady Preston. "Sadly, I do believe too many think like you do."

Clarissa was happy to learn that she was right and that Lady Preston had said as much, for they were interrupted by her butler just then, who came in and said, "I do beg your pardon, my lady, but you asked me to remind you when it was four o'clock."

Lady Preston stood. "Thank you, Connor. I am so sorry, Miss Ellison, but I have a lecture I am attending this evening."

Clarissa stood too. "Of course! I do beg your pardon for taking up so much of your time, and thank you, once again, for your advice. I will go see Lady Welles as soon as possible."

Only later, while Rebecca was changing for the evening, did she realize that she had forgotten to disabuse Miss Ellison of her mistaken notion that the Season was a competition. She would speak with her about it later.

CHAPTER TWENTY-FIVE

Ox still hadn't made up his mind how he was going to propose to Clarissa. Should he declare his intention to court her first? Ask her uncle for permission? Write to her father?

He was allowing all the possibilities to run through his mind as he entered Lady Haddington's ball that evening. He nodded to various acquaintances and maneuvered himself to avoid Miss Ricketts on his way to his usual stance against the far wall. As he did so, he noticed that Clarissa hadn't yet arrived. It was still early, and her aunt did like to make an entrance.

He had just decided to speak with Clarissa, herself, about it when he saw her enter the ballroom. Her aunt paused at the entrance, looked around, then seeing whoever it was she was looking for, was about to head in that direction. Surprisingly, she turned back to Clarissa before doing so. She must have said something, for the girl nodded and followed the woman farther into the ballroom.

He lost sight of them, much to his dismay. Knowing Lady Morley, she would probably completely ignore Clarissa as she chatted with her own friends. Ox decided to seek her out.

He found her and her aunt speaking with a woman in a peacock-blue turban sporting matching peacock feathers. She had a very pretty young lady with her, probably her daughter. She was blonde with cute freckles on her nose—to her mother's horror, he was certain. The girl didn't look much older than seventeen and spent a great deal of time staring at the floor.

The girl's mother caught sight of him hovering nearby, deciding whether he should join them. Her eyes widened, and Ox prepared himself for the usual look of fear he was normally greeted with. Strangely enough, instead of taking a step back, she gave him a welcoming smile.

Clarissa turned around and did the same.

"Good evening," Ox bowed to Lady Morley. "Miss Ellison." He took her hand and placed a light kiss on her knuckles as he bowed and she curtsied.

"Oh, Lord Uxbridge, how delightful to see you this evening," Lady Morley said. "Maria, may I make you and your daughter known to the Earl of Uxbridge?"

"We would be delighted," the woman answered, her feathers waving gently above her head.

"Lord Uxbridge, this is my dear friend the Viscountess Stokes and her lovely daughter, Miss Emmaline Stokes."

Ox bowed to them both. "It is a pleasure to make your acquaintance."

"And yours, my lord. Lud, it's been so long since I was in Town that it seems as if every which way I turn I am meeting someone new," Lady Stokes said.

"How long has it been, my lady?" Ox asked politely.

"Well, Emmaline is eighteen, so I suppose it must be eighteen years," the woman laughed.

Ox turned to smile at the girl to allay the terror she must be feeling, being so close to him. Strangely, while she was looking up at him, it was with interest rather than fear. The girl blinked her big blue eyes at him and gave him a shy smile.

Ox was flummoxed. He wasn't entirely certain what to do. Never had a young lady simply treated him as if he were any other gentleman.

"My lord?" he heard Clarissa say. She must have said something, and he'd missed it. He turned to her. She did not look happy. In fact, despite the fact that her mouth was slightly turned up in a pleasant, polite smile, her eyes flashed with... anger? Dare he hope—jealousy?

"I do beg your pardon, Miss Ellison," he said. "I missed what you said."

"I merely asked how you were doing," she said, her voice pitched a little lower than usual. Goodness, she *was* angry.

"I find myself in dire need of the company of a beautiful young woman and, er, perhaps a turn about the room. Would you honor me, Miss Ellison?" he asked, holding out his arm to her.

She softened immediately, and Ox did a little jig in his mind. Turning to the other women, she said, "If you wouldn't mind excusing us?"

"Oh, not at all! Why, no one could pass up an invitation like that," Lady Stokes said with a giggle.

After they'd gotten out of earshot of her aunt, she turned to him. "How are you, truthfully?"

He lowered his eyebrows, trying to discern her meaning. "I am well. And you?"

She nodded. "The same."

She turned and began looking around the room. Ox was pretty certain who she was looking for. "He's not here," he told her.

She looked up at him curiously.

"Drayton," he said, answering her unspoken question.

"Oh! Yes, I know," she answered.

"You know?" His friend wouldn't have told her and not him, would he? Or perhaps Miss Buttery-Clements had said something to her?

"Yes, I—" She clamped her mouth shut only to add a quiet, "I shouldn't say."

Ox leaned down toward her. "You know about Dray and..." He deliberately left the rest of the sentence unsaid.

"Miss Buttery-Clements?" she finished, speaking equally softly. She widened her lovely green eyes. "Yes. I take it you were made aware?"

He nodded. "Heard it from Lord Aston."

"Are-are you all right?" she asked hesitantly.

She sounded upset. Well, she must be, knowing she was thrown over for another. Or, in her words, that she'd lost the game. He sighed, feeling bad for how she must have been hurt.

"I? How are you?" he asked. And then he added, purely out of curiosity, "How did you learn of it?"

"I accidentally saw them leave," she told him. "I was just walking up the street."

"Really?"

She nodded. "So, we are both left to search out others, I suppose."

This was it, he realized. This was his opportunity to say something of his feelings. To tell her, well, if not precisely how he felt—admitting he loved her seemed inappropriate at this time—but at least asking if she might be amenable to a courtship.

He'd just opened his mouth to speak when she said, "My lord, you have been so kind to me..."

Ox closed his mouth. Was she going to ask him? He doubted she would be so forward as to hint at a courtship—not that he would mind in the least.

"Would you mind very much introducing me to any other gentlemen you think might take an interest in me?" she finished.

He froze. He couldn't help it. He simply stopped walking and stood stock still.

She misinterpreted his reaction. "I am coming to terms with the fact that Miss Buttery-Clements has clearly won the Season, but I wonder if it's possible for me to come in second."

She wanted someone else. Anyone else. Anyone but him. His chest tightened. His throat closed, and it was all he could do for the moment to continue breathing.

When he could manage it, he growled out a "No!" before walking away.

CHAPTER TWENTY-SIX

Clarissa couldn't believe it. No? No, he would not even help her find another gentleman? Whyever—

And then she thought about it. Perhaps just the thought of marriage upset him so much now that he could no longer have Miss Buttery-Clements. She wondered if he'd truly loved her. Clarissa knew that the thought of Lord Uxbridge with anyone else made her chest ache. She'd almost dragged him away from her aunt's friends before he had the opportunity to meet the beautiful Miss Stokes. But perhaps he felt the same about Miss Buttery-Clements—furious that his closest friend had snatched her from right under his nose. The poor man. No wonder he was short-tempered.

Clarissa's heart went out to him. How she longed to chase after him. To pull him into her arms and soothe away his hurt. But she was certain she would be rebuffed, and that would hurt her more than nearly anything.

But they were friends. Perhaps he would see it as a friendly gesture, then she could at least know the pleasure of—

"You seem to have the worst luck with men," a snide voice said from just beside her.

Clarissa nearly jumped. She tried to control her rapidly beating heart and face Miss Ricketts with equanimity. "Good evening, Miss Ricketts."

As the girl looked down her nose at Clarissa, an idea sparked. Miss Ricketts chased after only the most popular, eligible men. Surely she would be able to introduce Clarissa to someone. And, honestly, the longer Clarissa stood about thinking of Lord Uxbridge, the less she wanted to meet anyone else, and the harder it was for her not to simply make a fool of herself and go running after him.

"Miss Ricketts," Clarissa said, "you are a discerning person. Might you be willing to introduce me to some gentlemen?"

The girl frowned and opened her mouth to say something, but then she seemed to think better of it. Instead, she allowed her eyes to roam about the ballroom. She paused, as if she found who she was looking for, and then locked her arm with Clarissa's.

"Right this way. I see the perfect man for you."

Miss Ricketts stopped in front of two gentlemen. One was a middle-aged man with dark hair that looked in dire need of some attention, preferably a wash and then brush. It was clumped together with grease and in disarray. The other was a slightly younger man with smiling eyes and the brightest red waistcoat Clarissa had ever seen. She wondered if he felt the need to compete with the soldiers in their red coats.

"My lords," Miss Ricketts oozed.

They broke off their conversation to bow to her.

"May I present Miss Ellison?" she asked, looking in particular at the greasy-haired man.

"Please do!" that gentleman answered.

"Miss Ellison, Lord Metworth and Lord Drakestone."

Clarissa curtsied to the two men and then silently cursed as the orchestra, which had been taking a break, suddenly began playing the opening notes of a cotillion.

"Miss Ellison, it is a pleasure. Would you care to dance?" Lord Drakestone said, his words slightly slurred. Either he was attempting to hide an accent, or he was drunk.

"Oh, I—" Clarissa started, wondering if it was possible to say no.

"Of course she would. Why, my lord, she and I were speaking just over there when she asked me to introduce her to you," Miss Ricketts said with enthusiasm.

It wasn't precisely the truth. Clarissa had not asked to be introduced to him, but to a gentleman. And here she was, introduced. She supposed she might as well dance with him, and then perhaps she could ask their hostess to find a proper, eligible gentleman to introduce her to.

She smiled, placed her hand on his sleeve, and allowed him to lead her out onto the dance floor.

The moment the music started in earnest it was clear the man was drunk. He wavered on his feet and nearly lost his balance a few times. He did, however, manage to pry from her that this was her first Season.

"Do not tell me that a beauty such as you is having a hard time finding a man to marry you?" he asked, smiling slyly at her.

"No, not at all," Clarissa answered. "I was in hope of a proposal from one gentleman, but then sadly, he chose another," she admitted.

The man *tsked*. "Bad luck, that."

"Indeed."

"And your mama has found you no one else?" he asked before spinning around once more than was necessary.

"I am here with my aunt," Clarissa explained. "And unfortunately, she does not know very many eligible gentlemen," she said, fibbing a little. Her aunt did know some gentlemen, but they were all younger sons, although she had introduced Clarissa to one gentleman farmer who had come to London to look for a wife. It wasn't that these men weren't pleasant, but they were all looking for a wife with a significant dowry. Once they heard that hers was almost nonexistent, they were no longer interested in her.

"You poor thing," Lord Drunk... er, Drakestone answered. "And your aunt is...?" His eyes roamed the ballroom.

Clarissa looked about but could not immediately locate her aunt. She did happen to see Lord Uxbridge standing against the wall as usual. "I'm afraid I don't see her. I'm certain she is about somewhere."

"Really?" He narrowed his eyes. "I mean, yes, yes, of course. She is certainly here somewhere."

By the end of the dance, she wondered if she was going to have to help the gentleman off the dance floor.

"Blast, but it is hot in here," he said, taking her hand and tucking it around his arm. He stank of liquor.

"Er, yes, it is rather warm," Clarissa agreed.

"Let us go outside for a breath of fresh air, shall we?" He didn't give her the chance to answer, but somehow whisked her most efficiently out the doors and onto the balcony.

She hoped the cooler air would sober him, but he seemed to list a little toward her as he dragged her toward the garden.

"It is a lovely garden. Shall we go for a little stroll?" he asked.

"I don't know, my lord, I should probably..." Clarissa tried to tug her hand free from under his arm, but he grabbed her hand with strength she wouldn't have guessed he possessed, so she could not.

"Now, now, my dear. We are just going to go for a little walk. It will feel good, I promise you." Already he sounded less intoxicated. Perhaps the fresh air was helping him to sober up.

"Very well, a short walk, perhaps, but then I really need to get back to my aunt," Clarissa agreed, not that she felt she had very much choice in the matter. His grip was becoming even more firm.

They headed off to the right, down a path with pretty torches lighting the way. But then the lights stopped, and it was suddenly very dark.

"I think we should turn around, my lord," Clarissa said, once again trying to pull her hand out.

"No, no, just a bit farther," he said. He sounded completely sober now and seemed to be walking with great purpose, as if they were not so much on a stroll but going someplace.

It turned out they were. Much to Clarissa's surprise, when he suddenly stopped, placed a hand along the back wall of the garden, and pulled open a door Clarissa hadn't even noticed.

He shoved her out and then grabbed her, pressing her back against the wall.

"What..." Was all she was able to get out before his lips were pressing against hers, and then not only his lips, but his entire body.

What in the world was Clarissa doing with Drakestone? The man was a rake, a drunk, and a cheat.

He watched as the fellow stumbled his way through the cotillion, with Clarissa, at times, having to save the man from falling onto his face. What in heaven's name had driven her to choose Drakestone of all the men in the room? Why was she dancing with him? Ox couldn't stop watching, although he tried.

Once the dance was over, he would rescue her from that lout. Hell, he'd even dance with her himself if it came to that—whether she wanted him to or not. Introduce her to other men! The idea still burned inside him.

Ox turned back toward the dance floor just after the music had ended, but didn't see Clarissa and Drakestone. He bolted from the wall where he'd been standing and searched about for them.

There!

Drakestone had Clarissa's arm tucked around his, and he was leading her out toward the garden. Oh, there was no question that Ox would allow that man to take his love outside without him. Ox followed.

"Oh, Lord Uxbridge," a woman's voice said as he made his way across the room. He turned and saw Lady Stokes smiling at him.

He paused to bow to her. "I must beg your pardon, my lady. I, er, I am otherwise occupied at the moment." He turned and headed back toward the doors. Clarissa and Drakestone were gone.

Ox did his best not to break into a run. He walked as quickly as he could in an attempt to catch up to them. Pausing, he scanned the couples on the balcony taking the in the air. Clarissa didn't seem to be among them.

Could he have taken her into the garden along the lit pathways? He did not like this at all. Not. At. All. He suppressed a growl of anger as he headed into the garden.

He turned left and jogged down the path a little way, but there was no sign of them, so he turned around. This time, he did not hesitate to break into a run.

He ran past the point where the torches ended, thinking he heard Clarissa's voice, but then there was silence. He stopped, breathing hard. His heart was pounding, making it difficult to hear anything. He focused on just listening.

The music from the ball, the muffled sounds of the people behind him, a giggle from a bush he'd passed. He moved forward, farther into the dark.

And then he heard it. A brief shout. It sounded like Clarissa, but it was broken off, stopped. By a hand? By a mouth?

A low guttural sound came from his throat, or perhaps it was his heart. He ran forward, but the path came to a dead end. He spun around. Where were they?

Backtracking, he looked left and right, but to his right was nothing but the back wall of the—a door? Had the lout taken her out of the garden?

Ox felt along the wall. He'd just found the handle when he heard "Get your hands—"

He burst through the door and, in one swift motion, grabbed Drakestone by his collar, pulling him away from Clarissa.

"Hey!" the man protested. "What the hell—"

"What do you think you're doing?" Ox said, his voice low. He gave the man a shake, but really, he wanted nothing more than to punch him in the face. And the stomach. And the kidneys. And the throat. He wanted to beat—but Ox was too aware that Clarissa was standing right there watching him. He could see her in his peripheral vision. She either had her hand to her mouth or was wiping her lips, probably the latter if Drakestone had kissed her.

"Get off me!" Drakestone squirmed, trying to break free of Ox's grip.

Clarissa stepped forward, and before Ox knew it, her fist slammed into Drakestone's face. Ox let the force of it take the man down.

He turned and saw her lift her chin with satisfaction, but then his eyes were drawn downward to her gown, which was hanging off one shoulder, exposing her soft, delicate skin.

"Why, you little bitch!" Drakestone spat.

Ox didn't remember anything after that.

A voice broke through the red haze of fury. "My lord! Lord Uxbridge! Jonathan!"

Ox was breathing hard. He'd drawn his arm back to land another blow to the man's face, but he found it caught.

"Jonathan, stop! You're going to kill him!"

Clarissa's words broke through the haze.

Ox looked down. The man's face was a bloody mess. He was bleeding from his nose and mouth, and his eyes were closed. There might have been blood coming from a cut to his left eye as well. It was hard to tell.

And suddenly it all came rushing back. The blood. The anger. The yelling. Ox had been a boy, but he'd been a strong one. Always much bigger than the other boys his own age, he'd been teased and teased until one day he'd finally snapped.

His tormentor's face had looked like this too, only there had been the addition of a pool of blood around his head from when Ox had bashed it against the ground.

Ox had never seen him again. He'd heard it had taken months for him to recover fully.

With a shake of his head, he dispelled the image of that boy. Slowly, he got to his feet. And then... Clarissa. Dear God, she had seen him... she had witnessed...

He remembered her ripped dress and tore his coat off, but he couldn't face her. He couldn't. He dropped it on the ground and then ran.

Clarissa picked up the coat, keeping her eyes averted from the bloody mess that was Lord Drakestone. She put it on as she followed in the same direction Lord Uxbridge had flown.

She found her way around to the street where the coaches and their drivers waited until they were required again.

She approached one young man, perhaps some gentleman's tiger. "I beg your pardon," she said, trying to keep the trembling under control—when it had begun, she couldn't really say. She wasn't cold. In fact, she thought she was perspiring a good deal. But still, the shaking would simply not abate. The young man turned around. "Would you be so kind as to find Lady Morley's coach and inform the coachman I need him to take me home?"

The boy took one good look at her, nodded, and went running toward the coachmen hanging about.

Chapter Twenty-Seven

The following morning Clarissa was still sitting in front of the fireplace—where she'd been all night—when a maid came in and informed her that her aunt wished to see her. At least the trembling had stopped, but she still felt hollow. Tears had not come. She was certain she had been through every emotion—fear, anger, pride that she might have been the one to break the man's nose, even relief that Lord Uxbridge had shown up when he had—but there had been no tears.

Clarissa sighed and nodded. "Please send Annie to me, to help me dress."

"Yes, miss." The girl bobbed a curtsy and disappeared.

What Clarissa really wanted was a bath. Even though she'd scrubbed her lips numerous times last night, she could still feel that disgusting man's mouth on hers and smell that stink of alcohol and sweat.

She gave herself a shake. She didn't have time for a bath.

Half an hour later, she entered the drawing room, where her aunt was speaking with the housekeeper. Upon seeing Clarissa, however, she dismissed the woman.

"Who gave you permission to leave the ball last night? It wasn't me. And according to Lord Morley, it wasn't him either." The woman glared angrily at Clarissa.

She sank into a chair, unbidden. "My apologies, Aunt. I was taken suddenly"—she paused and then continued ironically—"and violently ill."

Her aunt's aggressive posture softened. "Oh, dear, yes. You do not look well at all. Was it something you ate? Dinner did not sit comfortably with your uncle, but he was not made ill by it, thankfully."

"If you don't mind, Aunt Lily, I would like to return to my room to rest," Clarissa said, deliberately not answering her.

The woman waved her off. "Yes, yes, of course. It is a good thing we had no plans for the evening."

In his bedroom, Penley removed the bandage the valet had insisted upon the night before.

His man peered at Ox's cut and bruised knuckles. "Well, it's a good thing it was a tree you hit, my lord, and not whoever made you so angry. I have heard that they have bags full of sand at Gentleman Jackson's, which are much easier on the hands."

Ox hated lying to the man, but he simply could not have told him the truth. And he was glad he hadn't when the article about Lord Drakestone had been front and center in the newspaper that morning.

It was a relief to read that the man was still alive. And thank goodness, he had been unable to speak and name his attacker after he'd been found.

Ox flexed his hands. They hurt but were usable. He supposed that had something to do with the odd-smelling concoction his valet had put on them before wrapping him up tight the night before.

"Thank you, Penley," Ox said. "I shall keep that in mind next time I am driven to hit something." He got up and went down to his study. He debated paying a call on Drakestone, then figured that would cause more talk than just leaving him alone. Hopefully, the man was intelligent enough not to divulge who had beaten him. He should be aware that nothing good could come of that.

Ox could still see Clarissa standing there in the moonlight, her gorgeous auburn hair half-fallen down, her pale green gown hanging off one shoulder, the shine of tears and fury in her eyes. Ox chuckled to himself as he recalled her surprising and unexpectedly strong hit to Drakestone's face. In his shock, Ox had let go of the man, who had gone sprawling onto the paving stones with the force of her punch.

But when Drakestone had cursed at Clarissa and made to get up, Ox had seen red.

Ox's thoughts shifted to Clarissa. Was she all right? Had that bastard had a chance to truly hurt her? He wished with all his heart to go to her, but he couldn't. He knew what he would find if he did so. Fear. Eyes wide with terror. Steps back if he were to step forward. And that would only be if she even agreed to let him into the house.

No. He would not, could not stand to see that in her eyes.

It was such a shame her brother had left the previous morning. If he'd still been here, Ox could have sent him 'round to see how she was doing. But now... he didn't know what to do. Now she knew what he was capable of.

With that image staying stubbornly in his mind's eye, Ox needed something to distract him. There was only one thing that did.

Hours later, a soft knock on his studio door jolted him from his work. Thank God, he'd been dipping his brush in paint. Otherwise, the portrait would have had a pink streak going across the entire thing.

"Jonathan?" His mother stood in the doorway.

"Yes, Mother, is there something you need?" he asked, putting down his brush to ensure there were no accidents.

"Are you all right? Penley told me about your injured hands, and now you've been in here all day. You've missed luncheon and tea."

Goodness, much more time had passed than he'd realized. He pulled out his watch. Half past five!

He shook his head. "I do beg your pardon, Mother. I had no idea. I've been so focused on my work."

She took a few steps closer to see what it was he was painting. "She's beautiful."

Ox admired his work and thought he'd done a pretty good job at capturing his subject.

"Lady Preston sent a footman around this morning, but I told him you were not to be disturbed."

"Lady Preston?" Of course! What an idiot he was. "Lady Preston!" He jumped to his feet. He would write to her and ask her to call on Clarissa. She would be able to find out how Clarissa was doing.

"Er, yes, Lady Preston," his mother repeated.

"I need to write her a note. Er, to thank her for inquiring," he said, making up something on the spot.

"Jonathan." She put a hand on his chest to stop him. She then took his right hand in hers and looked at the bruises, which were an alarming shade of purple. "You did not hit a tree, did you." It wasn't a question. It was a statement. "That man, Lord Drake-whatever."

"Drakestone," Ox provided.

"You were the one who beat him. All I want to know is why," she said gently. There was no fear or anger in her voice. No disappointment either.

Ox dropped his gaze to the floor.

"He was attacking Clarissa," Ox admitted. He then looked up at her. "You should have seen the facer she landed on him, sent him straight to the ground."

Lady Uxbridge smiled. "I expect nothing less from Frederick's sister." But then she turned serious. "But you still felt the need to hit him."

Ox nodded. "He was going to get up and—I don't know if he would have hit her or what, but I didn't wait to find out." He swallowed. "He hurt her. Her... her dress was pulled down and... and..." Ox put his fingers onto his closed eyes, feeling the prick of tears.

"Shh..." His mother pulled him into her arms. He had to bend down to rest his head on her shoulder, but he still savored her comfort, just as he had when he was a child.

After a few minutes, once he'd regained control, he lifted his head. His mother captured his face in her hands and looked up at him. "I'm proud of you, Son. You defended a girl's honor, and you had the self-control to stop once it was done."

He shook his head. "She stopped me. Clarissa. She grabbed my arm and made me stop before I killed him."

"Well, however it was done, you *did* stop. She may have reminded you of the need, but *you* did it," she insisted.

He thought about it. Maybe he did. When he'd beaten that boy, so many others had tried to stop him, but he had just gone on, regardless. This time... this time, all it had taken was her calling his name and a light touch. That was progress, he supposed.

"I need to write to Lady Preston and ask her to check on Clarissa. I need to know that she's all right."

His mother nodded and stepped out of his way.

Chapter Twenty-Eight

Lady Preston,

It is imperative that you visit Miss Ellison today. Please do me this favor, and I will be forever grateful.

Ox

PS: Please send me word of how she fares.

PPS: She may explain why I have asked this of you.

Rebecca frowned at the note she had just received. She looked up at the clock. It was nearly six and certainly well past regular visiting hours. On the other hand, Ox's note did sound urgent.

With a swift decision, Rebecca found Connor and requested her coach be brought around. While that was happening, she ran up to her room, made sure her dress wasn't too wrinkled and her hair in place. She put on her hat and gloves, grabbed a shawl, and went down to await her coach.

Not much later, she was knocking on the Morleys' door.

It was opened by the butler.

"I am aware that this is an odd time, but if you could please inform Miss Ellison that I need to have a word, I would greatly appreciate it." She handed the butler her card.

"I am very sorry, my lady, but Miss Ellison has been indisposed all day. I doubt very much that she would be able to see you," the man told her.

This was worrying. "Then it is even more important that I see her."

The butler gave a small shrug, as if to indicate that he did not understand women, and let her into the house.

"Please tell her that I would be happy to visit with her in her bedchamber if that would be more convenient," she told the man as he headed for the stairs.

He gave a nod to acknowledge her and then went up.

He wasn't gone long. "If you would follow me, my lady," he said, giving her a slight bow.

She followed him up to the second floor and to a room at the end of the hall.

After a brief knock, he let her into the room.

Miss Ellison's bedroom was a lovely pale pink with matching curtains, two chairs in front of the fireplace, and darker rose silk covering the walls. Miss Ellison stood by the fire.

"I am so sorry to disturb you, my dear," Rebecca said as she headed straight for the girl. The butler hadn't been wrong. She did look ill. Her face was starkly pale. At least her eyes looked clear, and she was dressed in a pretty sprigged muslin gown that looked well-worn and loved.

Miss Ellison curtsied. "Not at all. Please do forgive me for not inviting you into the drawing room. I'm certain my aunt is there, and I'd rather not disturb her," Miss Ellison said, indicating Rebecca take a seat. "May I offer you some tea?"

"Oh, no, thank you."

Once Miss Ellison had seated herself, Rebecca took out the note from Ox. As she handed it to the girl, she said, "I just received this from Ox. Perhaps you can explain it to me?"

Miss Ellison read the note, immediately pulled a handkerchief from a pocket, and dabbed at the corners of her eyes. "He is so kind. So good," she said.

"He most certainly is, but what shall I tell him?"

She sniffed. Keeping her gaze on her hands in her lap as she fiddled with her handkerchief, she said, "I am fine." She looked up then and met Rebecca's eyes. "Please do assure him that I am well."

"I'm certain he'll be relieved to hear it."

The girl dropped her gaze once more. "You want to know what happened."

"If you wouldn't mind. I'm afraid I am fearing the worst," Rebecca told her. What in the world *had* happened? Had she and Ox fought? Had he proposed, and she said no? Had he learned of her gambling and become enraged?

"Oh, no, not the worst. Lord Uxbridge intervened before that."

"Intervened?" Now Rebecca was completely confused and became even more worried. That news article about Lord Drakestone sprang into her mind.

Miss Ellison nodded. "I was introduced to a... a man last night at Lady Haddington's ball. After we danced, he said he wanted a breath of fresh air. I thought that was an excellent idea because he was clearly intoxicated."

"Oh, dear."

"He insisted I go out with him, but then he dragged me through the garden and out the back door." Miss Ellison's voice became softer.

Rebecca put a hand to her mouth but managed to keep herself from gasping.

"He had only managed to press his mouth to mine and had started tearing at my dress when Lord Uxbridge—"

Rebecca couldn't hear any more. She jumped from her chair and pulled the girl into her arms.

Miss Ellison held on to her as if the world were ending. Shockingly, she did not break into tears. Perhaps she had already cried herself dry.

They stood there for a few minutes before Miss Ellison said, "Lord Uxbridge punched him until he was bloodied and unconscious."

Rebecca tightened her grip, but Miss Ellison pulled away.

"He stopped before he killed the man."

"Well, thank God for that," Rebecca said, now certain of who the man was.

Miss Ellison nodded, sniffed, and then went over to her wardrobe. She pulled out a man's coat. "He left me his coat and then ran off. I didn't even get a chance to thank him."

Rebecca took the coat when Miss Ellison offered it to her. "Would you like me to return it? Are you certain you wouldn't rather do so yourself?"

Miss Ellison looked up in surprise at that. "Go to a gentleman's home?"

Rebecca smiled. "With me to act as chaperone. And, if I'm not mistaken, I believe he lives with his mother as well. We could say we are there to visit with her."

Miss Ellison's lips parted, and a tiny smile began to creep onto her lips. "We could."

"Do you think you might be up to doing so this evening? I'm certain Ox would be very relieved to see for himself that you are—while, naturally, very upset—overall unharmed."

"I... I would like that," she said hesitantly but then added, "What about my aunt? I told her I haven't been feeling well, which allowed me to stay in my room all day."

Rebecca gave a little shrug. "I'll have a quick word with her while you get ready."

A real smile flitted on and off her face. "You are too good to me, my lady. I don't know how—"

"Pish tosh, this is what friends do," Rebecca said, waving away her words. "Come, show me to the drawing room and then splash some water on your face."

It was a little awkward simply walking into Lady Morley's drawing room where the woman was sitting with a book. A bit of explaining and some bending—although not breaking—of the truth, and Miss Ellison's aunt was giving her permission for the girl to spend the evening with Rebecca.

"I promise, the fare shall be light, and it shall just be the two of us sitting down to dinner," Rebecca was saying when Miss Ellison came into the room ready to go.

She had changed to a nicer gown and fixed her hair.

"Well, Clarissa, I do hope you are mindful of the honor Lady Preston is affording you," Lady Morley said, looking the girl over.

"Yes, my lady, I most certainly am," Miss Ellison said.

"Excellent. I shall see her home later," Rebecca said, heading to the door.

"Not too late," Lady Morley called after them.

They headed straight to Uxbridge house, Miss Ellison clutching Ox's coat in her hands. Wisely, she had left it outside the drawing room when she'd gone in to say goodbye to her aunt.

The Uxbridge butler was surprised to find visitors knocking at the door at this odd hour, but Lady Preston insisted that he check with the lady of the house to see if she would receive them.

When the butler returned and informed them that Lady Uxbridge would see them in the drawing room, Lady Preston gave a nod as if she had known this would happen. They were shown into the drawing room.

Lady Uxbridge greeted Clarissa with a hug. "Oh, my dear, I am so happy you are all right."

Being engulfed in the arms of this large, motherly woman, tears came to Clarissa's eyes.

"You poor dear, you are naturally still upset," Lady Uxbridge said, pulling away to look at her.

"No..." Clarissa managed to croak, her throat tight with emotion. She took in a deep breath and pulled out her much-abused handkerchief. "You must excuse me, my lady, it's... it's actually you both that has me shedding these ridiculous tears."

"What?" "Whatever can you mean?" Both ladies said at once.

A little laugh burst from Clarissa. She looked from one woman to the other. "I lost my mother a little over two years ago," she explained. "Ever since then, the responsibility of caring for my father's house and all my younger brothers and sisters has fallen to me."

"Oh, you poor child!" Lady Uxbridge exclaimed.

"That is an enormous responsibility for one so young," Lady Preston agreed.

"I have had the help of my sisters Diana and Eleanor. They are two and four years younger. It's just…" Clarissa looked from one lady to the other, trying to put her embarrassing feelings into words. "You are both so kind and understanding and…" She trailed off, not quite knowing how to finish her sentence.

Lady Uxbridge smiled. "Motherly?"

"Yes. I shouldn't need—"

"Now, don't you be silly," Lady Uxbridge interrupted. "We all need a little mothering now and then—especially when we've had such a terrible shock."

"And are in a strange, new place trying to manage on your own," Lady Preston agreed.

Lady Uxbridge looked a little confused at that. "You are staying with your aunt, are you not?"

"A more unfeeling, selfish creature I have never seen," Lady Preston said.

"She never expected to be responsible for bringing me out," Clarissa said in her aunt's defense.

"Nor wanted to, clearly," Lady Preston persisted.

"Well, never mind her," Lady Uxbridge said, waving a hand in the air as if trying to dispel a bad odor. "You have us, and although I do not go out into society, I am only too happy to offer my advice—even when it is unwanted. Just ask Uxbridge," she added with a laugh.

"Ah, speaking of Uxbridge," Lady Preston started.

"Oh, yes, of course. It is he who you actually came to see. Come." She led them out of the ground floor drawing room and to the back of the house.

"He is in his studio," she explained. "Been there all day."

"His studio?" Clarissa asked.

"He doesn't usually work at night—the light, you know—but when he's upset or anxious, he retreats to where he is most comfortable and happy. We all do, I suppose."

They followed the lady into an ordinary-looking study filled with books and a large desk with neat piles of ledgers and papers.

In the far corner, a door hung open.

They came around to the other side of it to find a small room, practically a closet. Lord Uxbridge was sitting at a rough, paint-splattered wooden table pushed up against the window. There were three lit candelabras surrounding him as he bent over something so small Clarissa couldn't even see it over his left arm, which rested on the table.

He was not wearing a coat, but a white smock with the sleeves rolled up above his elbows. His head was dangerously close to the candles sitting at the top of his table by the window. His concentration was so intense he didn't seem to have noticed their arrival.

Lady Uxbridge waited until he lifted his right hand and then clicked her tongue. "Uxbridge, you are going to set your hair alight."

He jumped a little, then lifted his head to look at the candle just in front of him. "I will do my best..." he started, then turned to look at her.

He jumped to his feet. "Clarissa! Lady Preston! What—"

"We came to show you that Miss Ellison was doing well," Lady Preston said. She was standing just behind, in between Clarissa and Lady Uxbridge.

Clarissa took a step closer, peering at what he'd been working on. She was shocked to find that it was a very small painting of herself. It couldn't have been much bigger than three or four inches in height and three inches wide. Despite its size, it was incredibly detailed and was a remarkable likeness.

"Oh, I, er..." He paused, and she looked up at him.

"That's incredible. I didn't know you painted. And it's so small!" she said in awe.

"Er, yes. Miniatures," he admitted with a guilty little smile.

"He is very talented and gets quite a few commissions," his mother said proudly.

"It's just a hobby," he added quickly.

Clarissa could hardly take her eyes from the painting. He'd been working on her gown, having finished her face and hair. The level of detail was fantastic, down to her diamond earrings.

"I would have never expected something so small could be so precise," Clarissa said.

"I have to say I'm not at all surprised," Lady Preston said. She'd come closer as well and was peering over Clarissa's shoulder.

Clarissa turned to the lady, who was smiling broadly.

"Why?"

"He is a Gemini. They excel at such dichotomies. Gemini are twins. Two sides of the same person. To the world, he is a bold, sociable gentleman. In private, an artist."

Lord Uxbridge just shrugged and began to roll down his sleeves, covering his powerful forearms. That made Clarissa wonder what he would look like without his shirt altogether. Just the thought made her warm.

"They are also drawn to others who are very different from themselves—like you, Miss Ellison," Lady Preston continued.

"No need to blush so, Miss Ellison," Lady Uxbridge said, a broad smile on her face.

Clarissa put her hands to her cheeks. They were hot. How embarrassing!

"You are lovely when you blush, but perhaps not quite such a deep pink," Lord Uxbridge said, clearly teasing her. "I am happy to see that you are doing well," he added on a more serious note. "I've been worrying all day." He slipped past Clarissa and Lady Preston, so they all moved into the larger room instead of being crammed into his small studio. Much to

Clarissa's shock, he began to unbutton his smock. Underneath, he had on only his white shirt. The image of him without it that she had shoved away resurfaced again. He was so large and muscular, and his chest was broad—perfect for laying one's head against to be engulfed in his arms.

"Why did you not visit her yourself?" Lady Preston asked, breaking Clarissa out of her daydream.

Now Lord Uxbridge's cheeks flushed. "I... I was afraid..."

"Of what?" Clarissa couldn't help but ask when he stopped.

He looked at her, worry in his eyes. "That you would be afraid of me," he admitted.

Clarissa frowned. "Why would you think so? I have never feared you."

"You saw... Oh, Miss Ellison, I am so very sorry you had to see me hit Drakestone." His gaze dropped. "You have seen me at my worst. I am not proud of what I did."

"But you saved me from that monster!" she exclaimed.

He looked up at that, a little smile playing on his lips. "I think you might have been quite capable of saving yourself. At least, you got a good start on doing so before I intervened."

Clarissa couldn't help her own smile coming to her lips. "You don't grow up with three younger brothers and learn nothing of how to defend yourself."

"And so glad we are that you did," Lady Uxbridge said. "But sometimes you need a big, strong man to finish the job."

"And Lord Drakestone will recover," Lady Preston added, looking at his lordship.

He nodded. "Thank God for that. I've never liked the man, but I didn't want to kill him." He turned troubled eyes on Clarissa. "You stopped me from doing that."

"I just brought you to yourself. You are usually a very gentle man, but you seemed to lose yourself in your anger."

He nodded. "I could not bear to see you threatened."

"You were wonderful," Clarissa said, her voice somehow not working quite right. She looked up into his deep blue eyes, seeing something she had no name for, but it certainly made her heart pound. He stared back at her as well. His expression was serious, but kind. She almost felt as if a magnet was drawing them closer to each other. She'd even taken one step closer to him when one of the ladies cleared her throat, making Clarissa jump. Goodness, how long had they been staring at each other? It felt like a moment and a lifetime.

"I do hope you both will join us for dinner," Lady Uxbridge said. There was a broad smile on her face, as if she were delighted at the prospect of having guests.

"Yes, indeed, do stay. I will just, uh..." he said while placing his smock on his desk chair. "I will finish getting dressed. If you ladies will excuse me." He walked quickly from the room.

Chapter Twenty-Nine

Ox joined the ladies in the drawing room. They were all sitting happily chatting, each with a glass of madeira. He was just about to help himself to some brandy when the butler came in to announce dinner.

As the only gentleman present, he paused for a moment, wondering who he should escort to the dining room. Precedence said it should be Lady Preston, but his heart wanted it to be Clarissa.

His mother saved him from the dilemma by taking Lady Preston's arm, saying, "There is no formality here, just a comfortable family meal. Come, Lady Preston, let me show you to the dining room."

Both women smiled knowingly at him, making him chuckle and shake his head. He held out his arm to Clarissa.

As she gently laid her delicate fingers upon it, she said quietly so only he could hear, "Goodness, now there are two of them!" At that, he burst out laughing, causing the two older ladies to pause and turn back toward them.

"No, no, carry on," he said.

The butler had cleverly set the table so that the four of them would sit two to each side of the table, rather than Ox at the head and his mother at the foot. As the table sat ten comfortably, that would have left entirely too much space between their guests. In this current arrangement, they could all sit comfortably together.

Ox sat Clarissa next to his mother and took the seat opposite her. Oh yes, he liked this very much.

The cook had somehow worked a miracle, and the food presented looked as if the ladies had been expected all along. The conversation was an idle discussion of who was at which party and who had danced with whom. Ox didn't participate much, not that the ladies seemed to notice. He just sat, looking across at Clarissa. There was such a wonderful sense of completeness seeing her at his table. It was as if it was meant to be—even down to the fact that she and his mother were getting along so well. This, right here, was what made him happiest.

As the dishes were cleared away and pudding placed on the table, along with some fresh fruit, Lady Preston was saying, "Sir Phillip escorted her to the British Museum just last week." Ox had no idea who "she" was, but Clarissa's response caught his attention.

"Oh, I would so love to go to the museum. I've never been there."

"You've never been?" he asked, surprised.

"No, we've been so busy since I arrived, and Aunt Lily doesn't enjoy the museum. She doesn't see the point of it—or so she told me," Clarissa told them.

Lady Preston clicked her tongue disapprovingly.

"Why, Uxbridge must take you," Lady Uxbridge exclaimed. "He was just there showing dear Frederick around."

"Frederick?" Clarissa asked, turning toward his mother.

"Why, yes, of course. Your br—"

"Mother!" Ox said, quickly cutting her off, but it was too late.

"My brother? My brother, Frederick?" Clarissa asked, her expression beginning to look thunderous.

"Oh, dear," was all his mother could say,

"Frederick was here? When? Why didn't he come and stay at my uncle's?" The words flew out of Clarissa's mouth. She was so angry! So... upset. Goodness, she could barely register what she was feeling, her mind was so filled with the thought that her brother had been in London, and she hadn't seen him.

"You have every right to be upset, Clarissa," Lord Uxbridge started.

"Miss Ellison," she nearly growled. "I have not given leave for you to call me by my given name."

She could see him clench his jaw for a moment, but then he got hold of himself. "I do beg your pardon, Miss Ellison."

"Frederick was afraid you'd send him right back home if you knew he was here," Lady Uxbridge said.

"Of course I would have!" No, she should not shout or speak harshly to this lovely woman, Clarissa reprimanded herself. "I do apologize for my tone of voice, my lady. I should not have spoken to you thus."

Lady Uxbridge patted her arm. "It is quite all right. You are upset."

"I would still like to know why my brother was here..." Her voice trailed off as she remembered her brother's threats to come to speak to their uncle about paying his tuition. But those had been just empty threats, hadn't they?

"Perhaps you know already," Lord Uxbridge said quietly.

She looked up at him. "His tuition?"

He nodded.

"But then why didn't he come and speak with my uncle? Or did he and was sent home by him?"

"No," Lord Uxbridge answered, holding her gaze. "He didn't because I explained to Mr. Ellison—"

"Lord Haversley," Clarissa corrected him. "My brother holds my father's lesser title."

"Oh! He never told me," Lord Uxbridge said, looking a little confused. "I called him Mr. Ellison the whole time he was here, and he never corrected me."

Clarissa could only shrug. "I don't know why not."

"Anyway, I explained to him that Eton did not accept students midterm, so whether or not his uncle agreed to fund him now, it wouldn't make any difference," his lordship explained.

"I did not know that," Clarissa said.

"Neither did he, but when I told him as much, I also offered to show him a few sights around Town so his journey wouldn't be for naught."

Clarissa nodded, but one thing still bothered her. "But how did he end up staying here?"

"Ah, that is a funny story," Lord Uxbridge said.

As they ate their dessert, he told them all about how he'd come upon the boy trying to decide whether he could knock on the Morleys' door, then his lordship's subsequent invitation.

By the time they repaired to the drawing room, Clarissa's anger was gone. She was still going to write Frederick a scolding letter, but she didn't feel as slighted as she had earlier. There, now that she was calm, she could even put a name to her feelings. Even that made her feel better.

"We cannot stay long," Lady Preston said, accepting a cup of tea from Lady Uxbridge. "I promised Lady Morley I would get Miss Ellison home early."

"Of course," the lady said graciously. They finished their tea and said their goodbyes and thanks, then Lord Uxbridge himself walked them to the door, where Lady Preston's coach was waiting.

The lady went out the door first, and Clarissa was about to follow when Lord Uxbridge placed a hand on her arm, stopping her. She looked up at him. There was an odd light in his eyes.

"May I call upon you tomorrow, Miss Ellison?"

"Of course." The words popped out of her mouth before she'd even given the request any thought. "I don't believe my aunt has any plans for us," she added, thinking about it.

His face lit up as if he'd just won some hard-fought game. "Thank you. Until tomorrow, then."

Clarissa gave a nod and then joined Lady Preston, who was waiting in the coach.

Why would Lord Uxbridge ask to see her? The obvious answer she dismissed with an ache in her heart but determination to be practical about this.

The main reason gentlemen asked ladies such a question was if they planned on proposing, but his lordship didn't like her that way. They were friends. That was all.

No, that couldn't be it. There had to be some other reason, she decided.

Clarissa hardly slept that night. She kept seeing Lord Uxbridge in nothing but his shirt and breeches. Those forearms! Who would have ever thought forearms could be so enticing? And yet they were—not just because they hinted at how strong and powerful the rest of his arm might be, but because they made her think about what he might look like without his shirt altogether. Just the thought made Clarissa warm with a funny feeling in the pit of her stomach. Was this desire, she wondered? She'd read enough novels to know of desire but had never thought it might feel like this—all tingly and hot.

She also thought about why he might have asked to call on her. Deep in her heart, she wished it might be because he was going to propose, but then she chided herself as an overly hopeful ninny. He had done nothing to indicate he felt anything more for her beyond friendship.

Yes, he'd beaten Lord Drunkstone senseless, but that was just him being the gentleman he was, protecting a woman. Any man would have done as much.

There was also that feeling she'd gotten when they'd danced at Lady Preston's, but that could have been—must have been—a figment of her overactive imagination. He'd given the same sort of look to Miss Buttery-Clements when he'd danced with her... No, he definitely wasn't coming to propose. One thing was certain, however. Clarissa had to thank him once again for saving her. She might have been able to incapacitate Lord Drunkstone for a minute or two if she'd kneed him in his privates—she'd seen what happened when her brothers wrestled and one accidentally hit the other there—but would that have given her enough time to run away? The point was moot now, for his lordship had come to her rescue, and as much as she hated needing to be rescued, it had been wonderful that he'd done so. It made her feel... cherished. Such an odd feeling, and one she hadn't felt since she was very young. Before her mother had become distracted by Clarissa's younger siblings, and she had been told that it was her duty to look out for them.

Clarissa set aside all her silly thoughts when she finally rose from her bed that morning, still a little bleary-eyed from lack of sleep. She made it down to breakfast just as the footman was beginning to clear it away.

"I'm so sorry, John," she'd said as she stopped him. "If I could just fill my plate, and then you can remove the platters."

"Of course, miss," he said, holding them out so she could help herself to a cold bit of scrambled egg and a slice of ham.

"Well, you seem to have regained your appetite," her aunt said, looking up from the newspaper she was reading—probably the gossip column because Clarissa couldn't imagine the woman had interest in anything else. Uncle Lawrence must have already gone to his study, for he was no longer at the table.

"Yes, my lady. I think the rest and light fare yesterday did the trick." Clarissa took her usual seat across from her aunt, wondering if she should tell her of Lord Uxbridge's intention to call. But then she remembered her aunt thought she'd had dinner at Lady Preston's the night before and knew nothing of their visit to the Uxbridges.

"Well, that's good. I thought I would pay some calls—" She was interrupted by the butler who'd come into the room.

"What is it, Jones?" the woman asked.

"I do beg your pardon, my lady, but Lord Uxbridge is here to see Miss Ellison," he informed them.

"What? At this hour?" She stole a look at the clock on the mantel. "It's barely ten."

"Shall I tell him that—"

"No," Clarissa interrupted. "I shall be happy to meet him, er, with your permission, Aunt?"

"But you've just sat down to your breakfast, and truly, this is such an odd time to pay a call," her aunt protested.

"I wasn't so hungry. Please?" Clarissa asked, giving her aunt a hopeful little smile.

The woman sighed and said, "Very well. Jones, show him into the drawing room, and I shall be there directly."

"Very good, my lady." Jones bowed and left the room as Clarissa began to shovel food into her mouth.

Her aunt just frowned at her and waited impatiently.

After two forkfuls of egg, a bite of buttered toast, and a sip of tea, Clarissa stood.

Her aunt did likewise and then led the way up to the drawing room.

Lord Uxbridge was standing by the window, looking particularly handsome in a deep-green coat and tan waistcoat with lighter green embroidery on it. The color matched his eyes so well. Even his blond hair was combed back neatly when usually it had a haphazard style to it.

"My lord," Aunt Lily said, entering the room, "What an unusual time for a call. Is there something we can help you with?"

He gave her a slight bow. "No, my lady, thank you. Actually, I came to speak with Miss Ellison if you wouldn't mind." He looked meaningfully at Clarissa.

Her aunt had begun to sit down when he added, "Alone."

She stood up again, her eyes widening. "Alone? But that is improper as you well know, my lord."

"Perhaps we could keep the door open a crack?" he suggested.

Clarissa's stomach tightened with anticipation—or perhaps she'd just eaten too fast.

Aunt Lily narrowed her eyes at his lordship, who just smiled in return. "Very well," she finally conceded. "I shall give you a quarter of an hour—"

"Half an hour," he bargained. His smile widened.

She inclined her head slightly. "Half an hour, but I shall be nearby."

Chapter Thirty

"Thank you, my lady." He gave her another bow and then followed her to the door. After she left, he closed it so there was only the slightest crack—not really enough for anyone to eavesdrop easily.

Clarissa sat on the settee, expecting Lord Uxbridge to take the chair to her right. He didn't. He sat himself right next to her instead.

"I am glad you're here, my lord," Clarissa started.

"Ox. Or if you prefer, Jonathan," he interrupted. "I would greatly appreciate it if we could be less formal with each other."

Clarissa opened her mouth but didn't know what to say. This was the second time he'd asked her to call him by his name. She still wasn't certain it was the right thing to do. She decided she would think about it later and continued with what she'd been about to say. "I wanted to thank you for saving me from that rogue the other night." She held up a hand to stop him from brushing aside his heroic actions as he'd done the night before. "I know how to defend myself, as I've said, but I don't know if I could have incapacitated him long enough to escape. You saved me. I've never wanted to be a damsel in distress, but I am grateful you were there to be my knight."

He smiled and even blushed a little. "I'm certain—" he started, but Clarissa cut him off.

"Just say you're welcome because, if you deny my thanks, I shall be very offended." She gave him a little smile so that he would know she didn't really mean it.

He chuckled. "I would never wish to offend you, so you are most welcome."

Clarissa nodded, satisfied that he now understood just how grateful she was.

"I believe I owe you an apology," he said, changing the subject. "I should have told you your brother was here. To be honest, I didn't because he was so happy, feeling like an adult, striking out on his own."

"But he is *not* an adult," Clarissa cried. "He's only fourteen."

"I know. That is precisely the age at which boys feel the need to prove themselves a man. They don't want to be seen as a child anymore. Believe me, I've been there."

Clarissa sighed. "And having his older sister hovering would have made him feel like a child—especially because I would have insisted he return home immediately."

"Precisely. And he did reach home safely, by the way. My mother and I received a very nice letter from him this morning, thanking us for our hospitality."

That made Clarissa laugh. "I'm sure Diana stood over him to ensure he wrote it."

"No, not at all. In fact, he said that he never revealed to his older sisters where he had gone. Apparently, they think he merely went to some cottage in the wood nearby."

Clarissa nodded. "The woodcutter's shack, most likely."

"Yes, that was it."

"Well then, I am pleased that he truly has learned some manners. "

"He is an exceptionally well-mannered young man. My mother and I truly enjoyed his company. We asked him to stay with us longer, but he didn't want to worry his sisters by staying away too long." His lordship—Jonathan?—reached out and took her hand. "I know I said this before, but you truly are blessed to have a family such as yours. I wish..." He paused to gather his thoughts.

Clarissa was impressed he could think at all. With her hand lost in the confines of his, she was having the hardest time thinking. All she could do was feel—warmth, gratitude, safety—and love for this sweet, wonderful man.

He'd lowered his gaze as he thought, but now he looked her straight in the eye.

"Miss Ellison, I would be honored if you would marry me and share your wonderful family and become a part of mine—small though it may be."

Clarissa was stunned and confused. "You want to marry me for my family?"

His eyes widened. "No! I do apologize. I, I botched that up, didn't I? I want to marry you because I love you."

Clarissa thought her heart might have stopped beating for a moment. She knew she'd stopped breathing, and strangely, her eyes pricked with tears. "You... you..." She took a breath. "I thought you didn't see me as a potential bride. I thought you just wanted to be friends. That's why I asked you to introduce me to other gentlemen."

Jonathan shook his head. "You were the one who suggested we be friends," he reminded her.

Oh, my goodness! Was that right? She couldn't remember but supposed it didn't really matter. "If I did, I was silly to have done so. And wrong. So very wrong. I love you, too."

In one swift movement, she was in his arms—and then not—as he pulled away to cradle her face in his large hands. Very slowly, he bent toward her. So slowly that she could have pulled away if she'd wanted to. She did not want to.

She sank into his kiss. She floated and lost all thoughts, everything. All she knew were his lips on hers. His sweet tongue running along the seam of her lips and then dipping inside her mouth when she opened them for him. Heat rushed through her. Oh, she could go on kissing this man forever. She even tentatively swept her tongue into him. He tasted sweet and oh so good.

Much too soon, he pulled away and then fumbled for something in his pocket. He pulled out a small velvet bag. From it, he shook out a beautiful sapphire and diamond ring. The stone wasn't a deep color, but a lovely blue.

"The color reminded me of your eyes," he said, reaching for her left hand. "And the diamonds will match your earrings."

Her earrings! Mention of them made her think of the evening she'd nearly lost them playing cards. She snatched her hand back before he could place the ring on her finger.

"I can't marry you!" she blurted out. At his shocked and hurt look, she amended her words. "Rather, you will not want to marry me. Not, not after I tell you something."

His eyebrows came down over his eyes. "What could you possibly say that would make me change my mind?"

"I-I'm a gambler. It's an addiction that runs in my family. My grandmother lost so much at cards she bankrupted the family. That is why my father never wants to spend any money—not on bringing me out into society, not on Frederick's education. Everything is reinvested into the estate or set aside for Frederick when he inherits."

Jonathan sat back, clearly stunned. Clarissa tried to swallow the lump in her throat. "I had to tell you. I couldn't keep that secret from you."

He nodded slowly and finally turned back to face her. "I appreciate your honesty. Have you played cards here in London?"

She nodded. "My aunt took me to a card party, but I left when the stakes became too high. And I went to another on my own. I wanted to win enough money to pay for Frederick to go to Eton—for one year at least."

Jonathan frowned. "How much did you lose? Are you in debt?"

"No! No, I won. But I can't—I can't keep the money. It's wrong. I tried to return it to the people from whom I won it, but Lady Shipton just laughed at me and wouldn't tell me their names—we all used aliases. I am planning on giving it to Lady Welles to give to those in need."

Johathan was looking less worried now. "And have you played again since then? Did you win this money in one night or over several?"

"In one night. I never want to play cards again. If I never hold another card in my hand ever again, I would be happy."

Jonathan took her hand again, igniting a spark of hope. "Then I don't think you have a problem, and therefore *we* do not have a problem. Clarissa, I love you, and I love you now even more because you have been so honest with me. That couldn't have been easy to say."

Clarissa dared a little smile. "It wasn't. But you still want to marry me?"

"I do." To prove his words, he slipped the ring onto her finger. It was much too big. She had very thin fingers.

He smiled. "We'll get it sized for you." He kissed her again, this time not as deeply, but a sweet kiss, nonetheless. He had drawn down his eyebrows once again when he pulled away. "You said you were *planning* on giving the money to Lady Welles?"

"Yes."

"You have not done so, yet?"

"No. Why?"

"I would be happy to take care of that for you. I see Lord Welles frequently and have recently begun going with him when he goes into the rookeries."

"Oh! That would be wonderful! I'll go and get it." Before he could respond, she jumped up and ran to her room. She was back with him just a minute later. "It is such a relief to get this taken care of," she said, handing him her reticule.

He took it, letting the weight of it pull his hand down. "My goodness!" He opened the bag and peered inside. "How much is here?"

"I don't know. I could never bring myself to count it," she admitted.

He weighed it in his hand. "It has to be at least a few hundred pounds!"

Clarissa shrugged. "Please, just give it to those who need it. And I promise to never gamble ever again."

He set it down on the sofa in between them before leaning in for another kiss.

"Well, well! What's this?" Clarissa's uncle's voice made them jump apart.

Jonathan stood and bowed to him. "My lord, I am honored to say that your niece has agreed to become my wife."

"How wonderful!" He came forward, his hand outstretched.

"I cannot believe it," Aunt Lily said from the doorway. "You actually won an earl!"

Clarissa stood up and laughed. Looking at Jonathan, she said, "Yes, I have won the greatest prize ever."

Epilogue

Ox eased himself onto the tiny chair at Gunter's. It was too cold for ices with the brusque September wind blowing outside. Thankfully, the shop also offered an enticing array of pastries.

Lady Preston reached a hand across the table and placed it on top of Ox's. "It is so good to see you, Ox. I quite missed you while you were on your wedding trip, you know."

He patted her hand fondly. "I would like to say that I missed you too, but then I would be lying. It is lovely, however, to see you too."

She laughed and pulled her hand back. "I am glad you didn't think of me. All your attention was where it should have been—on your beautiful new wife. And speaking of whom, how was your stay with the Ellison family?"

Ox sighed happily. "It was wonderfully chaotic. The first three days, all the children were on their best behavior, but slowly, as they became accustomed to me, they relaxed and began to behave as they normally would."

Lady Preston chuckled. "So, you do not regret marrying into such a large family?"

"Not in the least!" Ox said immediately. "They are everything I have always wished for."

"I am so happy for you."

He nodded his thanks. "We've engaged a nanny to take care of the younger children since Clarissa's closest sister, Diana, will make her debut next year and the little ones would be too much for Eleanor to manage on her own. She has only just turned sixteen, and then next in line is Frederick and then Helena, who is only eleven."

"Ah, and what is the news with young Lord Haversley?"

"He is settling into his classes at Eton very happily. We saw him there safe and sound. His excitement just at being at Eton was a sight to behold. He even got one boy, who was also starting his first year and not at all happy about it, to smile and begin to look forward to the start of classes."

"He sounds like a very engaging child," she said, as the waiter placed a pot of tea on the table between them and then a plate of select pastries Ox had ordered earlier for them to share.

"He is. In fact, nearly all the Ellison children are engaging in some way. They are smart, clever, and excellent sportsmen."

"It does truly sound as if you are quite enamored of them."

"I am. In fact, I don't believe I've ever been happier." He held her gaze with his own as he said, "And it is all because of you, my dearest friend."

Lady Preston smiled, her cheeks turning a very pretty rosy color. "I am just happy that you are."

"And how is your new venture going?" he asked, certain she wished to change the subject.

From the bright excitement that immediately began to exude from her, he knew he was right. "It is going very well. You, of course, know about the two other couples I was able to match this past Season."

"Of course," he nodded.

"Well, word has got around, just as I'd hoped, and I am beginning to get enquiries from anxious mothers and desperate fathers. They all want to hire me to find a match for their children—both sons and daughters. I am going to be very busy charting out their horoscopes this winter before I meet with each one in the spring. I'm hoping I can find a few pairs from those who have applied to me for help, otherwise... Well, we'll just have to see what next Season brings."

"And have you decided upon a name for this venture?" he asked.

"Well, I overheard Lady Wrexley speak with someone about me, and she called me the Zodiac Matchmaker, and I quite like that."

Ox chuckled. "Yes, that is indeed perfect. Well, I wish you all the best with this and I will look forward to watching as you find those destined for each other. I just hope the couples are easier on you than Clarissa and I were."

Lady Preston laughed. "Oh, I don't believe I can count on that at all. In fact, quite the opposite—I expect I am going to be getting a good amount of protest from those involved. But they will be happy in the end, I'm sure of it!"

About the Author

Meredith Bond's books straddle that beautiful line between historical romance and fantasy. An award-winning author, she writes fun traditional Regency romances, medieval Arthurian romances, and Regency romances with a touch of magic. Known for her characters "who slip readily into one's heart," Meredith's heart belongs to her husband and two children.

Meredith loves connecting with readers. Sign up for her monthly newsletter at http://meredithbond.com/blog/newsletter-sign-up/ to receive free short stories and get all her news before anyone else. And don't forget to find her on-line:

Website: http://www.meredithbond.com

Facebook:
https://www.facebook.com/meredithbondauthor

Amazon: http://www.amazon.com/Meredith-Bond/e/B001KI1SNE

Instagram:
https://www.instagram.com/meredith_bond/

Bookbub:
https://www.bookbub.com/authors/meredith-bond

Newsletter: http://meredithbond.com/subscribe/

Please don't forget to leave a review wherever you buy books.

OTHER BOOKS BY MEREDITH BOND

The Ladies' Wagering Whist Society
A Hand for the Duke
Jack of Diamonds
The Games She Played
A Trick of Mirrors
A Bid for Romance
An Affair of Hearts
Love in Spades
Token of Love
King of Clubs
Christmas in the Cards
Deck the Halls

The Merry Men Series
An Exotic Heir
A Merry Marquis
A Rake's Reward
A Dandy in Disguise
My Lord Ghost
My Gentleman Thief
Under the Mango Tree
A Spanish Dilemma

When Hearts Rebel

The Storm Series
Storm on the Horizon
Bridging the Storm
Magic in the Storm
Through the Storm

The Children of Avalon Trilogy
Air: Merlin's Chalice
Water: The Return of Excalibur
Fire: Nimuë's Destiny

Falling
Falling for a Pirate
Falling Through the Air

Chapter One: A Fast, Fun Way to Write Fiction
Self-Publishing: Easy as ABC
"In A Beginning", a short story featuring Lilith